THE
TAKEAWAY

THE
TAKEAWAY

Mark Harland

© Mark Harland 2020

Published by MVH Publishing 2020

A CIP catalogue record for this book is available from the British Library.

ISBN 978-0-9935895-7-7 (Paperback)
ISBN 978-0-9935895-8-4 (ePub)
ISBN 978-0-9935895-9-1 (Mobi)

Book Cover design by Black Swan Book Promotion

Book layout and design by Clare Brayshaw

Prepared and printed by:

York Publishing Services Ltd
64 Hallfield Road
Layerthorpe
York
YO31 7ZQ

Tel: 01904 431213

Website: www.yps-publishing.co.uk

IN MEMORY OF

Arthur Gordon Bedford
United States Navy
Purchasing Manager
China Fleet Club
HONG KONG
1970-1973

'Power grows out of the barrel of a gun.'

Mao Tse Tung 1966

AUTHOR'S NOTE

For many years Hong Kong was my home. I consider myself fortunate, indeed privileged, to have lived in the last and richest colony of the British Empire. My paternal grandfather was a Naval Officer stationed in the Territory before the First World War, my father was a Government Radio Officer stationed there during the Cold War and I myself returned to work there long before the Handover to China in 1997. And then it all came to an end.

Hong Kong was many things to many people. To ideological Communists it was the epitome of oppression, possession and capitalist avarice. To others, seeking political freedom and a brighter future for their families, it was a burning beacon of hope that they clutched in their hundreds of thousands. Both viewpoints had merit.

The negotiations that led up to the Handover were secret. Don't let anybody tell you any different. What did Deng Xiaoping say to Mrs Thatcher in Peking in 1982? Why did she really fall down the steps of the Hall of the Heavenly People following the negotiations for the future of Hong Kong? Maybe we will never know. One thing is for sure. Just as China reneged on the 1842 Treaty of Nanking, so it reneged on the Joint Declaration for the future status of Hong Kong. To many this was totally predictable and the

Handover was better described as a *'Takeaway'* – hence the title of this book.

When the late James Clavell wrote *'Noble House'* he said: 'I would like to offer this work as a tribute to her Britannic Majesty Elizabeth II, to the people of Her Crown Colony of Hong Kong – *and perdition to their enemies.* How prophetic.

This book is a novel set in Hong Kong a decade after the Handover but many of the happenings I know to be true. There will never be another Hong Kong and the plethora of people and characters that it spawned in its one hundred and fifty year history. One such character was Commander Arthur Gordon Bedford, United States Navy, to whose memory I dedicate this book. I should like to thank his wife Betty and daughters Susan and Alison for allowing me to 'insert' him into the plot.

The future of Hong Kong is still unknown.

PROLOGUE

Bekaa Valley
Southern Lebanon
8th October 1973

It was day three of the so called Yom Kippur War.

The Arab World was in vengeful mood and the Egyptian President, Anwar Sadat, had vowed to retake control of the Suez Canal and re-open it. On the holiest day in the Jewish calendar, the Day Of Atonement, Egypt launched massive pre-emptive raids across the Canal into Israeli occupied Sinai. In so doing he had set the whole Middle East alight.

The Yom Kippur War had been bloodier than the Six Day War in 1967. The Israeli Government was not in a mood to negotiate. The State of Israel was fighting on several fronts for its very existence. Attacked from the north at the Golan Heights by Syria it would do all in its power to prevent the Bekaa Valley in southern Lebanon from becoming a training ground for terrorists and insurgents striking at Jewish civilians with impunity whenever the fancy took them. Wave after wave of Israeli Air Force F4 Phantoms, their blue Star of David emblems glinting in the brilliant sunlight, had hit the valley that day with bombs, rockets and napalm. Casualties on the ground were high and many women and children were killed and wounded.

Over two hundred in one day alone. The Red Crescent field hospitals could barely cope with the incessant processions of maimed, burnt and horribly disfigured refugees who, for the most part, wanted only peace and stability for their families. They knew nothing about geo-politics, OPEC or the world price of oil.

Dusk brought with it a merciful release to the suffering of many. The bombing stopped but many still died of wounds received that day. The early evening prayers of the Faithful could not drown out the death cries of a wounded young Palestinian girl as she fought against nature to give birth before she left this earth. She succeeded and cradled her son for several minutes.

Just before she died she whispered a name to a nurse. 'Please, please! Let him be called Jamil. Jamil ibn Salim.' The nurse promised and within seconds the pretty Palestinian girl slipped into eternity. Such was life, and death, in the white heat of the Middle East in October 1973.

The girl, whose name was unknown, was buried the next day in a mass grave. She was just one of hundreds of innocent victims. She died not knowing that, in the world she had just departed, her progeny would one day become a man more feared than the Jackal and more revered in the Arab World than Arafat or Nasser. Jamil was orphaned after five minutes of life on this earth. His father, Abdullah ibn Salim, had been killed on the first day of the War.

Jamil grew up in the squalor of deprivation and despair that epitomised the lot of the displaced Palestinians of the last three decades of the Millennium. But life for him would be different. He wanted to be somebody and to achieve something. His schooling in the camps was rudimentary but the staff of the international relief agencies taught him English and French as well as his native Arabic. By 1997 he would have degrees in Business Administration and Computer Science from Beirut University. By 2000 he was running his own business in imports and exports, again based in Beirut. His company specialised in 'aviation and defence electronics' and demand for his services grew and grew.

His company raised millions of dollars for the Palestinian cause at home and abroad. He charged huge sums to those who could afford his services and little or nothing to his Islamic brothers who couldn't. He channelled vast sums into trying to solve the social problems of the Gaza Strip and his mantle took on that of the Robin Hood of the Middle East. But by 2001 Jamil was on the CIA's list of suspected international terrorists. Rumours abounded that he was personally responsible for the shooting down of several airliners in Europe and the Middle East. He denied any involvement after all accusations of atrocity. He was an accomplished liar.

He had friends in high places. At his twenty fifth birthday he chartered a luxury liner for a cruise from Beirut through the Suez Canal to the port of Aqaba in Jordan. The guest list included Royalty from no less than ten Kingdoms and Emirates. Jamil's star was still rising and yet the CIA were more and more certain. Information was passed internally to the National Security Agency at Fort Meade, Maryland and thenceforth to trusted allies only. The net was inexorably closing in on Jamil.

After two more aviation 'accidents' resulted in yet more international outcries for him to be brought to justice, a plan was laid to recruit him for a special job. He would, via intermediaries of impeccable source, be offered fifty million dollars for a single job. To Jamil it would be the highlight of his career.

1

The China Fleet Club
Gloucester Road
Wanchai, Hong Kong

July 16ʰ 1914

Clement Arrigoni, Electrical Artificer First Class, Royal Navy, was in a pensive mood. The sun had just set over the Western approaches of Victoria Harbour. As he looked out of the second floor window of the Naval Canteen he could just make out the shape of Green Island, one of the Navy's two main ammunition and ordnance depots in the Colony. Then, traversing his eyes slowly and deliberately to the right in a sweeping arc he took in Stonecutters Island, the peninsular of Kowloon, Cantonese for 'Nine Dragons.' The mountain of Tai Mo Shan a dozen miles distant towered three thousand feet behind and above even Lion Rock, Kowloon's tallest and Number One Dragon.

In the tropics twighlight was short and fifteen minutes after sundown the sky was black. The temperature dropped a few degrees but the sapping humidity was incessant. The brass ceiling fans provided a modicum of relief but made his cigarettes, home rolled from Nosegay tobacco, burn even quicker. He got another beer from the Chinese bartender and returned to his window table overlooking the harbour. This was his last night in the British Crown Colony of Hong

Kong. He had been stationed here and up the coast on the China Station at Wang Wei for three years. They had been three of the most fascinating years of his comparatively young life. At thirty five he had already seen more of the world than most people see in a lifetime.

At Wang Wei, where he made the three day trip nearly every month, he had been responsible for maintaining the electrical equipment on the Navy's river patrol boats that protected British interests on the Yangtze River. He always enjoyed these diversions, particularly when it offered some respite from the heat of Hong Kong's summer. But the contrast with Hong Kong was extraordinary. The country was weak, impecunious and badly treated by the rest of the world. In China, if you were not a poor peasant, you were a privileged Mandarin. There was no in between. The most populous country on earth was going nowhere. By comparison, Hong Kong was booming, absolutely booming.

Clement Arrigoni sipped his beer and looked again across the harbour to the Nine Hills. In the harbour were two cruisers, a battle cruiser, and four destroyers. They were not just symbolic of the might of the Royal Navy and *pax Britannica*. They were also a symbol of the growing wealth of Hong Kong and the level of protection it deserved. Since the Treaty of Nanking in 1842 ceded the Island of Hong Kong to Britain in perpetuity the country's traders and marketeers had sailed by their hundreds from every quarter of the United Kingdom to establish banks, factories, dockyards and go-downs. By the turn of the century it was starting to look like the prosperous London of the mid eighteen hundreds. People were starting to get wealthy. Very wealthy. Not just British expatriates but entrepreneurial Chinese too.

He would love to stay in Hong Kong forever but tomorrow, shortly after sunrise, the battle-cruiser Tiger lying at anchor in the harbour, would be taking him home to England. His tour of duty was now complete. Britain was at war with Germany and although he didn't know it, ahead lay the Battle of Jutland, the Royal Navy's biggest battle since Trafalgar. The battle that Admiral Jellicoe said Britain must win lest he could 'lose the whole War in an afternoon.' But first he would have a short leave in London with his wife Emily and their young son John whom he had not yet seen. In those days the Forces were oblivious to family life. A monthly letter from Emily postmarked Lower Edmonton, London that took seven weeks by Royal Mail Steamer was the only link with home. A blurred dog eared photograph of wife and son that he kept in his wallet were the only visual reminders of his loved ones.

As the Tiger slipped her moorings next morning the sun was rising high above the Lyemun Channel separating Hong Kong Island from the Chinese mainland. 'Lai – moon' was Cantonese for carpfish and folklore had it that the fishing in the Channel was the best in China. Clement Arrigoni stood on the starboard decking beneath 'Y turret' near the quarterdeck of the huge man of war as she gathered speed towards the east and the open ocean of the South China Sea. He took one last look at Victoria Peak that stood sentry over this rich and growing jewel of the Empire, wiped a tear of farewell from his eyes and went below decks. He would never see Hong Kong again but he had played his own small part in the establishment of a trading port and industrial city that in time would rival Sydney and San Francisco in majesty, money and sheer magnificence.

But even in his wildest dreams Clement Arrigoni, Electrical Artificer First Class Royal Navy, could not have envisaged just how rich the territory of Hong Kong would one day become. It would in time become the richest city in the Orient. A prosperous pimple on the nose of mighty China. And one day somebody would want it back. One day.

Kam Sang Restaurant
Kennedy Town
Hong Kong

December 10th 1982 – 1:00 pm

There was a distinctly cool wind blowing from the north. The winter monsoon was decidedly early this year. He hoped it wasn't a sign but like all Chinese a degree of superstition was in his blood. Jimmy Leung had had a message via discreet channels on the Chinese side of the border that his presence was required at a meeting. It sounded important.

Jimmy's driver dropped him off just outside the tram depot and he walked the last hundred yards to the Kam Sang restaurant. His new green Rolls Royce Phantom would have been just a little too conspicuous. This was a private lunch meeting with business associates. He was greeted by the head waiter who led him to a table in the corner right at the back near the swing doors into the kitchens. Another waiter threw a clean white cloth across the table and took his order for a Tsing Tao beer. He lit a 555 State Express and waited for the others.

Upstairs in a smoke filled private room belonging to the proprietor were three men, all in their fifties. The thirty year old tugboat *Wang Ho* had delivered them to a wharf a short walk from the Kam Sang an hour earlier. Scruffily dressed, they had posed as crew members but in fact were anything but. Travelling without documents they would be safely back in Canton shortly after dark that same day. None of them had ever been to Hong Kong. In fact none had ever left the People's Republic before.

Shortly after one o'clock a smart suited businessman called Harry Kwan alighted from the Kennedy Town tram after its busy half hour journey from Happy Valley. He had spent the morning in the Member's lounge of the Royal Hong Kong Jockey Club catching up on gossip and chatting with fellow racing enthusiasts. His eldest son Kelvin had stayed behind to meet with their own trainer from the family owned stables. He would catch up on the news later. Right now he had a very urgently convened meeting to attend. His friend Jimmy Leung had sounded very insistent on the telephone. Something must be up. He walked into the restaurant and spotted Jimmy sitting alone at the back. He ordered tea from a waiter and sat down next to Jimmy.

'This is a pleasant surprise Jimmy but why are we lunching here? It's bit grim! I thought the Hilton was your usual watering hole. This place is full of dirty coolies on their lunch break from the go-downs over the road.'

'Yes I know. Stop moaning, the food's very good. I've ordered some dim sum and steamed fish by the way for the both of us. Anyway just listen to me for a minute before the other three join us from upstairs. I'll keep it brief and to the point.' He did.

Harry Kwan was aghast at Jimmy's news but not totally surprised. On the Hong Kong side of the border the possibility had been mooted for some time but this was the first official corroboration that not only would there be tacit support from the other side in Guandong Province but physical assistance and hard cash. Money. Lots and lots of money. And gold.

Ten minutes later the three others from upstairs came down the rickety wooden staircase and Jimmy Leung introduced them one at a time to Harry Kwan. He didn't know if they were real names or aliases but he took them at face value. They certainly weren't tugboat crew. They spoke no English whatsoever, only Cantonese. Food arrived for all of them and they wasted no time in tucking into the delicious dim sum. One of the three appeared to be slightly older and assumed the role of spokesman for them all. He had met Jimmy in Whampoa, the port of Canton, many times over the last ten years when Jimmy had travelled on the cargo boats belonging to Leung Shipping. He gave his name as Cheung Chi-doi. He told Harry Kwan that they represented a much larger group of businessmen in the Pearl River Delta who envied the political and economic stability of Hong Kong. If only Guandong Province was the same. Some hope. Mao Tse Tung's so-called Great Leap Forward had been a disaster. The elderly Chou en Lai was a moderating influence in Peking but he could only do so much and his health was failing. The latest 'Five Year Plan' meant nothing. It would be the same as the last one, itself a carbon copy of the previous one.

The week before had seen a sea change in direction from Peking. The British Prime Minister had had a summit meeting with the Chinese Premier Deng Xiaoping in the Great Hall of the People. She had looked ill after leaving the meeting and had fallen down the steps leading from the Hall in front of all the journalists' cameras. It had taken days for the information to percolate down the bush telegraph to Guandong. When the information finally arrived it caused near panic in the Canton and Whampoa business community who had hitherto been allowed a degree of free enterprise and autonomy in what was still a rigidly controlled communist country. The news was quite simple. It had been surmised that the Prime Minister had asked Deng for a twenty five year extension to the Lease and had told him that Britain intended in any event to keep Hong

Kong Island as a colony which had been ceded in perpetuity under the separate Treaty of Nanking. Deng had told her that if they did then China would invade and destroy it in two days. He had meant what he said. The Prime Minister knew it. She was stunned. Her advisers had let her down badly. China was not Argentina.

Cheung Chi-doi told Harry Kwan that forty eight hours earlier the business leaders in Guandong had met in secret conclave in a disused go-down on the upper reaches of the Pearl Delta. A decision had been made. If there was support for the idea within Hong Kong and from genuine Hong Kong people, then a plot would be launched one day to overthrow the post-colonial administration after the Handover in 1997. A new country would be formed, free from Peking. It would be centred on the great Pearl River itself. It would take in the hugely successful Hong Kong and the Portuguese enclave of Macau. Secretly, it had even been given a new name already. It would be called the *Pearl Delta Republic.*

The restaurant emptied of diners over the next half hour leaving only the five of them and the proprietor locked the front door. He knew the score. The Kam Sang was a regular haunt for these sort of meetings. He brought them pots of green tea and a huge plate of sweet Chinese cakes and left them to talk alone. By five o'clock they were finished and wrapped up the meeting. The three mainland Chinese left the restaurant via the back door into the alley and the back streets teeming with humanity. In less than fifteen minutes the *Wang Ho* was steaming out into the western approaches towards the Pearl Delta. They left behind a battered old leather trunk with brass corners that had long since blackened. It was they said, their 'deposit' for the cause. Jimmy and Harry nearly left it behind. Just as well they didn't. Inside were twenty gold bars. A thousand taels.

At the current market price it was worth almost a million US dollars. Curiously each bar was stamped with a Hong Kong Government assay mark.

That gold proved to be the first of many hundreds of contributions over the next twenty five years from the boys across the border. The list of contributors grew and grew. Their names were kept secret. Hereinafter they were referred to by Harry and Jimmy as simply the *Guys from Guandong.'*

The gold was sold the next day and the first accounts to fund The Operation were opened at the Head Office of the Hong Kong & Shanghai Banking Corporation at No. 1 Queens Road. Harry delegated his son Kelvin to open a corresponding account at the Hanover Street, Edinburgh Branch of the Bank without undue delay. It was known as the Operational Account. One day 'Hanover' would become 'Handover.'

Harry and Jimmy decided between them that as Hong Kong had been born during the Opium Wars then it would be appropriate to give the operation the code-name *Operation Opium.* Should the name ever leak out then potential adversaries would mistakenly believe there was a narcotics connection. There wasn't. A new Bank was established to act as a front for the Operation. It was called Macmillan Rand.

In the immediate years ahead The Operation turned into a crusade. Former enemies became brothers in arms and casual friends became close friends. Between them Harry and Jimmy had a plethora of contacts, private as well as commercial. No stone would be left unturned in the quest for support, both personal and financial. Favours were called in all around the globe. From the U.S. From England From Scotland. From Australia. Representations were even made to the Nationalist Government in Taiwan. After all, they were under threat as well and one day a future U.S. Government might try to undermine them by doing an under the table deal with Peking.

The expiry of Hong Kong's lease was like a time bomb waiting to explode. Nothing could be done to prevent the Handover on July 1st 1997. However, behind the scenes a lot was happening. Guandong Province was prospering and growing like nowhere else on earth. The new Economic Zones were thriving and allowed to work along capitalist lines. What on earth would Mao have said to that? In June 1989 the mass killings in Tiananmen Square, the so called Square of Heavenly Peace, in the newly named Beijing caused shock waves throughout China – particularly in Guandong Province whose economic success was leaving the rest of the country looking distinctly flat footed. Or to be brutally honest downright backward. The Fat Cats in Beijing even erected a huge clock in Tiananmen Square that counted off the days, hours, minutes and seconds to the time that they themselves would become colonialists. The clock became an omnipresent reminder to the people of Hong Kong of the doom and gloom to come.

The subsequent political crackdown across the huge country served only to increase the resolve of the Guys from Guandong. Nothing, but nothing, would detract them from their aim. One day, after the Handover, when Beijing would be least expecting it, their own ill deserved spoils of Hong Kong would be taken from them. One day.

The threat of invasion from the north in retaliation would not materialise. There would be enough ackers in the kitty of Macmillan Rand to pay *anybody* off as and when necessary. Absolutely anybody.

Composite Signals Organisation Station
Tai Mo Shan New Territories
Hong Kong

Midnight

The Duty Officer switched his set off, rose from his executive type swivel chair and decided to get some fresh air. In any event it was time for his tea break and a fag. He'd prefer a Carlsberg or three but that would have to wait until he'd finished his twenty hour stint on watch and he started his three days leave. Ted Birch handed responsibility over to the most senior Radio Supervisor and walked outside into the clear cool air.

Cool it certainly was – barely five Celsius. The Station was sited at the very summit of Tai Mo Shan, the highest mountain in the Territory. It was the only place in Hong Kong where a frost had ever been recorded. When the ether was at night you could listen in to just about everything you wanted to. The somewhat primitive Chinese codes had been cracked by the boffins back at Government Communications Headquarters in Cheltenham and all gathered intelligence of note was passed on immediately to either U.S. authorities at Naha, Okinawa or more usually to Pine Gap and DSD (Defence Signals Division) in Melbourne, Australia. Little got missed. It worked well.

Ted walked around the perimeter enjoying the air and the cigarette. His mind started to wander. In another ten days he would be on Christmas leave in Ripon, Yorkshire. A log fire. Roast turkey. Chestnuts. Christmas carols. A half hour later he was back at his desk. A near frantic Supervisor, Tony Southon, almost screamed at him the moment he went back into the Ops Room.

'Where the heck have you been for the last twenty minutes?! Hell has just frozen over. The Pope's become a

Protestant. Taxes have been abolished. Ted, just get a look at these signals coming in from up Province. Wow! I've been on this Station since 1966 and I have never seen anything like these! Who are these guys, Ted?' There were no 'sirs and salutes' at Tai Mo Shan. They were all civilians – mostly Brits and only the odd Australian here and there. Tai Mo Shan had neither a bar nor a cricket pitch.

At that exact moment Edward Birch didn't know. *He'd never heard of the Guys from Guandong.* So much for a quiet spell to see out his shift. Ted Birch didn't make it to the carol service in Ripon Cathedral. His entire leave was cancelled. He had to make do with tea and corned beef sandwiches three thousand feet up a mountain.

Composite Signals Organisation Station
Little Sai Wan
Hong Kong Island
11th December – 1pm

Station Commander Jack Kirby was on his lunch break. He'd enjoyed a delicious chicken curry washed down with San Miguel beer in the Mess at Ariel House. He sat in one of the easy bamboo sofas on the verandah overlooking the lovely cricket pitch and beyond to the water's edge and the Lyemun Channel. It was a clear warm day typical of December weather in Hong Kong. Fifteen miles distant he could see Tai Mo Shan. With binoculars you could just make out the white golf balls protecting the radars and listening antennae which were there just as much to protect them from prying eyes as much as the typhoons that plagued this part of the world for four months of the year. Sometimes five.

The report on his desk that morning from TMS, as they all called it, was mind boggling. Problem was he didn't know what best to do with it. Ted Birch's boys had picked up a whole load of new traffic the night before that were doing his head in. The communications recorded weren't even encrypted for Christ's sake. This was just bog standard chattering Cantonese between several transmitters on frequencies not normally used by the Chinese military. In fact not normally used by anybody at all. Not ever. No, these people, whoever they were, were not military. Probably not official either. The D/F Station at Kong Wei up near the border had narrowed the transmitters down to seven or maybe eight sites all within two hundred miles of Hong Kong.

That the messages were sent at all was illuminating but the contents of the messages themselves were absolutely sensational. In twelve hours time Birch would be back on Hong Kong Island and he would convene a meeting of his senior linguists, Ted included, before sending any onward reports either back to UK or anywhere else. He'd already consulted his own station expert 'Monty' MacMahon who had buggered off to play golf at Fan Ling. He might have to call him back.

Jack Kirby tried to concentrate on the lively cricket match that was being played out on the lush pitch in front of him. Little Sai Wan (LSW) versus the Kowloon Cricket Club (KCC). Amongst his four hundred strong staff at LSW were a hundred or so Australians on secondment from the Royal Australian Air Force only ninety percent of whom were useful with a bat! Vic Johnstone and Colin Metcalf were at the crease carving up KCC's opening bowlers who looked like they'd been at an all night party. That's because they had. Sat on the verandah all padded up and ready to bat was the number three batsman, Mick Brisley, who had been at the same party as the opening bowlers and was mighty thankful that LSW had won the toss and were batting. Fielding down near the far boundary was no joke with a headache. Jack Kirby hardly noticed. His mind was somewhere he'd never been in his life. Not over the boundary. Over the border.

Kirby mused to himself. Oh blimey. None of the manuals prepared you for this. If Ted's boys had got it right then it seemed that some definite degree of subterfuge was taking place just over the fence in the PRC for which there was no explanation. But it was so amateurish in propagation. Had it been done for their benefit? Were they meant to pick it up? Was it a stunt? It seemed almost too simple for that. He tried to watch a little cricket. Johnstone was caught 'out' trying to hit the ball onto a passing Mitsui OSK Lines container ship out in the Lyemun Channel with a hay-maker of a shot that every schoolboy is told how *not* to play.

Brisley swallowed the last of his beer and trundled down the steps to replace him at the crease. He still had a headache. Brisley emulated the late great Don Bradman. He walked slowly out to the wicket to allow his eyes to adjust to the bright sunlight and as he did so a passing jumbo jet of Pan American Airlines moved slowly across the sky on its final descent into Kai Tak Airport. Flight PA01, the flagship round the world Clipper Service, was on schedule. The four huge Pratt and Whitney jet engines screamed to keep the giant bird in the air just above stalling speed as it clawed its way down to the safety of the concrete ribbon in the harbour three miles distant. The usual approach was over Kowloon but the northerly monsoon necessitated the 'walk' in over the water. Some pilots dubbed it the Jesus approach. That was the second passing plane during that over alone. One day in the not too distant future they would have to build a new much bigger and safer airport but in overcrowded and built-up Hong Kong where on earth would they manage to do that?

Jack Kirby watched the cricket until the end of play. He couldn't even remember who won. His mind was on other things. Should he tell Cheltenham yet or not. Probably not a lot of point at this stage. GCHQ's Director General Michael Merryweather would almost certainly be at Cheltenham Races today anyway.. They can wait until we know a bit more. In fact a lot more. He didn't want some desk bound tossers in Middle England telling him what do about the Middle Kingdom. He could predict what would happen if he informed GCHQ at this stage. All hell would be on. Merryweather would take the information to next Thursday's meeting of the Joint Intelligence Committee at 10 Downing Street. Nobody would know exactly what to do. The Foreign Secretary would tell the PM that it was *a most sensitive matter and we must be awfully careful Prime Minister not to offend Peking'* and then it would get passed on to some departmental mandarins who were more concerned with offloading the Hong Kong problem than trying to solve it. With the Christmas Holiday period coming up the issue would be in the gash bin within a couple of weeks. No, sod Cheltenham. In the meantime Anglo-Australian relations were at the top of the list. He'd go and buy Brisley a beer. He'd been out for a duck. Zilch!

Kirby convened the meeting in his office the next day at 10.00 am sharp. There were five men present. Himself, Birch, MacMahon (who had foregone his golf) another top linguist Murray Thomson and the head of the Australian Section, Squadron Leader Randy Baxter RAAF. They all knew why they were there and Kirby had spoken to all of them independently beforehand. Kirby opened the batting.

'Gentlemen, I don't have to tell you just how important this might be. I use the word *might* quite deliberately because quite frankly none of us can be certain as to the authenticity of these transmissions. The problem is that it is only a matter of days since the Prime Minister was in Peking talking to Deng Xiaoping about the future of the Territory post-Handover in 1997. That's fifteen years hence but it seems that all sorts of commercial interests have started to come out of the closet like long leases on land and property that necessitate some sort of understanding in the very near future if the Handover is to proceed smoothly. Unfortunately the so called Foreign Office Mandarins are about as much use as a chocolate fire-guard when it comes to dealing with China. Let's face it, since the frigate HMS Amethyst had to fight her way out of the Yangtze single handed in 1949 London have got it wrong every time. Over Korea. Over Anthony Gray. Over the riots here in 1967. Over Vietnam. Over trade. You bloody name it. But it's we who are the Government's eyes and ears – that's what we get paid for. So, the big question is, are these transmissions genuine or designed to deceive us?

One by one the other four gave their honest opinions.

The general consensus was that in all probability there was *something* major afoot in Guandong Province that was not unconnected with the recent Prime Ministerial visit to China. The implications were either huge or a storm in a Chinese teacup. Kirby shredded the memo from Birch and in effect the meeting had not taken place. Three days later Kirby flew to Naha, Okinawa for his regular bi-monthly meeting with his opposite number Al Geister from the NSA at Fort Meade, Maryland. The normally routine meeting between the two men, always informal but usually mildly interesting, took on a whole new complexion with Kirby's news. They had a long talk about the 'Guandong Transmissions.'

Geister's laid back Californian demeanour blended well with Kirby's West Riding of Yorkshire grit. They were a good combination and fed off each other for ideas and interpretation of sometimes complex issues. But this was not normal stuff and they both knew it. They carried on their discussions over dinner in the base's Officer's mess that evening. By the time they'd finished their third coffee they had reached two important conclusions. Firstly, that these transmissions *were* significant and in all probability would be followed by others. Secondly, that it would be better, for the time being at least, if as few people as possible knew about it. If 'the file' was going to be buried then it might as well be in the hands of people who one day might have the nous to do something about it.

The next day Geister took the USAF 707 back to Langley AFB in Virginia via Hickam and Edwards. Kirby flew back to Hong Kong on a Northwest Orient regular flight. Kirby didn't tell Cheltenham. Geister didn't tell Washington.

When he died in his native Yorkshire shortly after his premature retirement on health grounds, Jack Kirby had done his bit for Operation Opium without even knowing it.

HMS Apollo Bay of Biscay
48° North 6° West

Lieutenant Bruce McCandless had just come off watch from the bridge of the Leander class frigate HMS Apollo. It was his first appointment as a Junior Officer and in forty eight hours or less they would be back in their base port of Plymouth Devonport. It had been a long and arduous trip for the ship and its crew from the Falkland Islands and the ship looked distinctly weather beaten and battle weary despite the fact she was only a few years old. The weather in the South Atlantic had been brutal and the ship had taken 'green water' over the bows for weeks on end. Only later would critical inspection in Her Majesty's Dockyard reveal the extent of damage to her hull. To make matters more uncomfortable for her crew, she was 'riding high' in the water having unloaded munitions and supplies to other ships of the Fleet still safeguarding the Falklands against another possible Argentine attack. It had taken many weeks to get all the materiel the eight thousand miles south. No point in taking any of it back!

Apollo had bunkered at Ascension Island on the long haul home and she would have to reach baseport without refuelling again. All the Fleet's supporting tankers were strung out like floating gas stations for three thousand miles south of Ascension. She was steaming at a comparatively leisurely fifteen knots to conserve fuel which served only to make the journey even longer. They had been just too late to see any of the action against Argentine forces having arrived in late June as part of the 'back-up' fleet which had allowed badly damaged vessels to return to the UK. Now it was their turn to come home. They had been away for six months and it had been the ship's longest continuous deployment since she was first commissioned. At least they would make it home for Christmas.

McCandless started to unwind in the wardroom with a large gin and his thoughts started to turn to home. A spot of well deserved leave first. If the ship was going to be 'in dock' for a spell he might be able to do a few other things he had put on ice for a while. He didn't know it yet but within three days McCandless was to receive the letter from 'Drafty' at Portsmouth detailing his next appointment. The sad reality was that battle casualties in the South Atlantic had opened up new opportunities. His ambition of following in his Grandfather's footsteps in the Submarine Service were closer than he thought. Within two months he would be serving in the new nuclear submarine HMS Splendid. If only he could have known at this juncture what his life and career had in store for him.

McCandless ruffled the auburn hair inherited from his Irish Uncle Henry and laughed loudly when he heard the punch line of a joke being told by one of the other officers in the wardroom. A good job the Captain wasn't present. He had been the butt of the joke but his strict disciplinarian and humourless nature did not blend well with the rest of the Officers who regarded his as a tyrant. McCandless had often thought what a jolly good job it was he hadn't been an officer in Nelson's Navy. He'd have been keel hauled twice a day every day for insubordination! He was always in trouble. Even his annual appraisal interviews were a chore and the jokes he cracked at these supposedly serious meetings were never appreciated by his superiors. To McCandless these gold braided self appointed Gods were the worst part of the Navy and reminded him of the luddite Board of Longitude that had dallied for years and years whilst they considered the skills of John Harrison, the most brilliant horologist in the world. Harrison had perfected keeping accurate time at sea for years but could not persuade these maritime dinosaurs to accept his proven theories. History would in time prove Harrison right but the dithering of the naval hierarchy cost the navy dearly in time and lives.

At his last annual appraisal at Portsmouth just before the Falklands issue blew up the interviewing Vice Admiral had asked McCandless what one single improvement he would make to the Navy if he were the First Sea Lord.. McCandless had taken only two seconds to reply. He looked the Admiral straight in the eye and suppressing his normally permanent grin kept a straight face.

'Well, Sir, I would immediately sanction the serving of Wrens (women sailors) on HM ships on a fifty-fifty personnel basis. All new ships to be built would be designed and constructed with double cabins. This would be especially important on submarines, Sir, like the ninety day Polaris patrols where quite frankly normal entertainment is sadly lacking. The boost to morale throughout the Fleet would be enormous, Sir. The old adage of 'rum, bum and baccy' would be replaced by 'rum, fun and baccy' and the face of the Navy would change for the better for ever. It will also assist in recruitment in the years ahead. Young. heterosexual men would not refrain from joining up fearful of going blind within the year from too much....'

McCandless didn't finish his sentence. The Admiral brought his fist down sharply onto the table top. Bang!

'Let me tell you, young man, that what you have just said will never, ever happen. Not in my lifetime and not even in yours! Thank you. That will be all. Dismissed.'

McCandless's cards were marked. The Admiral added his own hand scrawled notes to the file.

Immature and disrespectful. Does not appreciate the finest traditions of the Senior Service. Obviously he fancies himself as some sort of maritime gigolo. The expansion of the nuclear submarine squadrons in the years ahead will the give the Draft Board ample scope to relegate this young man's undoubted talents to those parts of the ocean where his sense of humour and ardour can do the least damage.

He had given McCandless exactly what he wanted!

The wardroom radio was tuned into the BBC World Service and after delivering the shipping forecast from Faroes to Finisterre the announcer's BBC English *'This is London'* led you into the lilting opening bars of the beautifully haunting 'Lilibolero.' On the sea or under the sea, anywhere in the world, an English sailor felt as if as if he was watching cricket on a village green whenever he heard that tune. As the chimes of Big Ben faded the deep male Oxbridge voice continued.

'The news at eighteen hundred hours, Greenwich Mean Time, read by Philip Treleaven. The Prime Minister has returned to Britain from her visit to China and the Far East where she held talks about…'

The gong rang for dinner. 'Baby's heads' and 'bangers and mash with train smash' were on the menu. His favourites! What rotten luck they were both being served on the same day. He might try and bribe one of the cooks with a half bottle of Lemon Hart rum to repeat the menu before they hit Plymouth. He turned the radio set off. Nobody seemed interested anyway. What was all that crap about China?

2

London, England

July 1st 1996

The British Airways Concorde from JFK New York landed at Heathrow Airport at 4pm. Commander Gordon Bedford, US Navy Retired, was ostensibly on vacation. An unmarked black Jaguar took him and his wife Betty straight to the Mountbatten Hotel in Piccadilly.

The décor in the Viceroy Suite was impeccable. The many drawings, sketches and watercolors that adorned the pastel coloured walls told the history of Admiral Lord Louis Mountbatten's days of service in India and the Far East. The irony was not lost on the retired Commander.

That evening Bedford received three male visitors to his private suite, one British, one American and one Chinese.

Next day they took the Great North Eastern Railway from King's Cross north to the city of York for a reunion with old friends. Over the next two weeks they took in the English Lakes, Scotland and the whole of Yorkshire, Gordon's ancestral home.

They had some real fun in Yorkshire and even managed to find the old pub in Welburn near York, "The Farthing House", which had been owned by Gordon's grandfather Bartholomew in the closing years of the 19th Century.

The present day owners, John and Maggie Tate-Smith, were delighted to meet the pleasant couple from America. Intending only to drop in for a pint of ale and maybe a ploughman's lunch of bread and cheese they ended up staying for over a day. The Tate-Smiths were so interested in hearing stories of the Victorian Barthlomew Bedford that they invited them to stay overnight as guests. Thus far Bartholomew Bedford had been only a name on the property deeds. Thenceforth they could actually picture him as a real person with his handlebar moustache and gold pocket watch tucked into the his striped waistcoats as at 10 o'clock every night, in accordance with Licensing Laws, he bellowed out at the top of his voice 'Time, Gentlemen please' to indicate that the pub was closing for the night.

That night John Tate-Smith let Gordon perform that duty at 11 o'clock. Drinking hours had been extended by one hour in the 100 years that had passed but John still kept up the time honoured tradition. Gordon got a bigger kick out of that than anything for a long time!

Gordon mentioned that he had an old sepia photograph of his grandfather back home in Jacksonville and he promised to get it copied with a new computer enhanced process and mail it to them to hang on the wall of the pub's saloon bar. John and Maggie were thrilled.

John and Gordon drank Grouse whisky well into the small hours. The next day before they left for the Lake District, Maggie taught Betty how to make real Yorkshire puddings and promised to cook roast rib of beef and puddings on August 1st, Yorkshire Day, and invite some friends round to show off her new expertise. After lunch they all said their goodbyes and promising to keep in touch, set off north for the town of Kendal.

During the drive Gordon mentioned to Betty that he thought the name "Farting Horse" instead of "Farthing House" would make a great name for a chain of motels in Florida. In his mind's eye he had already designed the logo of a large palomino with its rear legs splayed and a blast of hot air erupting from under its raised tail. He decided that he would mention it to an old navy buddy on the USS Enterprise called Pete Schaefer who had just bought a run down motel near Cape Canaveral and wanted to give it a new image.

When he mentioned this to Betty she just looked him in the eye with that overpowering wifely look and said 'Gordon Bedford, you are *such* an asshole!'

It was indicative of Bedford's sharp mind that he could combine supine laid-back humour with business. Tomorrow however, he would have to put humour to one side.

Next day, while Betty sailed Lake Windermere on the pleasure cruiser Swan, Gordon drove the Hertz Rentacar to the nearby town of Barrow-in-Furness about an hour's drive away. Barrow was to the United Kingdom what Newport News was to the United States and it was home to Britain's biggest shipbuilders. He could see the yards from miles away as the winding road descended towards the town. The giant blue and yellow cranes were in perpetual motion as massive metallic sections were raised from the ground and gently lowered into place onto structures that would one day actually look like ships instead of giant Meccano sets.

Gordon drove past yard after yard where tankers, supply ships and landing ships of every size and description were slowly taking shape. British Nuclear Shipbuilders plc was doing quite well now that several of its competitors had either gone into liquidation or turned to building oil rigs. Its order book was full – well almost.

As he passed the huge covered yard that looked more like an aircraft hangar for jumbo jets than a dockyard Gordon smiled wistfully to himself. Jesus, if only these guys knew what was coming! This was the specialist nuclear submarine construction facility and inside the huge plant it was empty. Only essential utilities were turned on to maintain its safety and integrity. It had been over a year since the last of the four Vanguard class Trident missile submarines had been fitted and delivered. The profit on those contracts had just about covered the lean times that followed. The post Cold war peace dividend had bought problems to many industries. Gordon reflected that it was exactly the same back in the States. Here in Barrow if the Government didn't stop pissing about and order some new subs soon there were bound to be big cutbacks and job losses. The Board of Directors was getting very worried.

After checking in at the main security gate Gordon was shown to a reserved parking space almost at the front door to the main office building. He was expected.

The Sales and Marketing Director, Albert Armstrong, who's great-grandfather had founded the yard back in 1888, warmly welcomed the American visitor to his office. A call from London the previous day had asked if he would kindly receive a courtesy visit from a retired US naval officer who was on vacation in the area. It was not unusual to be visited by 'old sea dogs' who were writing their memoirs and wanting to obtain details of their old ships that had long since been turned into razor blades. However it was odd to be visited by an American. He suspected that Mr Bedford had probably served as a liaison officer on a British ship and wanted some material for a book.

After the usual introductions and pleasantries Armstrong's secretary came into the room and asked if they would like tea or coffee. By now acclimatised to being in 'Olde England' Gordon asked for tea which took the pretty young lady by surprise. She thought that all Americans drank coffee.

From Armstrong's office window on the fifth floor you got a good view of the slipways and beyond them to the grey painted hangar that wasn't making any money.

The panelled office walls were festooned with photographs of ships that had been built by the yard for a hundred years. The earliest ones were more brown and white than black and white and were of the old Dreadnoughts and battle-cruisers that represented the days when Britannia really did rule the waves and the orthodoxy of *pax Britannica* guaranteed safety for the Empire and perdition to her enemies.

Albert Armstrong was a nice guy. He was sixty four and retirement at Christmas was looming. He was the last Armstrong on the Board of the Company which was now part of a gigantic defence corporation that made everything from frigates to tanks to submarines to walkie-talkies. In his pin stripe suit he looked every bit a Fifties industrialist. That's because deep down he was. They chatted quietly for five minutes or more about the 'good old days' when ships were made of steel not plastic and had real guns fired by real men, not computers.

A gentle knock at the door announced that the pretty Rebecca was bringing in the pot of tea for two and the fig biscuits that she knew were his favourite. Albert often wondered if he would get the same service from his wife Mabel after he retired. Some hope!

After they had finished the tea and biscuits both men lit up. Gordon on his Dunhill and Albert on his cherrywood pipe.

'Make smoke! Make smoke! they chirped as they imitated an old fashioned destroyer Captain trying to hide his vessel from enemy eyes. Albert Armstrong was enjoying the company of his American visitor and sought some advice on what to see and do on their planned holiday to Florida next January to mark his retirement. They were already on first name terms.

' I'm awfully sorry, Gordon. How rude of me. I'd almost forgotten that you're here for your benefit not mine! How can I help you? Some photographs perhaps or some technical information on a particular ship? Our archives are extensive and survived the Second World war absolutely intact. I'm sure that …'

Gordon Bedford took another long draw on the Dunhill and it burnt right down to the filter in so doing making even more smoke.

'Albert, my friend, I am going to solve you the problem of that empty grey hangar I can see over your shoulder about a mile away.'

Six butts in the ashtray and a quarter ounce of Three Nuns Purple later Mr Albert Armstrong was the happiest man on Earth. He could retire at Christmas with a clear conscience. The jobs of all his men were safe.

They parted with a warm handshake and the mutual promise to meet up in Jacksonville next January when they could 'make smoke' and talk about proper ships until the Grouse ran out. In Gordon's house the Grouse never ran out.

As he left the yards behind him and drove back to Lake Windermere to pick up Betty, Gordon just couldn't stop thinking about the palomino with the sphincter problem.

Next day they turned up the Motorway and headed for Scotland. Betty shopped for America in Edinburgh.

She bought enough jumpers from the Edinburgh Woollen Mill to deprive at least a hundred sheep from their winter protection and had to arrange for them to be shipped back to the States.

While Betty emptied the family credit cards on Princes Street Gordon drove north to Balhousie Castle, Perth for lunch with Major General Alan Archibald Ferguson.

The business in Scotland completed they drove south roughly following the coast and spent a few days in Scarborough on the Yorkshire Coast. Betty remembered the movie 'The Graduate' and the charming Simon and Garfunkel song 'Are you going to Scarborough Fair?' There wasn't a fair anymore but there was a branch of the Edinburgh Woollen Mill and she bought a whole load more jumpers that she had meant to buy in Edinburgh.

Gordon drunk Grouse with his old pal George Lister at the North Cliff Golf Club. They had met years earlier when George had been seconded to the US Navy Supply Corps when he was just a very junior officer. Gordon's family links with George's native Yorkshire had ensured a long friendship.

On their last Day in England Gordon had one meeting in the morning at a Chinese restaurant in Soho while Betty shopped at Harrods in Knightsbridge. Souvenirs for daughters Susan and Alison back in Cincinnati were obligatory.

The voyage back to New York on the Cunard liner QE2 was a dream.

A week later the souvenirs were duly delivered to Cincinnati in the shiny dark green bags with the famous company logo on the side that was recognised the world over.

When Gordon asked Alison what she thought they would look like with a farting horse logo on the bag instead she pulled a face at him and said 'Dad, you are *such* an asshole!' Coming from the youngest daughter that was a bit grim.

Jacksonville, Florida
January 8th 1997

Gordon Bedford and Albert Armstrong 'made smoke' and got drunk drinking Grouse. Betty and Mabel exchanged knitting patterns.

3

London

March 17th 1997

At one stage it had appeared that HMS Astute would never be built. Promised for years as the first of a new class of nuclear submarine to replace the Swiftsures, many believed that the order would never come.

All the usual excuses had been trotted out – budgetary constraints, Ministry of Defence cash flow problems etc. With the sacred cow of 'Eurofighter' taking up a disproportionate amount of the defence budget for the next ten years, once again it was the Navy that was expected to bear the brunt of the squeeze. Wasn't it ever thus?

Then, against all expectations, and out of the blue, the Conservative Government of John Major on March 17th 1997, its last effective day of office, announced a contract to build Astute and two sister boats Ambush and Artful at a reputed cost of £2 billion pounds. More than a few eyebrows were raised at the cost. With talk of two expensive new carriers for the Millennium where on earth was the money coming from?

The announcement, which was made in a Commons Written Reply, went largely unnoticed. Next day's newspapers were full of the forthcoming General Election which Major was expected to lose. He did.

All three boats were to be constructed, fitted out and commissioned with a minimum of fuss. In line with tradition affiliations would be made with Army Regiments. *HMS Astute* with the King's Own Scottish Borderers, *Ambush* with the Black Watch and *Artful* with the Argyll and Sutherland Highlanders. The shakedown cruises would be to the Bahamas Grand Banks missile range where their systems and missiles would be thoroughly tested.

On a misty Scottish morning in early October 1998 the British nuclear submarine HMS Splendid had slipped her moorings at Faslane naval base on the Firth of Clyde. Gently she nosed her way out into the Atlantic. She was on a mission. Her commanding officer was one Capt. B.V.McCandless

Crossing the Atlantic Ocean she paused briefly en route to check out satellite and associated data link systems connected to her new Tomahawk land attack missile system. The first test firing in California was only days away.

Should the test prove successful then all of the United Kingdom's submarine fleet would, in time, be equipped with this most lethal of long range weapons. It would provide the Royal Navy with the ability to hit a target with a thousand pounds of high explosive to an accuracy of six feet from almost a thousand miles away.

Transiting the Panama Canal she then slipped beneath the waves and headed west north west into the Pacific towards her destination more than two thousand miles away. Four days later she broke surface twenty miles south of San Diego Naval Base. The crew quickly struck up a jack-staff on the bow to fly the Union Flag and a small White Ensign fluttered from her conning tower.

A school of dolphins rode the bow wave for almost an hour. It was a good omen. As the boat slowed to enter harbour a lone piper in full Scottish Highland regimental regalia appeared on deck and started to play a long, gut churning lament. The piper was from the submarine's affiliated Regiment. All Scottish based submarines had a similar affiliation. It was tradition.

Welcoming United States Naval officers stared incredulously at this most bizarre of spectacles. The seeds of revenge were being sown that day. Not even McCandless knew that. Yet.

Port Loma Submarine Base, San Diego, was home to the boat for the next few days. The wives and girlfriends of many of the crew had flown out to California for a vacation. For a few of the crew it was their first successful deployment on a submarine and in the highest tradition of the Submarine Service they were presented with their famous 'dolphin' badges in a glass of grog which they had to drink in one gulp, retaining the badge in their teeth. All the men did so with alacrity. It all augured well for a successful mission. McCandless was happy.

Three days later, with all preparations complete, the single test Tomahawk missile was gingerly lowered by crane into the submarine's weapons hatch on the forward casing. It was the first of sixty five such missiles that the Ministry of Defence was purchasing for the Royal Navy. Less than twenty four hours later the missile impacted its target – a mock up communications station on San Clemente Island eight hundred miles away from the launch point. A member of the crew casually remarked that it was the first time since the Revolutionary Wars that explosives fired by the British had landed on American soil.

Three weeks later HMS Splendid sailed back into her Scottish base to a tearful welcome from the crew's families. They were home in time for Christmas.

HMS Splendid had been the first so equipped, successfully firing her first test missile into San Clemente Island off the coast of California on the 18th of November 1998. With much technical help from the U.S.Navy and the blessing and acquiescence of the Pentagon, the Royal Navy had proved itself capable of handling this most lethal weapon of war.

Little or no assistance would be needed subsequently. Within two years the United Kingdom would have equipped at least half of its submarines with Tomahawk. The Pentagon knew that this would ease the stretch on the US Navy and the British boats would share the burden of patrolling the world's trouble spots. That was the primary reason for the handing over of the technology. The "special relationship" was in good shape and nowhere did it manifest itself more than in the co-operation between the two navies. It was not uncommon for the United States Secretary for the Navy and Britain's First Sea Lord to discuss ship deployments when *they* thought it necessary. In their view they didn't need to inform their superiors about a lot of things. Presidents and Prime Ministers are mere politicians after all. Eventually they either retire or get voted out.

A Memorandum of Understanding would be signed, and a contract effected, that would ensure U.S. technical backup and servicing arrangements for the Tomahawks for at least ten years. Only a handful of people in the whole world would realise the significance of this deal when it came. To the Guys in Guandong it would mean *everything*.

4

Talk of the Town Nightclub
Excelsior Hotel

With a swoosh, the Otis elevator's doors opened at Level 34, the very top of the Excelsior Hotel.

'Good evening, Sir.' The beautiful Chinese hostess bowed her head ever so slightly when speaking. 'A table for two?'

'Three please. Another gentleman will be joining us shortly.' Commander Gordon Bedford USN Retired, led the way to a vacant table overlooking the Royal Hong Kong Yacht Club and the rest of the magnificent harbour.

Gordon Bedford was sixty five and the opportunity to visit his old haunts was too good to miss. He had known for a long time that he would be back one day – he just wasn't quite sure when. Gordon was five ten and still quite lean. His dark brown hair had thinned a little with age but he had grown a moustache since leaving the Navy and it suited him. He drank Grouse Whisky when he could get it and Jim Beam when he couldn't. He smoked too much and his little cough was in fact the first signs of emphysema.

Gordon was much more than just a sailor. He was a businessman and had a Masters Degree in Business

Administration from Harvard and graduated from Annapolis in the Class of '55. After service in several Fleets including the Sixth and Seventh, the offer to take up a shore post in Hong Kong was a dream. He was the luckiest guy in the whole of the Navy.

His companion was a young Royal Naval Commander, Bruce McCandless who was in Hong Kong 'on vacation' from England. He had served in Hong Kong before a year earlier when his former boat, HMS Peacock, had been based at the temporary HMS Tamar on Stonecutters Island which would be handed over to the communists within days.

Both men were in civilian clothes. They had only met that afternoon but already assumed the easy conversational style of old friends. Bedford lit up a Dunhill and McCandless chewed on a stick of complimentary chicken satay whilst they waited for the two cold beers they had ordered.

'So when were you last here in Hong Kong, Gordon?'

'Not since '85. As the resident USN Commander my official title was Officer in Charge, U.S.Navy Purchasing Department, China Fleet Club. We called it a PX, what you guys call a NAAFI I believe.

After promotion to full Commander at Yokosuka, Japan I was retired early but on a full pension. I returned to Cincinnati, Ohio where the girls finished High School. After that I moved to Jacksonville, Florida on medical grounds. Warmer climate!'

'Why an early retirement?'

'Well, Bruce, it may be hard for you to believe but in the early Seventies Hong Kong was awash with US Navy personnel on R & R, rest and recreation, from the Vietnam war. All those guys were on combat pay and the amount of money that went through the PX at the China Fleet Club was staggering. A million dollars a day easy. All the goods sold there were supplied by local traders, mostly Chinese. Some with mainland connections.

If you wanted it, you could buy it. Rolex watches, diamonds, cameras, jade, Tientsin carpets, ivory – you name it.

Nixon had lifted the trade embargo with Communist China after all that 'ping-pong' diplomacy crap in Peking and everyone was making a fortune. Problem was the whole thing was unaccountable because it had gotten so big. There were false allegations that I was being paid big sums under the table to favour certain traders and suppliers. Bottom line is that I was replaced by some Bible Belt turkey who went to church three times a day, didn't drink or smoke and who wouldn't mix with his suppliers.'

'Was that such a bad thing?'

'Too right! Nobody was getting any "tea money" and the whole business shrank. Turnover went down by 80% in one year.'

'Off the record, were you on the make?'

'Never. Bruce, I would never discredit the Navy. I'll say this. I lost count of how many times I was approached with truly lucrative offers to swing contracts. Even my wife Betty was approached. Naturally I had to tell the authorities. The Navy got shit scared and decided to promote me home. End of story.'

In his own mind McCandless gave Bedford the benefit of the doubt.

Bedford knew that his big pay-off would come from the Chinese 'Guys in Guandong' long after he had left the Navy. His 'finders fee' for McCandless was a million dollars, payable in July 2007. That would be OK. The Navy would not object to that. Just a little boost to the pension fund!

'So why are we both here today Gordon? The Navy offered me a free 'liaison' trip prior to the Handover. I wasn't going to say no to that. Why are you in HK precisely, Gordon?'

'I am here to meet you and introduce you to the gentleman now walking towards us.'

Rising from his chair Gordon Bedford stretched out his hand to the elderly Chinaman who grinned broadly to reveal several gold teeth.

'Hello, Gordong, my good old friend. Long, long time no see. We both get too fat now old men. Ha ha!'

'Jimmy, you old asshole. Nice to see you again! Jimmy this is my English friend Bruce McCandless. This is the guy who I think might be able to help you.'

Jimmy Kam-Fai Leung was now sixty seven.. Twenty years earlier he had run his own shipping and trading company. Born in Canton in 1930 he came to HK after the War against Japan. He came with family money determined to build a big company. He sure did.

Jimmy was 100% Chinese, whether communist or capitalist didn't matter. He was one of those types who had a foot in both camps and he was equally at home in either. In the late Sixties and early Seventies his firm had supplied the American Navy PX with everything that came in from China. Mostly jade and ivory. The mark-up was one thousand percent. Jimmy became a millionaire. His masters and suppliers in Guandong likewise.

During his long stint in Hong Kong Gordon and Jimmy lunched weekly every Friday at either the Hilton, Jimmy's choice, or the Swiss Inn in Wanchai, Gordon's favourite. They developed a rapport that was probably unique in the whole world. Both their masters knew it.

As the sun set over the harbour to the west, lights appeared as if by magic across the whole of Hong Kong. With darkness a veritable fairyland unfolded in front of them.

The trouble was that the information that both men imparted to McCandless over the next hour made him feel as if he was in just such another world. In one month's time HK would be handed back to Mainland China. The tea money would finally stop. Forever.

For Lt.Bruce McCandless R.N., the world would never be quite the same again.

By 9.00pm an unmarked car collected him from the Excelsior and drove him through the cross harbour tunnel to Kai Tak International Airport. At 11.00pm he was London bound on Cathay Pacific flight CX255 – the non stop red eye flight to Heathrow. He would not set foot in Hong Kong again for a long time.

During the fourteen hour flight McCandless could think only of what Bedford and Leung had told him. Some 'liaison trip' that was! He wasn't even allowed to stay for the Handover Ceremony in a few weeks time. Now he knew why.

Apart from the Prime Minister and His Excellency the Governor, McCandless was the only Briton thus far to be told of the plan. His assistance was essential. So was his silence.

The Excelsior Agreement was an unofficial trilateral accord between certain officers in the United States and United Kingdom Governments and representatives of the Regional Guandong Government. Its aim was simple. To overthrow the Peking backed Hong Kong Government at the most opportune moment after the Handover.

One day, if all went to plan, Hong Kong would once again become governed by 'foreign devils' – all in the interests of making money.

The plans had already been laid for co-operation from inside Guandong Province. Deng Xiaoping was already dead and the hard liners in Beijing would find it increasingly difficult to prop up their cronies in Hong Kong.

The ultimate prize was the creation, effectively, of a new democratic country comprising the hugely successful Guandong Province, the former British Colony of Hong Kong and the Portuguese Territory of Macau.

The Guys in Guandong had had enough of communism, Beijing and the ageing, senile and dynastic Politburos. They wanted money and Independence.

They wanted to give birth to the *Pearl Delta Republic.*

McCandless was the insurance policy. In a years time, for sure, he would be the Commander of the Third Submarine Squadron. The NSA would make sure of that come what may. They hadn't invested hundreds of millions of dollars from 1960 to 1997 for nothing. They had already funded all of the United Kingdom's intelligence operations in Hong Kong during that time. A few more million bucks here and there meant nothing.

After McCandless had left the Excelsior Gordon Bedford drank some Grouse with Jimmy Leung. In fact quite a lot of Grouse.

Neither of them had let on that they had known his father Victor McCandless for nearly two decades. Quite simply, he didn't need to know.

5

There had never been anything like it. Nor would there ever be again. This was the end of the British Empire. Handing over banana Republics to indigenous populations was one thing. Handing over the richest city in Asia to the last communist power on earth was quite another matter. The Last Governor was almost inconsolable as the Union Flag that flew over Government House was lowered, ceremoniously folded, and handed to him by a police officer. In a couple of hours time it would all be over.

Around the globe millions watched the build-up to the Handover ceremony on TV. In the United Kingdom, from Stornoway to Southampton and from Cornwall to Cromer thousands of retired sailors, soldiers, airmen, policemen and prison officers who had served in the Colony sat glued to their sets. A million memories came flooding back as every single one of them entered their own time machines and travelled back to different times and different days. Days of amahs. Of heat and humidity. Of green tea. Of Star Ferries, fire crackers and typhoons.

But in Hong Kong the Good the Great and the Gormless were gathering on the new parade ground to watch history being made and history being destroyed. The old Prime Minister, the new Prime Minister, the Prince of Wales and the entourage of countless 'hangers on' clung on to their umbrellas. The Gods and Ghosts of Tai Mo Shan looked down upon them all and wept. It rained cats and dogs throughout the entire evening. For the incoming Confused Confucian Communists this was very, very bad joss.

The feng shui could not have been worse.

With seconds to go before the Treaty of Nanking became a worthless document the Honour Guards of the Black Watch, the Senior Highland Regiment, and a Guard of the Royal Navy performed their unenviable duties. Tung Chee Wha assumed executive power in Hong Kong at the stroke of midnight on June 30th 1997 and over 100 years of British Imperial history came to an end.

Ten miles to the south, on the other side of Hong Kong Island, things were a little bit different.

At 1.00am on July 1st, the Royal Yacht Britannia, escorted by the frigate HMS Chatham, sailed east through the harbour and Lyemoon Gap as they did so passing less than a mile away from the former British/NSA intelligence gathering station known as Little Sai Wan.

Still just inside Hong Kong waters they passed Waglan Island, uninhabited save for a handful of Royal Observatory weathermen who manned the typhoon tracking station. At its closest point to the island, Chatham slowed down to a steady ten knots. Six members of the SBS, the Special Boat Squadron, clambered up the netting cast over the ship's starboard quarter. Their Gemini inflatable was winched on board. They, not the Official Guard, were the last British forces to leave Hong Kong.

'Mission accomplished, Sir. All safely back on board' barked the sergeant to the Officer of the Watch.

With the six Navy men were two senior officers of the Black Watch Regiment. Looking more than a little green from the choppy ride in the inflatable the pair of them looked grim. Whilst the eyes of the world had been on the Handover Ceremony on the Harbour-side, they had been performing a very private regimental task at Stanley Prison.

In the mid – Seventies two of the Regiment's junior privates had murdered two HK Chinese taxi drivers who had tried to rob them. Soldiers who had taken too much booze were easy targets. It was commonplace. Both pleaded alcoholic amnesia but were charged, found guilty and sentenced to death. Fortunately for them the then Governor commuted their sentences to life imprisonment in Stanley Prison. Privately, the Ministry of Defence in London told the Black Watch that arrangements would be made for their Regiment to be the last to garrison Hong Kong – in 1997. The idea was for both men to be 'sprung' on the last day of colonial rule rather than leave them to the Communists. A deal was done.

At midnight precisely the two officers arrived at Stanley Prison having walked less than a mile from the small pier at St Stephens beach. At the end of Tung Tau Wan Road they walked past the sentry box which appeared unmanned. Passing the old Stanley Club building on the left they approached the huge white painted walls of the prison's inner compound. Nobody seemed to be about at all. Was everyone watching T.V.? Maybe so. Still, it was a bit spooky. Ten minutes later there was still no sign of the two Scotsmen, now in their early forties. They waited.

At 12.15 am a Chinese Army Officer appeared from the gatehouse. His English was not good but he needed no interpreter.

'You wan your two squaddie now OK? Here you can have.'

The tailgate of a Prisons Department truck dropped down noisily. Two limp bodies dressed in full regimental ceremonial dress rolled from the back and onto the tarmac. Both had been shot in the back of the head with one bullet, Chinese executional style.

The two bodies were left behind. Britain was no longer the ruling power.

By dawn The Royal Yacht Britannia and HMS Chatham had joined up with the other naval units that comprised exercise Ocean Wave '97. Within a day the Last Governor disembarked from Britannia in the Philippines and flew back to London. All *he* had to do now was write and sell his memoirs.

It was all over bar the shouting.

Sixty miles to the northwest, in the City of Kwangzhou, formerly known as Canton, seventy year old Cheung Chi Doi had an early night. He hadn't even bothered to watch the Handover on TV. In the morning as the first shafts of silvery light brought dawn over the Pearl River he would take his caged songbird to the park and practice his 'Tai-Chi' like he did every morning.

6

Barrow in Furness
Cumbria, England
July 1st 1997

At 10.00 am the Finance Director's telephone rang. It was their London Bank. The FOREX clerk was most polite.

'A substantial foreign credit has come in overnight for your company, Sir.' Albert Armstrong had tipped him off that an inward foreign transfer was imminent but the amount shook him rigid. Surely that couldn't be correct. He queried it, certain that a decimal point had been misprinted.

'Yes, Sir. I can confirm the amount. Let me repeat. Four eight five decimal five seven million Australian dollars. Today's sterling rate is two point four four dollars. Shall we convert for you or retain the dollars on account at six percent per annum?'

'Convert please and credit our Head Office sterling account.'

''Thank you, Sir. Consider it done. Goodbye.'

He picked up an internal telephone to Albert Armstrong's office. He didn't seem at all surprised at the news and lit his pipe. The first stage payment had been made to British Nuclear Shipbuilders in Barrow -in-Furness. The origins of the international bank transfer seemed a little hazy. Why Melbourne for God's sake?

The first stage of 'Operation Opium' had begun.

Sion, Switzerland
Same date

On Saturday mornings only a handful of staff were in attendance. The OstenBank Privat S.A. had clients the world over but Sundays were the only concession to the observance of a Sabbath by its Lutheran Partners.

Heidi Muller always worked Saturday mornings and she received a whole day off midweek to compensate. It was always fairly busy in her section – Inward Remittances – as it was the first working day after the Muslim weekend. They had many Arab clients. In fact on Saturdays there was rarely any business other than from the Middle East. She was surprised, therefore, to print off an electronic transfer of funds for a new account with funds originating in Edinburgh. New clients were permitted to allocate three letters and four digits to their designated account. The annual rate of interest for these ultra-confidential accounts was only a half a percent. The client was lucky. Some banks charged a negative rate of interest. Such was the price to pay for guaranteed anonymity of gains, ill gotten or otherwise.

Ten million US dollars had been transferred in. The chosen combination was LSK2007.

The second stage of Operation Opium had begun.

7

Fort Meade, Maryland

2nd April 2001

It was late. Most of his colleagues had gone home. Manning the National Security Agency was of course a twenty four hour operation but even its Chief had to have some time to himself. He would read through the files one more time and then drive home to the Baltimore suburb of Glen Burnie and supper with his wife Gaynor and two teenage kids.

Malcolm MacCullum was a deeply troubled man and right now he felt very, very alone. Nothing could have prepared him for the office that particular morning. They say that every job has its Monday morning but that cliché was a touch understated today. He had skipped lunch and had drank far too much coffee for his own good. His doctor had told him to reduce his caffeine intake and quit smoking with his mild angina condition. He had coped surprisingly well with the latter but, hell, a few coffees? Come on man!

The crisis had started, for him at least, with a phone call from the "office" to say that his driver would be picking him up an hour earlier than normal, six o'clock, and that he would be briefed en route to Fort Meade by an aide. It had been the quickest yet longest day of his life. The President himself had spoken to him on an encrypted line as soon as his feet hit the office. In a nutshell the position was this.

Hours earlier a Navy intelligence gathering plane operating from Kadena, Okinawa and monitoring broadcasts off the coast of Guandong Province in Southern China had been forced to make an emergency landing at a Chinese Air Force base on Hainan Island. It seems that a Chinese fighter had deliberately collided with the Aries EP-3, and badly damaged, the plane's captain had to either land it on Chinese soil or ditch and risk the lives of his twenty three crew on board. The Chinese pilot, who's name was given as Wang Wei was missing, presumed dead.

To say that the situation was tricky was like saying that treacle was a little sticky. Less than three months into his term the President was keen to be seen to be surrounded by a good and experienced team of advisers. He went on TV and played an open hand. He admitted he was 'troubled' by the Chinese actions and asked for a speedy return of the aircrew to their native land. It didn't happen.

Military considerations apart, MacCullum knew that there was an added factor to the equation. Approximately every forty eight hours ever since the handover of Hong Kong back to China, specialist Navy planes had made the tortuous patrol from Okinawa a thousand miles to the southwest, had loitered on two engines to conserve fuel, and then returned to base. Less than a dozen people in the whole of the United States military and intelligence establishment knew why. But he was one of them.

For the tenth time that day he opened and read the file compiled by Al Geister back in January 1983. Eighteen years ago for Christ's sake. The file had lain dormant at the NSA for years, having simply been filed alongside other speculative items. It had not been inputted into any database on his specific orders. He read Geister's notes that had been heavily influenced by the input of several British intelligence officers. The names of Kirby and Birch were mentioned several times. One thing was certain. – nobody had told Washington. Of that he was sure. Should he tell the President now? Probably not. Best to wait a while to see how the political situation developed over the next few days. Besides, the President probably didn't even know where Guandong was until yesterday. He checked Human Resources records. Geister was still alive but retired in Sausalito, California. He might be worth a call or even a visit. He might know more than he was prepared to put in the file. Perhaps best to wait a few more days.

The situation deteriorated markedly. By the following weekend the Chinese had still not released the US crew which included three women, all linguistic experts. The President had tried all the diplomatic channels available to him, including some that would normally have been a no no. Chinese Premier Jiang Zemin was seemingly determined to make him look like the new kid on the block, which of course he was. In the meantime, unbeknown to the American public, the Navy surveillance flights from Okinawa continued exactly as before.

The President was both bemused and angry. The hawks on his right were telling him to block China's application to join the WTO, the World Trade Organisation, and to lobby the International Olympic Committee into making sure that Beijing didn't get to host the 2008 Olympics which were so important to them. Just when he thought that progress had been made Jiang decided to go off on a tour of South America.. He was taking the piss. The US refused to apologise for its plane being inside international airspace and without the apology China refused to release the crew, let alone the plane. Stalemate. The only people who were laughing were the makers of the yellow ribbons that Middle

America were tying around 'the old oak trees' in their thousands. Zemin held all the cards and both sides knew it. Patience was the name of the game.

Several more days passed. Nothing happened. MacCullum decided still not to tell the President. He did however book a short weekend vacation to San Francisco, taking his wife and family with him. Geister's home was less than a half hour's drive away from 'Frisco and on the Sunday he would take a little sojourn – alone.

It was a short and pleasant drive over the Golden Gate bridge to Sausalito. In the Sixties and Seventies the little town had gotten a reputation as a bit of a hippy retreat but in recent years had taken on the more conservative mantle of a yachtsman's retirement haven. Al Geister's house was not difficult to find from the directions he had given him over the phone. Al had been taken my complete surprise on taking the call from MacCullum the day before. They had worked together on a special project in 1997 just before he had retired and he was pleased to see him again. Taking two cold beers from the refrigerator they sat on the teak decking overlooking the bay and the myriad of pleasure boats enjoying the holiday weekend.

MacCullum's suspicions had been right. There was a lot more information that was not on file and over the next hour Al Geister regurgitated verbatim almost the entire conversation that he had had with Jack Kirby in Naha, Okinawa in January 1983. He certainly had a remarkable memory but there again, that was part of his job. When he left just before sundown to return to Frisco MacCullum knew that he had a much better grasp of the situation then anybody else in Washington. He was equally certain that within a few more days the crisis would almost certainly be over. If their interpretation of the situation was correct then sooner or later the continuing intelligence flights would receive a message for their ears only. Probably just before the Easter Holiday period, not that that meant anything to Confucianists.

MacCullum returned to Maryland. The short break had done him good.

The very next day, Tuesday April 10, a hundred nautical miles south of Hong Kong, the Navy E3P Aries was flying on a heading of 'two five o' towards Hainan Island. That day they were monitoring certain new frequencies with particular care. Instructions from on high. The captain set the plane onto a roughly circular course with a diameter of about fifty miles. There was lots of radio traffic from planes heading to and from Hong Kong's new airport at Chek Lap Kok. It was all routine. They had five hours loiter time on the two inboard Allison turboprops. Then it would be '080' and home to Kadena Air Force Base and a well earned rest.

'OK crew, we'll do one last orbit then head for home' the captain announced just before sundown. It was just after six in the evening. Three hours later the computer discs were downloaded and sent to Fort Meade on secure satellite links. Another two hours later and confirmation of certain transmissions was lying on MacCullum's desk. Al Geister was right. The Guys from Guandong were still in business. Washington still didn't need to know. Not yet.

The next day Chinese Foreign Affairs spokesman, Sun Luxi, speaking live from Beijing, announced that the full American apology had been well received and that the next day the twenty three US nationals would be allowed home. Sure enough, that same night a chartered Continental Airlines 737 was dispatched from Guam to Hainan to fetch 'our boys' home. The crisis had lasted twelve days from start to finish.

Like Jimmy Leung had said back in 1982. There would be enough money in the coffers of McMillan Rand to pay off anybody. *Absolutely anybody.*

On the day that the American crew were reunited with their families, Beijing took the deliberate measure of announcing to the world that Squadron Leader Wang Wei, whose body was never found, had been made a Revolutionary Martyr. In Communist Chinese terms this was akin to Sainthood and meant that his wife would receive a State pension and that his six year old son would in future be able to attend a special private school in Beijing. This would ensure that he would get his pretty little head stuffed with shit and noodles at the same time.

8

Riyadh, Saudi Arabia

5th May 2001

It was the biggest party in the Royal Kingdom for many years. The official opening of the Al Faisaliah Centre was going to put Saudi Arabia back on the map. It was the tallest building in the world – if you counted the spire on the top. It beat the rival Kingdom Centre across the city by a only a few feet and the only reason that both got built was because two rival Crown Princes vied with each other to build the biggest building on earth. Money was no object. Top crude oil was pushing thirty bucks a barrel and Saudi Arabia had only to open the taps to buy whatever it wanted.

At twelve noon King Fahed cut the customary ribbon in the festering heat of the midday sun on the immaculately green astroturf lawns surrounding the Centre's base. To the millions watching worldwide on TV it would look like real grass. The Saudis had heard that the Chinese Olympic Committee had actually painted brown grass green to impress visiting delegations from Geneva and had simply taken the idea a little further. Maybe you can't buy astroturf in China! The King and all Crown Princes there present walked slowly along the endless yards of temporarily laid green carpets that led into the shaded interior of the massive artifice. This was the Saudi equivalent of the 'red carpet treatment', the colour green being next to God in Islamic ideology. The officially invited dignitaries and their guests, all three hundred and eight of them, shuffled noisily behind into the lobby like a human centipede. Ten minutes later and the entire throng was in air conditioned bliss as aides with clipboards scurried around peering at guest's ID tags trying to match the names to the computer generated lists. It was typical Saudi chaos and it took almost an hour for everybody to be directed to an elevator for the eight hundred feet ascent to the Banqueting Hall on the seventy seventh floor. In the centre of the elevator lobby was an onyx plinth six feet by three and a foot high. Mounted on it was a half size statue of a racehorse moulded in solid twenty four carat gold. The caption, written in Arabic and English, informed you that it was in memory of '*Al Ghawar*' the Crown Prince's favourite racehorse that had died of equine green grass disease only a month earlier. It had won the Dubai Gold Cup the previous year and was like a son to him. The Prince had been in mourning from that day to the present. The statue was a public display of grief and opulence on a scale that only Saudis could afford.

The guest list, all male in Saudi tradition, was an impressive role call of a kind of Islamic edition of Who's Who. Every Sultan, Emir and Sheikh from every Gulf State was present. That alone accounted for over two hundred. There were also several dozen western guests from the many Embassies and Consulates in the city that now regarded itself as the unofficial capital of the Islamic World. Scores of waiters bearing trays of 'mocktails' – alcohol free cocktails –mingled with the assembled whilst they waited for the set piece speeches and the banal humdrum of social intercourse minus women and drink. Everybody seemed to be a smoker. It was a macho habit that all Arabs had picked up from the early days of Aramco's and BP's explorations several decades earlier. The whole country had gone from sand dunes to skyscrapers in two generations. At least the British and US representatives had the consolation of knowing that in two hours time they could enjoy the liquid contents of the diplomatic bags that came in thrice weekly from D.C. and London.

Eight delegates had been shown into a separate elevator back on the ground level. They had been taken straight to level eighty and the private offices of the Crown Prince who owned the building. It was not an error. It was quite deliberate. As the Master of Ceremonies commenced the official reception on level seventy seven, forty feet above them a meeting of a rather different kind was about to commence. It was the first convention of the newest and the most secret organisation in the world. It was also the richest. For reasons of security it had no name. Its committee comprised of eight men at any one time. Eight countries belonged and for security reasons only one delegate could attend any given meeting. The Chairman, speaking in mid-Atlantic English, was sat at the end of a long boardroom type highly polished Italian table. Out of immediate sight, behind a screen, were interpreters who translated the Chairman's words into the several different native tongues of the delegates, the words being relayed via infra red headphones. Spanish. Arabic. Burmese. Cantonese. Japanese. French. Malay.

Seated and silent, wearing headphones, they looked like a multi ethnic Parliament of an artificially created country. Eight sects, eight languages. In reality they had far more power and influence in the world than any single state, even a superpower. Between them they controlled ninety five percent of the world's narcotics. James Bond, eat your heart out. This was real stuff.

The Chairman, who was Caucasian, opened the meeting. Instantly little red lights on the side of the headphone earpads flickered into life indicating that the interpreters had started their work and that the voice activated equipment was operating smoothly. They all nodded when the Chairman welcomed them to the meeting. Nobody took notes. It was forbidden.

'Gentlemen, I thank you for attending today. The official opening of the Al Faisaliah Centre has afforded us the opportunity to gather under one roof without undue suspicion but I must first tell you that security is paramount. When we have finished our business in less than twenty minutes time you will all, together, descend to the ground floor and then be shown to another elevator to take you to the function room below. You are all wearing legitimate ID cards, albeit in false names, and if any questions are asked you were shown to the incorrect elevators previously and had to be redirected. That explanation will not be queried. Only the engineers who designed and built this place know their way around yet. It's all so new.'

'Now, to business. The knowledge I am about to impart to you is known to but a dozen men in the world. You will all know that the US President, Powell, has recently confirmed his country's commitment to the National Missile Defence System. It is more commonly referred to as the Son of Star Wars.' He paused momentarily to allow the interpreters to put this into the seven other languages. They seemed to be moving at different speeds. It took only a few seconds in French but the red light was still flashing on the headset of the delegate from Hong Kong. He hoped this wasn't going to be a problem.'

'To continue. Son of Star Wars, which we are going to call *Sirius* amongst us, after the brightest star in the whole galaxy, is going to be the biggest and most expensive defence project that the world has ever undertaken. Current estimates are publicly put at 200 billion dollars. However, our own sources inside the US Treasury inform us that it could be double this sum eventually. It is starting to scare the living shit out of the economists on Capitol Hill and certain Congressmen have started to question its value. Senior members of the Administration have been ordered to embark on a world-wide campaign to persuade doubting friends and allies to back the scheme. A big push has been made in the United Kingdom because without the two major ground radar stations there the system is a non starter. Other states have simply been asked to contribute vast sums of money towards the cost.

The Chairman pointed across his right shoulder to emphasise the point he was about to make. 'See the twin towers of SAMA a couple of miles over there in the haze?' That's the Saudi Arabian Monetary Agency. We know for a fact that they've been asked to contribute five billion. Washington has reminded them how vulnerable they were when Iraq fired scud missiles at them in the Gulf War and it seems like they've taken the bait. The Saudis are gonna pay up.'

He paused again. An interpreter seemed to be having trouble with translating 'living shit' into Japanese and the delegate from Kobe was whispering into his chin mounted microphone for confirmation. Eventually he seemed satisfied and the red light stopped flashing. At this juncture all the delegates appeared puzzled and the Chairman recommenced.

'So, what has *Sirius* got to do with us? Everything my friends. Everything. So much money is being pumped into *Sirius* already by the US military that we are already beginning to see the benefits. Joe Public in the US doesn't realise it yet but in the Caribbean and the Gulf of Mexico we are starting to have an almost clear run. It is almost what the British had in the Mediterranean for a hundred years. *Mare Nostrum.*' He grinned to himself, knowing that would really test international linguistics. He was right. All seven lights flashed for almost twenty seconds. US Navy anti drug patrols have been severely curtailed as their vessels have had their sea time reduced to cut costs. Their use of submarines is now almost non existent and their Coast Guard vessels are much, much slower than the new purpose built fast and long range boats that we have had constructed to order in the Odessa shipyards that welcome our business and foreign currency. In short, gentlemen, the US Navy is starting to run out of money to fight us! Our profits are increasing almost daily.'

'We have to make sure that *Sirius* goes ahead. It is the best thing to happen to us for many years. Only one man in the world stands any chance of stopping Sirius. That person is none other than the Chinese President Jiang Zemin. He has warned Washington that if the project goes ahead there will be dire economic consequences for the US and he has backed this up by cancelling a huge Chinese order for Boeing 777 airliners. The two Senators for Washington State where Boeing is based have made urgent representations to Powell. He's starting to have second thoughts. We simply cannot allow this to happen. *Sirius* must go ahead. That Son of a Bitch Zemin has to be stopped.'

The Cantonese translator was in trouble again. 'Son of a bitch' had come across as a Running Dog and had totally confused the man from Hong Kong. 'Running Dog' was an old Maoist epithet. Was somebody making insinuations against him? He was embarrassed and didn't like it. He was losing face and starting to sweat. He was a senior member of the 14K Triad and wasn't used to looking stupid. The Chairman rescued him and acted swiftly to bring the meeting back on track.

'I have therefore asked the delegate from Hong Kong, the Special Administrative Region of China, to assume a crucial role in our planning. Only he can help us all. Will you my friend?'

All eyes turned to him. The Chinaman beamed like a laser. This was his moment. He thumped the table and blurted out rapid Cantonese. It took only a second for all present to hear his positive response in their headphones. The others all clapped their hands in appreciation. The meeting closed. All was well. It had taken only a quarter of an hour for Jiang Zemin to acquire the most powerful people in the world as an enemy.

On the flight back to Hong Kong the man from the 14K started to put his plan together. He already knew which person in the world to approach for this special assignment but the problem was how best to do it. To all intents and purposes he was all but unapproachable. There again, maybe not. Suddenly he had an inspiration! That golden horse in the Al Faisaliah Centre had given him an idea. Back at his apartment in Kowloon, after sleeping off the jetlag, he made a few phone calls. It was time to call in a favour or two.

9

John Ross had taken the call on his cellphone. Very few people had the number – only his secretary and closest associates. It had been another long day in the competitive world of international reinsurance and most of his business partners around the Pacific Rim were a few hours ahead and already away from their desks. He was just about to leave his Hollywood Road office and head downtown for 'Happy Hours' drinks in the Chinery Bar at the Mandarin Hotel when the call came in. It was Kelvin Kwan.

'John, hello. We need to meet quite urgently, certain people need our help. You still have those connections in Dubai don't you? Good. Let's say, half an hour then. The Hot Lips Bar on Kowloon Side at six thirty? Good . Thanks then. See you shortly.'

John Ross hailed a cab right outside the office. He was lucky considering it was rush hour. Fifteen minutes later he was at the Star Ferry terminal. He paid off the cab and walked towards the newspaper stall. He bought a copy of the evening edition of the China Mail and joined the snake of humanity that formed an orderly queue for the First Class section. He put his one dollar coin into the brass indentation of the shroff's collection booth and pushed his right knee against the metal turnstile to move forward. Ouch! The cashier had not yet released the lever and he bruised his knee. He thought they always did that when a Gweilo, a foreign devil. was going through. Just a little reminder that in the post imperial orthodoxy the white man no longer held the upper hand. No matter. He walked slowly up the stairs to the upper terminal which would allow him access to First Class, reading the front page as he did so.

The Hang Seng Index, Hong Kong's equivalent of the Dow Jones, was up over four hundred points on the day. Civil Servants were to get a five percent pay rise. The recent RTW Exhibition – 'ready to wear' – had netted a billion dollars worth of orders. The rents for the new Government Housing Estates at Tung Chung had been announced. The winning ticket for the Government Lottery had not yet been claimed. The estimated cost of the new Revolutionary Plaza office complex was given as over a billion dollars. Every single story was about money! Ross had long since considered that Hong Kong was the world's biggest monument to the Seven Deadly Sins and nothing would change his mind.

The ferry from Kowloon, called Meridian Star, nosed into the berth, its front propeller acting as a reverse thruster, slowing the boat down from ten knots to zero in less than the length of the vessel. The normally bluegreen sea turned into cream as the screw bit into ocean. Ropes affixed fore and aft, the steel gangplank came crashing down and several hundred passengers alighted seemingly all at once. Ross boarded and found a convenient seat four rows in from the embarkation plank. He moved the seat backing back so that it faced the other direction. All Star Ferries were double ended and went backwards and forwards across the harbour all day without actually turning round. A whistle blew, ropes cast off and the engines started.

The eight minute crossing gave Ross time to muse on Kelvin's call. The Hot Lips Bar was not his favourite and simply leant credence to his Seven Deadly Sins theory. Why on earth did he want to meet there? The warm easterly breeze ruffled his hair as he gazed across at the expanse of the harbour and the now disused runway of Kai Tak Airport. What would they do with it? There would be some sort of scam involved that's for sure.

Ten minutes later Ross was walking down Ashley Road towards the intended venue. Dusk had fallen quickly during the harbour crossing and behind him the mountains of Hong Kong Island twinkled like giant Christmas trees as the lights of a hundred thousand offices and apartments were switched on. He made his way into the Bar as a tarty looking Chinese woman in her early thirties bade him 'Good evening' and smiled the thousand dollar smile. No thanks mate! Ross had a luscious Irish secretary to entertain him and she came as part of the compensation package. He didn't need to pay.

Kelvin spotted him from a distant table and waved him over.

'Hi, John, this is my associate Ronnie Yip.' They shook hands perfunctorily without any warmth. Ross thought that if that was his real name then his cock was a lighthouse. He was right.

Kelvin continued. Ronnie's in exports mostly to the Middle East. He's just got back from a trip to Riyadh, Saudi Arabia. He's in construction equipment mostly. Power tools and the like.' Another tale. Another lighthouse.

'John, I've told Ronnie that we will do all we can to help him with his problem. You'll have to excuse me but the wife and I have a dinner engagement tonight – a fund raising dinner for the Community Chest at the Mandarin. I hate them but you know what Alice is like. All the dressing up and chit chat. She loves it. I'll have to leave you two. Put all your drinks on my tab OK? John and Kelvin shook hands and in seconds he was alone with Yip. This was not the first time Kelvin had put him on the spot and it probably wouldn't be the last.

Ronnie Yip's English was not good. Rudimentary at best. His parents had come into Hong Kong in the Sixties to man the explosion in the textile workforce and their first home had been a twelve foot square cubicle in Block D of the Wong Tai Sin Resettlement Estate only a short distance from the edge of the airport runway. He had attended a charity sponsored school which functioned in three separate sessions. He attended the morning sessions which had given him ample scope to extend into other non curricular activities in the afternoons and evenings. By the time he was fifteen Yip was the bagmaster for a number of gangs that organised protection rackets against shopkeepers. That was just the beginning. At eighteen he became the youngest member of the notorious 14 K Triad Society and at twenty one their number two in northeast Kowloon. That province was the richest as it took in the walled Kowloon City into which the police did not venture. Unofficially its sovereignty was outwith the lease and it traditionally still belonged to China. In reality it belonged to the 14K. Most of Hong Kong's narcotics trade was conducted in the walled city. By the time he was twenty five, Yip was a millionaire living in style in a three thousand square feet apartment at Kings Park, Kowloon. He rewarded those who had been the kindest and most loyal to him. His parents and his school. But he never ever looked back.

'Mr Ross. Kelvin tells me that you have horse racing connections with the Arab peoples – Saudi Yan. Yes?' The conversation continued along equine lines for a little while.

'I need a special person to be recruited for a special job. Another beer, Pang Yau?'

In his own sweet way Yip was the Chinese contemporary of Jamil ibn Salim. By the time the two men had finished three beers the fate of Jiang Zemin had effectively been sealed. There was a lot of work to do, by himself and Ross, and the planning would have to be meticulous. Ross left the meeting alone. An hour later Yip left with the girl at the door who was by now wearing a two thousand dollar smile. Yip was nothing if not generous.

Ross walked back to the Star Ferry terminal deep in thought. Mmm. Yes I think I know the way forward on this one, he mused to himself. He would need Imogen's help but didn't he always. For lots of things. Tomorrow he would put in a call to Dubai. Leaving the ferry on Hong Kong side he called Imogen on his cellphone and arranged for them to meet for supper an hour later. He would take her to her favourite Indian restaurant, Gunga Din's, and put an idea to her. He thought it would appeal to her and give her a few days break outside of Hong Kong at the same time.

10

London, England

The Royal Overseas League is unique in the whole of London. Quaintly set in a beautifully tranquil corner of the city overlooking Green Park and beyond to Buckingham Palace, it is the very last bastion of Empire.

The Patron is, of course, the Queen and one is reminded of this fact as soon as one enters the lobby. 'Members will take note that Her Majesty will take tea at the Club on Thursday and all Members will wear jackets and ties etc. etc. announces a Notice from the Secretary. By order!'

First time visitors can be excused for thinking that they have been transported back a hundred years in time as they observe panelled walls sporting tiger's heads, photographs of Maharajahs, Nawabs, District Commissioners and former Viceroys of the Indian sub continent. Even the names of the banqueting rooms took you back in time to another more glorious age. The Hall of India. The Hall of Pakistan.

The First Sea Lord found the League to be a most convenient venue for quiet lunches and meetings where he did not want the whole world to be present. He was not personally a member as such but the "Hon. Sec." was a retired R.N. Commander now in his early sixties who had found himself a cosy sinecure. It was a simple matter to be given the nod by the commissionaire after a discreet word from the Commander.

Today he had some special guests and after a few pre-lunch gins in the bar overlooking the colourful gardens and the Royal Park he ushered his party downstairs to the dining room. As they walked down the wide sweeping staircase the three first time visitors, particularly the American, were impressed by the hand carved wall plaques that adorned the walls as they made their way to lunch.

Every former Dependency, Colony and Dominion was represented. Many of the names had been forgotten by most young people. Basutoland. Nyasaland. Burma. India. Pakistan. Malta G.C. Gibraltar. Jamaica. Zanzibar. The Falkland Islands. Malaya. Ceylon. The names seemed to go on forever and they were still only half way down the stairs.

Adjacent to the last step, was the last wall plaque. By the look of the highly polished, hand rubbed hardwood it was the most recent to be added to this litany of Empirical History. With its Union Flag, Chinese Dragon and Chinese sailing junk embossed on solid rosewood the numbers 1-9-9-7 were inlaid with Mother of Pearl.

It was indeed the Pearl of the Orient. The Crown's richest jewel.

It was Hong Kong!

The Members' dining room was now almost deserted. Only one party remained, sipping gently on the last of the post-lunch coffees. The First Sea Lord directed his party towards a reserved table where they sat and removed the silver rings from the white linen napkins.

The Head waiter, an Australian on an exchange visit to London from the Club's Sydney equivalent, brought them menus and they ordered without further ado. Two lamb, three beef. The massive joints looked absolutely succulent on the solid silver carveries that another waiter wheeled to their table. The Last Governor ordered the wine – two bottles of Bordeaux. He figured, correctly, that the other four didn't know a good wine from a glass of beer.

The Australian gave them his compliments and excused himself. He didn't want to dilly dally any longer. England were playing the Aussies at Lords and he had already missed the first session.

As an ex-colonial the Last Governor of Hong Kong was not an infrequent visitor to the League. but he was meeting the other four for the first time. Sat around the table were Peter Fitzgerald, Head of the NSA, Admiral Sir George Lister, the First Sea Lord, and two naval Commanders-Richard Ribchester and Graham Sefton.

The meal almost over, Graham Sefton lit a cigarette and inhaled deeply. He looked worried and perplexed. Ribchester was similarly glazed. The First Sea Lord grinned and refilled his glass, yet again, with twenty year old port. Portugal hadn't been England's oldest ally for nothing, he thought.

The Last Governor scraped the last of the brie from his plate and on to the last cream cracker.

Fitzgerald looked puzzled. 'Do you mean to tell me that this entire matter was decided upon several years ago in Hong Kong?'

'Absolutely. The only problem is that the two main decision makers who originally sanctioned the plan are no longer in power. John is in the Upper House and powerless and your predecessor, Malcolm MacCullum, is no longer living. However I still think that the Excelsior Agreement should stand.'

Fitzgerald swallowed hard. Mere mention of MacCallum's name had hurt. His sudden and recent death from a cardiac arrest had propelled him into the top job as his successor. They had been friends as well as colleagues and he knew that Malcolm had groomed him for the job.

'The bottom line is that we can't do a lot about the guys in China anyway. There has been positively no contact with them for years but you know what that lot are like. Time means absolutely nothing to them. Nor do changes of Governments. Shit, they don't change administrations like we do. They don't understand the concept of executive decision making now or then. I suppose you could say that they don't have to suffer the weaknesses of democracies!'

'While Governor of Hong Kong I had privileged access to private papers left behind by several predecessors. You would not begin to believe some of the deals that were brokered between Hong Kong and the Regional Commissars in Guandong Province.'

'Like what?' muttered Fitzgerald. He knew of course that there had been contact with the Guys from Guandong during the Hainan Crisis but decided to say nothing. MacCullum had updated Geister's files and shown them to him and him alone.

'Well take the situation in June 1967 for a start. The Red Guards were marching all over China waving their little red books. Our security forces were obscenely stretched in case of an invasion. The carrier HMS Hermes, with her nuclear capability, came up from Singapore and stood off but had to return for a long overdue refit in UK. The Fleet Air Arm was already in terminal decline.'

'The then Governor, Sir David Trench, requested another 2,000 troops in case of need. Guess what? Request denied. Aden was about to be evacuated meaning no troops were available until Christmas at the earliest. D'ya know what Trench did?

'Nope . But I think you're about to tell me.'

'Well at the time Hong Kong was suffering from its worst drought since records began. All the reservoirs were practically empty. Water was rationed like you would not

66

believe. The 'Guy on the Shau Kei Wan Tram' only got running water for four hours every four days. With riots in the streets and bombs everywhere life was hell. There was a long standing contract with the Chinese to buy millions of gallons of water, to be pumped through on August 1st.'

'So, you've lost me.'

'Well what Trench did was to arrange, unofficially of course, for twice as much water to be bought at twice the price, the second tranche following five months later on January 1st – all to be paid for in gold. He knew damned well that the second payment would only ever get into the hands of the Commissars themselves and that there would be no chance of an invasion before pay day.'

'Did London know about this?'

'Probably not. But it demonstrates that deals can be done under cover. The water was delivered, the gold was paid over to a fishing junk in the Pearl Estuary and everyone was happy.

According to Trench's Papers, the only one contact ever made was with one guy who came over on the train from the mainland. In those days the Kowloon Canton Railway came right down to the Star Ferry in Kowloon although the trains themselves stopped at the border at a place called Lowu and passengers had to walk off the communist train and then board a separate Hong Kong train. Only goods trains were allowed straight through mostly carrying pigs. Millions of them. I wouldn't be at all surprised if the guy in question came across on a freight train. A sweet and sour pork special! Somebody at a newspaper called the *Ta Kung Pau* set up the meeting. That's what I mean about Excelsior. The whole bloody thing was agreed years ago but the chances are it still stands as far as the Chinese guys are concerned. We can't stop now.'

At 3.00pm they wrapped up the meeting.

The First Sea Lord's official car took him to the MOD in Whitehall via the Naval Club in Mayfair first where he drank even more port.

The Last Governor was also heading for Lords cricket ground and invited Fitzgerald to join him. He politely declined. Only Limeys could name a sport after an insect! Instead he took a taxi to the US Embassy. He had some thinking to do and some calls to make. Jesus, now he understood the expression that there's no such thing as a free lunch!

Sefton and Ribchester walked independently to Green Park Underground and took separate tubes to Paddington and Kings Cross respectively. Sefton arrived at Plymouth later that evening and Ribchester at Barrow in Furness the following morning, overnighting at his mother's house in York en route. He did not sleep well.

Artful was fitting out with Tomahawk at Devonport. Ambush was about to embark on builder's trials in the Irish Sea in two days time.

11

Palm Beach Hotel
Larnaca, Cyprus

It was early May and Jamil ibn Salim's personal secretary had taken a call from a company in Hong Kong a week earlier. He had been out of the office at the time but intrigue alone made him return the call. He had never done business in the Orient. Jamil was totally magnetised by the beautiful female voice five thousand miles away. His command of English was good enough for him to detect a trace of an Irish accent. He had done business in Ireland, *unofficially*, before. Not even the C.I.A. knew about that.

Imogen Ireland had been impeccably briefed by her boss, John McMillan Ross. and introduced herself as Mr Ross's personal secretary. She told him that his name had been mentioned to Mr Ross by Sheikh Al Mohammed bin Turki when he was last on a horse buying trip to Dubai earlier in the year. Jamil's senses quickened at the mere mention of the Sheikh's name. He regarded him as one of his closest confidants although they seldom met in person. Mohammed bin Turki had been a guest on his birthday cruise. He had promised to repay his hospitality 'a thousand times over.' Was this it? It must be.

Imogen turned on the charm to Jamil and he found himself being seduced by her sultry, sensuous voice.

Mr Ross, she explained, had a job for him to do in eight weeks time in Hong Kong. The price was fifty million U.S. Confidentiality would be guaranteed. Was he interested? Asking Jamil if he would like to make fifty million was like asking a cat if it liked cream. A meeting was set up in Cyprus for a week later between Jamil and John Ross to discuss the details. Ross had no intention of going. He would leave Jamil to the gorgeous Imogen.

The large privately chartered motor yacht had taken only ten hours to reach Larnaca from Beirut. The weather had been good and the sea quite calm. Lebanese businessmen were a common sight in Larnaca. It had been widely assumed that a more stabilised Beirut would have once again assumed the role of banker to the Arab World but it didn't happen. Lots of Arab money had gone to Cyprus. After passing through the rudimentary immigration office at the harbour a private car took Jamil out onto the road to the resort of Ayia Nappa. A few miles out of town stood the Palm Beach Hotel which was thronged with hundreds of early summer tourists, mostly English and German. It had been a good choice of venue. He would not be easily recognised by foreign tourists. In any event he easily passed for a Greek or Italian with his olive skin, dark hair and laid back Mediterranean demeanour. The Armani jacket and Gucci loafers accentuated the Latin image. He had even shaved off his moustache to remove the final hint of Arabism.

The car pulled up at the main door of the hotel and Jamil alighted. He told the driver to return for him in three hours. That should be enough time.

Jamil walked into the white marble lobby which was teeming with sunburnt tourists. Blond girls were everywhere. From Dorking to Dusseldorf and Harlow to Hamburg, their two weeks would be remembered for two things. Sunshine and sex. Back in Beirut Jamil could have his pick of dark skinned, dark haired women. But he had never slept with a blonde European. He started to wish he had booked into the hotel instead of staying on the boat. He was a little early for the meeting and decided to get a beer in the bar just off the lobby. He ordered an Amstel beer and opened a new pack of his favourite Gauloise cigarettes. This place was heaven – so many blonde girls in one place. His imagination started to run riot. With his money he could buy any woman he wanted. He remembered that movie back in the Nineties called An Indecent Proposal. Everybody had their price. He could offer a hundred thousand dollars to any of these English or German girls for a week of sex. It would take them two or three years to earn that back at their office job in Berlin, Brighton or wherever. He decided to return here for a few days of fun and sex later in the summer when there would be even more blondes on vacation. Finishing his beer he strolled into the lobby and made for the main reception desk. The pretty head receptionist's name badge on the lapel of her smart green jacket announced her name as Helen Nicolides. She was about twenty five and obviously a Greek Cypriot.

To Jamil she was just a peasant with a desk job. He addressed her in very bad Greek in a contemptuous arrogant manner, not even removing a cigarette from the corner of his mouth. She maintained her composure and spoke back to him in English, guessing his understanding of Greek was inadequate. Back in Beirut he would have sworn at her. He was told to take a seat in the lobby – Mr. Ross's secretary would not be long. He queried her statement. He explained that he had an important meeting with Mr Ross, not a sidekick. Helen Nicolides just smiled for at that instant a beautiful blonde girl in her mid thirties tapped Jamil on the shoulder. He swung round, startled.

'Mr. Salim, how do you do. I'm Imogen Ireland from Hong Kong.' They shook hands limply. Jamil was stunned. 'John Ross sends his profuse apologies. Commitments in Asia have prevented him from making this trip. I have full authority to act on his behalf. The Hotel is very busy with tourists isn't it? Can I suggest that we go to my private suite and order room service?'ē Jamil was putty in her hands.

'Yes, of course, thank you.' He followed her across the lobby towards the elevators. This was a whole new experience for him. In his world women always followed the men. They made polite conversation during the short trip to the top floor. He had been mildly irritated when this unknown quantity had asked him to extinguish his cigarette in the sand filled ashtrays prior to entering the elevator but she had asked him so nicely he couldn't refuse.

'Is this your first visit to Larnaca, Mr Salim? I have always found Cyprus to be a most useful stopover en route to business trips in the Middle East. *So* welcoming.' Her lips rounded on the word *so* as if she was kissing the air in front of her face. Imogen Ireland's face was truly beautiful and Salim knew it. She had a full, almost round face but with well defined cheekbones but what struck you first were the eyes. They were a deep, deep blue. Like cobalt. Unusually for an Irish girl she was blonde and as Jamil was six inches taller than her he could clearly see that she was a real blond. No dark roots on this one. He was wondering if her pubic hair matched the lustrous mane on her head when suddenly they were there. Bing! The elevator doors opened automatically.

She stretched forth her hand inviting him to ascend first. He took one step then realised that perhaps he should show some deference to a beautiful lady.

'No, please. After you.' Jamil ibn Salim had never done that ever before in his entire thirty three years. As Imogen walked passed him he caught the unmistakable whiff of his favourite perfume. Private Collection by Estĕe Lauder. It heightened his senses immediately. It was the one scent in the world that could arouse him at twenty paces.

There were only four suites at this level that occupied the entire floor. They were all named after Greek Gods and Goddesses. Imogen's suite was named after Diana, the Goddess of Hunting. She swiped the electronic keycard through the scanner and the lock clicked open. Opening the heavily carved wooden door to reveal a magnificent interior, she entered the suite first and beckoned him to follow. He did so without hesitation.

'My favourite drink, Mr Salim, is an Australian chardonnay called Wolf Blass but it's not easy to obtain here. However some of the local wine is very good, the dry whites particularly. Shall I ask room service to send up a bottle on ice or are you going to give me all that Islamic nonsense and order an orange juice?'

For the first time in her company Jamil grinned broadly. 'I do drink alcohol Miss Ireland and yes the local wine will be fine. Thank you.' She picked up the 'phone and dialled room service.

'Let's deal with the business first, Mr Salim, while we wait for the wine. As I mentioned to you I have full authorisation from my Directors to act on their behalf. Quite simply the position is this.'

Imogen Ireland explained the deal in its simplistic terms. 'A particular aeroplane has to be shot down in flight at a particular time. There must be absolutely no chance whatsoever of survivors. The principle passenger on the plane will be the Chinese Head of State, Jiang Zemin. He must die on that plane. Period. As agreed the price is fifty million dollars. Ten up front payable to your company to preserve the business façade and the next forty payable to the Palestine Red Crescent.'

Jamil smiled inwardly and shuffled on his chair. This was beyond his wildest expectations. To a man as rich as Jamil the fifty million meant nothing. It was peanuts. The forty million to the charity that brought him into this world would be a godsend to them. He never forgot the debt of gratitude he owed the Red Crescent and annually he made large donations from both his personal and company assets. But the real reason for his happiness stemmed from his knowledge that his Arab brothers, in Saudi Arabia especially, were worried sick about the international price of oil being controlled one day from outside the world of Islam. He had been told after the last meeting of IOPS – the Islamic Oil Producing States- that the one country in the world who might outsmart their long term objectives was the People's Republic of China. What an opportunity this presented! With Zemin dead, China could dissolve into chaos. Inshallah!

Geopolitical considerations apart, Jamil had a personal reason for a chance to get his own back against the Chinese. Three years earlier he had been at a clandestine meeting in Peshawar, in northern Pakistan, at the request of several trusted associates. It had been an arduous journey just to get there via Lahore and Islamabad and he had expected a job of some kind to be on the table. Instead he had been threatened by some third rate Chinese diplomats from the Chinese embassy in Islamabad. They badly needed his expertise for a special project which they said must take priority over anything else he had in mind. The job was to take place inside Sinkiang Province within two months and if he declined to take it then his supply of sophisticated hand held anti-aircraft missiles would cease. A furious Jamil had overturned the table around which the parties sat. Nobody, but nobody dictated their terms to him like that. Two days later back in his Beirut office he cancelled his company's contract with Szechwan Aviation which had been China's 'legitimate' business front in the Middle East for many years. He had heard later that pressure for the deal had come from the top, that is Zemin. Revenge would be doubly sweet.

Imogen opened a brown leather document wallet and removed a plain white envelope. Lifting the unsealed flap she slid out a thin pink document that resembled a travellers cheque and held it up for him to see. It was a cashier's cheque drawn on the Edinburgh Office of the HSBC Bank in the sum of ten million dollars. The payee was his Beirut company A.A.A., Al-Aktar Aviation.

'This is the deposit, Mr Salim,' as her pink tongue curled out between her glossed lips to moisten the gum on the envelope. For a small envelope it was a huge lick. The infidel bitch was teasing him! Imogen leant forward across the small coffee table that separated them by only six feet and placed the envelope gently on his lap. Only a blind man would have failed to see the stirring in the crotch of his cream linen slacks.

As we agreed previously the remaining forty will be paid with a similar cheque after the job is done and then we....' She was interrupted by the ring of the door bell as the room service waiter entered. He deftly placed the ice bucket with the wine into the centre of the small table, removed a corkscrew from his jacket pocket, opened the bottle and offered her the cork. She laughed out loud, much to the embarrassment of the waiter who left as quickly as he had arrived.

'Why did you laugh at the waiter?' asked Jamil who by now was detecting that this blonde was definitely going to be a handful if he was to succeed in seducing her.

'I wasn't actually laughing at him, Mr Salim. It had just suddenly occurred to me that he might think I was a prostitute about to entertain a rich Arab client. Now we couldn't possibly have that could we? She took another bigger brown envelope from the wallet and passed it straight to him.

'These are your instructions for the job. I want you to read them now and commit the essential details to memory. The rendezvous co-ordinates in particular. It will take you at least ten minutes to read the dossier. In the meantime I need to take a shower.' She took a glass of wine with her and disappeared into the bedroom in a haze of perfume. Jamil read the file.

She had teased him to distraction. When she emerged twenty minutes later she wore only an almost see-through peach coloured housecoat, her hair still damp from the shower. He pretended to be still reading the dossier but his eyes lifted and gazed towards the vee of her long legs as she walked slowly towards him. He couldn't see any pubic hair through the thin material. She must be a real blonde, he thought to himself. At that precise moment in his life Jamil would have paid ten per cent of that deposit to screw her.

Imogen curled up on the sofa with her replenished glass of wine, the housecoat tantalisingly covering her torso as she drew her knees up towards her midriff. Jamil craned forwards as much as he could dare but still his imagination would have to outweigh the actual. Jamil tossed the dossier onto the table. 'Easy, money. But how much will you cost me tonight, Miss Ireland?'

'I'm not available tonight, Jamil' she said, using his first name for the first time. 'But listen. After the operation why don't we meet up in Singapore and you know, take things from there. I am sure I would find your company fascinating. The stories you have to tell must be legendary. I promise you I'm a good listener, particularly when I don't have work to worry about and I can really *relax*.' The stress on the last syllable left Jamil in no doubt. This lady was up for it.

'If you call my Hong Kong office number, the same one as before, I can fly down for a few days break. But I must warn you, Jamil, with the right man I am *absolutely* insatiable.'

'How much?'

'I'm not a whore, Jamil. If you do the job properly, nothing. If you botch it, I want the ten million back. Do we have a deal? His visible erection told her she had a deal.

'Jamil raised his glass. 'Cheers. We have deal!'

Imogen raised hers. *'Daiymi.* May it always be as nice.' My God, this bitch even knew some colloquial Arabic. As soon as Jamil left the suite she called Ross in Hong Kong. All was well.

On the short voyage back to Beirut Jamil ibn Salim could think of nothing else but what he was going to do with his blonde Irish lady in Singapore. Inshallah! God willing!

The next morning from the office of Al-Aktar Aviation he started to put together the necessary plans to complete the business in the Far East. Via trusted associates in Limassol, Cyprus he chartered the 6,000 ton freighter 'Aphrodite' on a 'bareboat' charter basis without crew, for sixty days from June 1st. Nothing would be left to chance. A new hand picked crew would be hired from Jeddah, Saudi Arabia for the entire sixty day mission. They would be very well paid and would keep details to themselves. Secrecy was essential. His normal business affairs frequently took him to Jeddah in any event and his movements would not betray his intentions.

He decided not to contact his friend Sheikh Mohammed bin Turki. Instead he would thank him personally for the introduction when next they met – probably at the Dubai Gold Cup. Yes, he would wait. By then he would also be able to boast of another conquest, inshallah!

Planning every detail with immaculate precision, his company press officer circulated a rumour that he had developed an illness and that he was planning to spend two months at a private Swiss clinic. He was looking forward immensely to the task ahead, and earning the next forty million dollars for the Red Crescent. Most of all he was looking forward to Singapore and bedding his first blonde. Furthermore, if the operation was a success she would not cost him a cent. Not yet anyway.

12

Baltimore, Maryland

Dawn was just breaking over the Atlantic as the still new looking RAF C17 Globemaster of 99 Squadron ZZ171 dipped unnoticed into BWI, Baltimore Washington International Airport, and taxied to a standstill on a deserted apron. The trans-Atlantic flight from RAF Brize Norton in Oxfordshire was bang on time.

Within an hour three of its male occupants were 25 miles away eating an early breakfast of eggs Benedict in the mess at Fort Meade, Head Quarters of the NSA, the National Security Agency. The only Government Department that was not financially accountable to Congress. It had no official budget. It was allowed to spend what it wanted to. And it did.

Peter Fitzgerald was Head of the NSA. At 53 he had a wealth of experience in naval matters and was one of the very few ex-military personnel to make a successful transition to a civilian job. Assigned to Norfolk, Virginia throughout the Eighties, he bore none of the Vietnam scars and conscience that had affected the careers of so many good men in the Pacific Fleet.

After attachment to CINCNAVEUR in Naples for three years he was promoted to Admiral and 'retired' into a desk job in Maryland. Very few people knew the exact role of his new job. His rank was quietly dropped and adopting the title of plain 'Mister' he slipped into comparative obscurity. Whilst the Freedom of Information Act had allowed Directors to open doors, even if it was just a crack, in a departure from tradition his military title was not used as a matter of standard practice.

Fitzgerald felt comfortable in the company of three other sailors and opened up a little. He expanded his personal viewpoint that the signing, in 1946, of the Signals Intelligence Treaty between the UK and the USA had been a wonderful accord. Pre-dating even NATO, the agreement more usually referred to simply as the acronym *UKUSA,* was the very basis of the friendship between the two English speaking countries who had done so much to bring freedom to so many. So had other English speaking countries and accordingly Canada, Australia and New Zealand had all subsequently become full members of *UKUSA..* It not only covered the globe but penetrated into deep space. In its field of signals monitoring it had no competitors that could come even close. The Treaty allowed all member countries to share the vast amount of information and signals intelligence – SIGINT- as if it were all in a communal pot. Billions had been spent on the most sophisticated computer system in the world called PLATFORM to make it all work. The equally impressive software system that allowed ladles to be dipped by members into this pot was called ECHELON. Nobody seemed to know why. The responsibility on the shoulders of Fitzgerald as Director of the NSA, America's representative within *UKUSA,* was truly awesome.

The First Sea Lord drained the last of the fresh coffee from his cup. 'You know, Peter, if this comes off then we are either heroes or in deep shit. Possibly both. Neither the President nor the Prime Minister are privy to all this. You do know that don't you? We can tell them afterwards.'

'I know you're right deep down. The creation of the Pearl Delta Republic is a huge prize. It will stabilise the whole Region, generate peace and prosperity for generations and hopefully will go a long way to solving the problem of Taiwan. It will weaken Beijing for ever.

'Peter, as I see it it's too late to go back now. I think we should stick to the Excelsior Agreement. You don't have to tell the President everything yet you know. Besides if at all goes pear shaped we can call it all off and explain away the whole thing as an exercise of some kind can't we?'

'Yeah, you're right of course George. OK let's put the final details together now. Call in your two colleagues and let's crack on.'

Commanders Graham Sefton and Richard Ribchester entered the room and shook hands warmly with Fitzgerald. All four had met before in London. Lunch with his former Excellency, 'The Last Governor', at the Royal Overseas League had proved to be a momentous day for all of them.

The details of their 'compensation packages' put together, two days later they flew home.

Peter was very generous with the NSA's money. He could afford to be. Officially it had no budget and any request for funding was never refused. Since the Cuban Missile Crisis in 1962 America had been paranoid as a nation about security. In the minds of Joe Public the FBI and the CIA looked after America but in reality in a world of deep space satellites and computers that performed their functions in billions of a hundredth of a second, it was the NSA that was America's first line of defence. The taxpayer didn't know it but the NSA together with its overseas bureaus cost more than the FBI and the CIA combined.

'George, one question, is this scheme crazy? Or is it gonna work? Are we doing the right thing?'

'Peter, that's three questions. The answers are no, yes, yes in that order. McCandless is the best and we can count one hundred percent on the other two. On that you have my personal guarantee.'

'That's good enough for me.'

13

It was June 1st and HMS Astute had been at sea for a week, working up and getting some of her new crew used to the demanding routine of a nuclear submarine. McCandless had had command of the boat since acceptance by the Navy. It was his baby and he loved it. If necessary he would spoon feed it.

The boat was two years old but still smelt new – like a new car with cellophane wrappers still around the seats. She had been delivered by her builders on time and to budget. Seven thousand five hundred tons and ninety seven metres of magic. The ultimate submariner's toy and a hundred years and a million light years away from the first E Class boats that first served on the China Station before the First World War. How times had changed.

McCandless was in the know about everything. Operation Opium. The Excelsior Accord. And the more secret arrangements pertaining to Jamil ibn Salim. After leaving British waters Astute sped across the Bay of Biscay and headed for Gibraltar where she would pick up some fresh stores and the crew would get a break for a couple of days. It would be their last recreation for at least six weeks, possibly longer.

At dawn on the 4th of June Astute slipped her moorings on the North Mole and glided silently out into the Straits.

With the Rock five miles behind her she dived to four hundred feet and increased speed to her maximum forty one knots. The brand new Rolls Royce PWR2 reactor, specially designed for this new class of boat, did not miss a beat. She was at least five knots faster than the boats of the previous class but you didn't read that in Jane's Fighting Ships. It simply said – 'maximum speed in excess of 30 knots.' Exactly. Next stop was Port Said and the entrance to the Suez Canal. She travelled alone.

A thousand miles behind her the rest of the units comprising Exercise Ocean Wave were steaming at a more leisurely twenty knots. These were the carrier Ark Royal, on probably her last global deployment, the tanker Wave Knight, supply ships Fort George and Fort Austin, the frigates Kent, Portland and Cornwall, the destroyers Edinburgh and Glasgow and as had now become the custom, a French warship, the frigate Econit. Officially part of the Exercise, Ambush and Artful were "accompanying" the fleet. In fact they were ahead of it and were only a day's sailing behind Astute. This was Britannia's annual fling. *Pax Britannica novus.*

In the afternoon of June 10th McCandless ordered Astute to periscope depth. In reality the 'scope' was an electronic mast and highly classified. They were in the Red Sea heading south south east and approximately half way between The Canal and the exit to the Gulf of Socotra and the Arabian Sea. The transit of the Canal had passed routinely save for a short delay in the Great Bitter Lake while a tug had towed a clapped out Liberian tanker away from the convoy that took ten hours to emerge at the Gulf of Suez. That was now six hundred miles behind them. Sonar had reported a surface contact three miles ahead.

'Up scope! Reduce speed to sixteen knots.'

The brilliance of the reflected sunlight took McCandless by surprise but in seconds his eyes adjusted. He saw what he wanted to see. Ahead of them was the Cyprus registered vessel Aphrodite. Excellent. Everything was going to plan. 'Down scope.' The next time McCandless saw the Aphrodite they would both be in the South China Sea.

Twenty days is a long time at sea in a surface vessel. In a submarine it is numbingly soporific. Astute would normally have a crew of over a hundred but for this mission she and her sister boats had a reduced crew of sixty six. This ensured a degree of comfort and space that would not normally be achievable. It would also reduce the casualty figures in the event of a loss of the boat. The crews weren't told that. The reduction in crew numbers was largely effected by the removal of the older members and most of those with wives and families. Should the question ever be asked as to why the boats were lean manned in the extreme, then the bog standard reply was this was simply an 'upgraded proving cruise' just a step up from builder's trials. It was of course a lie.

Submariners have different ways of killing time on voyages such as this. Some read books. Others write books, or at least keep diaries. In years to come any such diaries of this voyage would be dynamite in the wrong hands. Or even the right hands. Day after day all that changed was the boat's position on the chart. Inexorably, relentlessly, Astute sped eastward for the most part avoiding the shipping lanes that criss-crossed an increasingly busy commercial world.

As they headed almost due east across the Indian Ocean they passed by the former British air base on the Island of Gan. The island itself lay half a degree south of the Equator and as they deliberately 'crossed the line' those crew who had not ventured south of zero degrees before were given the traditional King Neptune ceremony. It helped to pass the time. From time to time faxes were received via satellite links bringing family news for the crew. McCandless never ceased to be amazed at the sheer variety of the family messages they received. Football results. Cricket scores. Children's drawings. Exam results. News of Grandad's efforts in the local leek growing competition. Imprints of toddler's feet covered in dye to show how much he or she had grown since Daddy had been away. You name it. All incoming family news was censored. No bad news that could upset a member of the crew was allowed. If the postman had made a wife pregnant then he wouldn't know until he got back to base.

As a bachelor McCandless had neither the worry nor the delight of family news. Some colleagues described him as a 'loner' but that was unfair. All submarine commanders are loners in that the responsibility for boat and crew bears heavily on their shoulders alone. The responsibility he bore quite easily. However from time to time he envied the majority of his crew who knew that at the voyage's end a wife and family would be waiting at the quayside.

Astute slowed down. She had made good time and was on schedule. A brief stop at Sembawang Dockyard in Singapore was required to collect documents but only a handful of the crew would disembark and then for only an hour or two at the most. On the last night in the Malacca Strait McCandless ordered the boat to surface and two at a time the crew were allowed up to the conning tower for some fresh air. Unfortunately an electrical storm brought heavy rain which made conditions unpleasant and the idea was abandoned after only half the crew had been up. At four in the morning on the 28th of June they were alongside at Sembawang. By first light they were once again at sea heading '044' into the South China Sea at full speed.

For McCandless it was almost like going home.

14

The Great Hall of the People
Beijing, China

According to the 1954 Constitution, Government in the People's Republic of China is through the National People's Congress indirectly elected every four years in proportion to population. The Central Committee can interpret laws passed by the Congress, issue its own decrees and even nominate the State Council. In practice, however, the inner *Standing Committee* does what the hell it wants.

The dining room had been reserved for the working lunch of the Committee. It had been planned for weeks. It was an imposing room but still somehow retained the almost Maoish plainness of the proletariat. The round heavily carved rosewood table was set for only four people. On the pale pastel yellow walls were countless portraits of Chinese patriots, some famous, some infamous and many unknown to the outside world. Periodic discolouration on the walls announced where some had been removed as their views and position had changed with China's history. Gone were the Gang of Four including Madame Mao and Liu Shao-chi. Lin Pao, Mao's self appointed successor was still there. So was Chou En Lai, Sun Yat Sen. and Deng Xiao Ping. The biggest portrait of all was, of course, Mao Tse Tung himself. It dominated one entire wall, the mole on his cheek as distinctive as Gorbachev's port wine stain. Not that Mao would have approved of any analogy or comparison. He had esponged any revisionist or bourgeois leanings that he thought epitomised the Soviets. Mao predicted that the world's countryside, that is the developing nations, would overcome the world's cities, that is Western Europe and the U.S., and that the triumph of world communism was inevitable.

Lunch was served at 1 o'clock precisely, the striking of the huge metal gong reminding Zemin of the start of so many western movies he had seen on videos. The pork, noodles and vegetables were served and eaten in almost total silence. Lunch was not the primary object of the meeting. It was simply a lubricant.

The four Members of the Inner Standing Committee were almost at the end of lunch. It was hot. Baking hot. Temperatures in the high thirties Celsius had come early to the Capital City this year. Perhaps it was an omen. The archaic, floor standing electric fan rotated slowly through its one hundred and fifty degree arc giving each diner a few seconds relief from their suffering until it traversed along to the next perspiring octogenarian. This was democracy Chinese style. With noodles.

Only the four members present were privy to the Operation despite the fact it had been planned for years. Today was make or break. Should they do it or not? They had to decide now. For Operation Long Swim, it was now or never.

President Zemin gave his final analysis to the other three.

'Look. There may never be another opportunity. We all know that despite the fragile peace in the Middle East the price of oil is still decided by a bunch of Arab Sheikhs. It has been ever thus since Yamani was President of OPEC in the early Seventies. This is our big chance. Our geologists have told us that the Spratly Islands in the southern South China Sea have huge potential for oil. Early findings are that we could treble our output when combined with our own mainland fields in Sinkiang,Kansu and Chinghai and the other offshore fields. With our known population in excess of 1.4 billion we need that oil just as much as the Japanese needed raw materials in 1941. That's why they attacked the Americans at Pearl Harbour. It's not as if we are attacking any major power. China has laid claim to the Spratly Islands for over twenty five years. OK, so have other countries like the Philippines and Vietnam. The fact is the islands lie on *our* continental shelf. It's not called the South *China* Sea for nothing, Comrades.'

'The timing could not be better. Even if the Americans wanted to stop us, which I doubt, the fact is that the major units of their Seventh Fleet are at Hawaii for the Independence Day celebrations. You know how pathetically sentimental they are. With the Middle East always unstable their Fifth and Sixth Fleets are always at full stretch, particularly since the Suez Canal became 'off limits' to them after the Arab terrorist attack on one of their destroyers in 2000. That was indeed a good investment, Comrade Chiang.' Zemin nodded towards the Defence Minister. Chiang was still slurping loudly on the last of his lunch and did not even look up.

'We have to move in now. Comrade Chiang, what is the military situation? Is it a clear position?'

Defence Minister Chiang cleared his throat of the last of the plum pancake that he should not really have eaten. At eighty one he was the youngest of the Committee. In fact he was the youngest member of the entire Praesidium.

'The Southern Red Fleet is ready to sail from Swatow tonight. Six transports with two thousand troops and supplies escorted by six frigates and destroyers and two Kilo Class submarines deployed ahead. The latest information is that the South China Sea is almost clear of foreign warships. As you all know we declined to give diplomatic clearance to the British this year for their naval vessels to visit Hong Kong during their annual exercises. Soon they will know why. There is of course the American destroyer en route to Vietnam but with good joss it will soon be disabled or perhaps even sunk after it has passed through the minefield our "fishing boats" have laid in its path. The American ship might even think they have hit one of their own mines left over from the Seventies. Comrades, everything is ready. We just have to agree right now between us. The Fleet will sail at dusk subject to our orders. I have nothing else to add.' He chewed some more pancake.

Zemin glanced across the table towards the other two members of the Committee. They both nodded in mute acquiescence. In his book silence was tantamount to tacit agreement.

'Then, Comrades' raising his cup of jasmine tea, 'I give you a toast. Operation Long Swim.' They all raised their cups and smiled. 'Let the orders be given to sail tonight.'

The code-name Long Swim had been Zemin's own idea. It mirrored Mao Tse Tung's well publicised two mile swim in the Yangtze River in the Sixties and it recalled memories of the great Long March against Chiang Kai Shek's Nationalists who had been forced to flee to Taiwan. Yes, he was a happy man. Within a few days, a week at the most, China would have established control over territory that was rightfully hers. On Saturday, in Hong Kong, on the Anniversary of the Handover from the British, he would announce to the whole world what had happened. In the Sixties Mao had said that '*Power grows out of the barrel of a gun*' and that maxim would be as true today as it was then.

His announcement would also coincide with the Anniversary of Mao's magnificent Hundred Flowers speech in 1957. He swaggered slightly as he looked across the room to the *Portraits of the Patriots* and in his mind's eye he could foresee a glorious picture of himself a hundred years hence. In time people might even mention his own name with that same reverence and humility reserved for the Great Man himself.

Zemin drank the last of his tea too quickly and he spluttered and coughed sharply. He had only just got over a heavy summer cold and the last of the catarrh still troubled him. He rattled his throat to clear it and nodded towards the nearest spittoon on the polished parquet flooring. It was no ordinary spittoon. It was priceless and demonstrative of the riches that successive Politburos had lavished on themselves. The large porcelain bowl was a two hundred year old ceramic replica of the *Kiulung* – the Nine Dragons Wall in Peiping. To Chinese it was almost as sacred to them as the Wailing Wall is to Judaism. The Wall had been built in the Liao era in about the year 1000 A.D. by a member of the Manchu Dynasty from Jehol who had seized the throne. The wall was constructed of tiles in five bright colours depicting nine dragons leaping energetically over waves to catch a bouncing ball, the sun, signifying the reins of power. The brilliant glazed colours of the porcelain reflected the sunlight beaming through the open windows. The presence of *this* bowl at *this* meeting could not have been more apposite. The waves beneath the dragons were the waves of the South China Sea itself and in a few days those waves would have been safely crossed and the glory would be his.

With a loud expulsion of air from his mouth the green satellite commenced its short trajectory towards the porcelain receptacle. His aim was not good. Its orbit was a little too equatorial. The viscous green projectile landed on the side of the spittoon just below the rim and completely covered the orange ball the dragons were playing with. The sun. That great luminary. The reins of power. Zemin turned white and all but fainted.

It was the worst possible feng shui.

Only one other Member of the Committee had seen exactly what had happened. Ninety degrees further round the circular table, on the other side of the spittoon, another octogenarian gripped his chopsticks so tightly until his knuckles were almost as white as Zemin's face. Li Shau Kee, the Minister of the Interior, was at eighty three, a kindly, pious and humble old man. He closed his eyes in silent prayer for what he had just observed.

Even in atheist China there was a God after all.

15

The Black Watch Memorial
Aberfeldy, Scotland

June 30th – Midnight BST

It was still faintly light. At this latitude in the month of June it never really got dark. An unseasonal chilly wind was blowing up the Firth of Tay and it ruffled the ginger hair protruding from beneath the soldier's tartan keppie. At the stroke of midnight the lone piper , Private McPherson, started playing his lament. Major General Alan Archibald Ferguson, Officer Commanding, The Black Watch, snapped to attention and saluted.

When the piper had finished, the Chinese representative from the London office of the Hong Kong Special Administrative Region stepped forward and placed a floral wreath of Jungle Geraniums on the memorial dias. He took two steps backwards, straightened up and nodded his head slowly and distinctly three times. It was his way. An aide, also Chinese, removed a lighter from his jacket pocket and stumbling forwards in the gloom, appeared to kneel down by the wreath and struck up a flame which flickered in the breeze for several seconds.

The accompanying note was written in Chinese characters. Translated it read:

*'To the Black Watch, with thanks
from the people of Hong Kong.
Today we all get even.
Tomorrow is a new beginning.'*

The ecumenical Regimental padre spoke a short prayer. Amen. The Hong Kong representative made a short speech in Cantonese which only he and the aide understood. Two minutes later everybody had gone and all that was left to mark the ceremony was the wreath and an offering of still smouldering joss sticks.

During the drive back to Edinburgh, Ferguson reflected on the short ceremony and he mentally reminded himself of the favour he owed John Ross. They had met four years earlier when he had been battalion commander in Hong Kong. Ross had been a guest at the battalion's Burns supper on January 25th 1997 and they had remained firm friends ever since. After the dreadful events on the night of the Handover Ferguson had confided in Ross who had offered the Regiment his help if ever it were needed. It was. This arrangement was very private. Strictly between them, and them alone, it was known as the Caledonian Conspiracy.

Rumours circulating in various sections of the press had recently speculated that the Government was going to amalgamate the Highland and Lowland Divisions of the Army and that one, maybe two, Scottish battalions would be disbanded. If the Black Watch was to fold after three hundred years service to the Crown then he, Ferguson, would ensure that its most glorious act of war would be effected within the next twenty four hours.

Seven thousand miles to the east dawn was just breaking over the South China Sea. How Ferguson wished he was there himself to witness the events about to unfold.

16

South China Sea
16° North 11° East
June 30th – 0500 Local time

The planesman brought the boat smoothly to the surface at the Captain's command.

The boat glided almost silently to a standstill. All engines and machinery were turned off. Battery powered emergency lighting provided the faint red glow to read instrumentation.

The great metal fish was dead in the water and totally silent. £500 million worth of nuclear submarine, the latest in Britain›s arsenal, was a sitting duck. Fortunately her potential adversaries did not know she was there. Of the sixty six crew members only McCandless knew *why* she was there at exactly that time and position.

Nestling forward in the submarine's weapons compartment were eight Block III Tomahawk missiles, sixteen GEC Marconi Mk.II Spearfish torpedoes and eight sub Harpoon anti-ship missiles. Nuclear weapons apart, no submarine in the world had a more powerful or accurate destructive delivery system.

The sealed orders delivered by diplomatic bag to Singapore and collected at Sembawang forty eight hours earlier had given simple but exact instructions – to surface at a precise time and position and maintain radio silence.

If no physical contact had been made with her by dawn, she was to submerge and rejoin exercise Ocean Wave one thousand miles to the south at 'best speed'......in her case in excess of 40 knots. The orders had been signed by the First Sea Lord himself.

The warm waters of the South China Sea lapped gently against the dark grey hull. With the sound deadening anechoic tiles dulling the usually musical chimes, McCandless and his boat waited and waited.

Dawn finally came and with it sight of a ship's mast in the gathering light to the East.

At a range of about eight miles it started to signal by Aldis lamp.

E...X...C...E...L...S...I...O...R...

McCandless drew a sharp intake of breath.. He had waited years for this day.

The mast on the horizon grew in size and gained definition as it sped towards Astute at high speed. At a distance of about five miles McCandless could see that it was a large destroyer, almost certainly of the Arleigh Burke class. At two miles the light was just bright enough for him to pick out the pennant number on the hull. The number 53 told him the ship was named after the US Navy's founding father – John Paul Jones.

The Arleigh Burke class were designed and built in the 90's. They were excellent ships with a high all round capability but Congress had played hell at the high cost of ships that didn't even carry a helicopter. This perceived omission was corrected in the second batch of the class but the John Paul Jones suffered from this major drawback. The destroyer hove to some 500 yards from Astute and lowered a motorboat which quickly skimmed its way over to the submarine.

The lone passenger threw his kit bag up onto the sub's casing and quickly scrambled up the netting two crew members had assembled over the side.

'Welcome aboard, Sir' prompted one of the seamen as they snapped a salute to a senior rank of an allied navy. Commander Don Ramsay USN nonchalantly bid a casual returning salute that was more of a friendly wave than anything else. 'Good morning, Limeys. I hope you guys have got the ham and eggs on the go!' Ramsay's generous girth gave testimony to food in general and his words to breakfast in particular. U.S. ships being 'dry' he made up for his affection for Bells whisky with an excess of food instead. His wife, Anola, tried to put him on a diet every time he came home to San Diego. She was fighting a losing battle and she knew it.

Ten minutes later Ramsay and McCandless were alone in the Captain's day room. Bruce McCandless wiped the sweat from his brow and pulled a long slug of coffee from his Popeye mug. The situation was unreal.

'Well, Bruce, this is it. Operation Opium is go! The Excelsior Agreement is being adhered to come what may unless we hear to the contrary by midnight tonight. Less than a dozen people, on our side anyway, know about it. Fitzgerald has given it the all clear.

We have only scant knowledge of what's happening in Hong Kong. As we speak arrangements for the Anniversary of the Handover are proceeding as you might expect. The usual Chinese crap – barges of fireworks, celebration banquets at City Hall, PLA navy ships in the harbour dressed in red flags.'

'Jiang Ze Min is due to fly in to Chek Lap Kok Airport at precisely 6am tomorrow in time for the noon fly past of Chinese Air Force Migs. Later he will attend the Hong Kong

Derby at Happy Valley racetrack at 6pm. Can you believe these guys?!' The Master at Arms on the 'Paul Jones' is running an unofficial sweepstake on the Derby – guess what horse I drew? – Tai Tam Tiger.'

'By the way, I need ten minutes alone with your Principal Warfare Officer. You know why.' said Ramsay, removing a flat metal tin from his kit bag. The tin contained the discs loaded with the targeting co-ordinates for the Tomahawk missiles nestled snuggly down in the torpedo room.

'Sure, I'll get you taken to Lt. Carter immediately' confirmed McCandless, reaching for a telephone. In less than a minute a crew member knocked on the door and Ramsay followed him out.

Bruce McCandless sat on the edge of his bunk in a deeply pensive mood. He could scarcely believe what was happening. How and why had history chosen him to be in this situation?

The son of a Government Radio Officer attached to the Admiralty he had followed family tradition by going into the Senior Service. Dartmouth Naval Academy had not particularly suited him. Too much brass and bullshit. His file was peppered with comments from his superiors pertaining to a lack of deference to his seniors, irreverent remarks about the way the Navy was run and his cavalier attitude in general. However, he was a brilliant officer. His crew worshipped him and never questioned his judgement. They would follow him and Astute to the ends of the Earth or in his case the Ocean. But for this special mission he would probably have left the Navy already.

One thing bugged McCandless to distraction. He had not told the crew the full story.

Officially Astute was on Exercise Ocean Wave an annual global deployment involving a dozen or so surface ships and normally one submarine, not three. Unofficially and probably illegally, here he was with a half-billion pound submarine loaded with eight Tomahawk cruise missiles pre-programmed to hit one or more targets in Hong Kong within 24 hours. When he gave the order to launch the next day, the crew would believe that the targets were disused oil and gas installations on Pratas Reef several hundred miles to the north.

He hated deceiving his men but secrecy had been paramount all along. Only he and Ramsay were in the know. It bothered him.

Ramsay re-entered the cabin, a slight grin on his face. 'Shit, Bruce, ya know I couldn't help but smile when I fed that data into the system!

'Yes Sir! Somebody is gonna get his ass fried real soon when those little rockets. hit home.'

McCandless tried hard to disguise his surprise. To the best of his knowledge and belief the targets were inanimate objects not personnel. Maybe Ramsay didn't know himself. Maybe he deliberately hadn't been told. McCandless considered asking Ramsay an innocent question or two to try and smoke out more information – if there was any.

'Hopefully, Don, casualties will be absolutely minimal. Preferably zero don't you think at that time of day especially. According to the schedules the last flights are due out at 18:00 for a three hour break in arrivals and departures while Zemin is waived off by his cronies.

When the Tomahawks hit the two main runways, four into each at three minute intervals spaced 2,000 feet apart that will effectively close the airport to all but helicopter traffic for days if not weeks. Hitting home between 21:00 and 22:00 collateral damage should be nil. Shouldn't it?'

'Yeah, I guess. But Ribchester and Sefton have different targets. That I do know.'

'What...you mean...'

'You don't know?'

'Know what? I thought this was a solo operation...are you telling me that...'

McCandless never finished his sentence. The intercom above his head buzzed loudly. He picked up the mike. 'Yes. McCandless.'

'Sorry to trouble you Captain. We're picking up some interesting radio traffic via the radio buoy on the surface. It's most unusual to say the least. We think that....'

'I'm on my way up.'

Ramsay followed McCandless to the operations and communications room.

'OK, Sparks. give me the gen.'

'Well, Sir, two things. Firstly we are picking up a very high volume of Chinese naval traffic. From the signal strength it's all pretty close. Say 50 to 100 miles, we guess roughly to the north. From what we can gather there are some dozen surface units involved. It could be that there is some sort of exercise going on but...'

'Not this far south' interjected Ramsay. 'The gook Navy has never exercised further south than 15 degrees north. Never. What in hell's name is going on?'

Only one crew member spoke any Chinese – in his case a little Mandarin. With the headphones pressed close to his ears he was lucky to catch one word in ten, if not twenty.

The problem was that Mandarin was not the normally used language of the Chinese Navy. Pin Yin was the most common form of translation. Since the loss of Hong Kong and the associated intelligence gathering operations there, the UK and the US had been deprived of much expertise. Specialist linguistics was one of them.

'I'm sorry, Sir, I'm not getting much of this. I can say though that for sure there are at least a half dozen vessels here if not more. I can tell that from the different voices and nuances. I think I picked up the words fifteen and Spratly, Sir.'

'Fifteen what?'

'Sorry, Sir, I don't know. It might be knots, ships, a compass heading, a position – I can't be sure.'

McCandless stroked his chin nervously. 'Sparks, you said two things had got your attention.'

'Yes, Sir. Radio Hong Kong's English news bulletin at 6.00 am this morning has hinted at a major patriotic announcement tomorrow to mark the Anniversary.'

Ramsay's face went ash-white. 'Oh my God it's gonna happen tomorrow. We should have guessed.'

'Guessed what, come on spill the beans, Don.'

'Beijing has laid claim to the Spratly Islands for over ten years, as have other nations.

Geological surveys are promising to say the least. The global oil companies have their eyes on them for sure. They could be the next Venezuela! You know how volatile the world price of oil still is. The Communists are gonna invade the Spratly Islands tomorrow and Jiang Zemin is going to claim them for the Motherland in his big speech . There is no other explanation. Those ships up topside are an invasion force. Shit a few hundred men will be enough.'

McCandless knew in his heart that Ramsay was probably right. Astute was bang in the middle between the Chinese naval units to the north and the Spratlys about two hundred miles to the south. Problem is, Astute isn't meant to be there at all let alone be about to do what she is within the next twenty four hours. McCandless and Ramsay repaired to the former's private stateroom.

'Don, this situation is unreal. We can't come clean with Northwood, our UK command centre, because only the

First Sea Lord and the Prime Minister are privy to our real mission. Northwood think we are at least a day's steaming to the south on Exercise Ocean Wave. On your side only Fitzgerald and his immediate confidants, including the Navy Secretary, are in on this. Am I right?'

'Not quite. Your colleagues Ribchester and Sefton in command of Artful and Ambush respectively are both probably within 20 miles of here. I was about to tell you earlier when your squawk box interrupted. One sub couldn't guarantee to do the job. If one fails that still leaves two.'

'I'm not hearing this. You mean that....'

'Look, Bruce, ours is not to reason why OK. Before dawn earlier today I boarded both Artful and Ambush for a short time to feed in the launch codes for their own Tomahawks. They have their own orders to launch at 20.00 Zulu tomorrow. In all probability they are both on the bottom lying low until shortly before launch. Job over they are out of it! Back to Diego Garcia. End of story. Period.'

'So why the hell are you still on my boat?'

'The John Paul Jones is on its way to Haiphong for a goodwill visit. This gave it the excuse to be in this part of the world at this precise time. Since former President Bill Clinton's warmly received visit to Vietnam in November 2000 bilateral relations have been most cordial. The NSA persuaded the State Department to show some solidarity with Vietnam during the anniversary celebrations. After all Vietnam is one of the claimants to the Spratlys and there is no love lost between the two countries now – hasn't been for years. When you rejoin Ocean Wave you will drop me off at Darwin and I'll be back in San Diego by July Fourth and the usual parties.'

'So are you telling me that if all goes to plan, sixteen separate Tom...'

'Yep' Ramsay anticipated quickly. 'Sixteen Tomahawks will hit Hong Kong all together within one hour. Eight into Chek Lap Kok and four each into the two main suspension bridges that link the city to the airport itself. Jiang Zemin will be stuck on an island. He was due to fly out at 20:00 so we know he'll be there OK. That's when the local Chinese guys who set all this up move in. Our job will be over.'

'What about the loss of life when the bridges go down, the very people we are supposedly going to help might get killed....'

'Hopefully not. There are friends and agents in place that should prevent that. Buses will break down on the bridge approaches. That sort of stuff.' The 'friends and agents' were Ronnie Yip and Associates. Ramsay didn't know who they were. It wasn't his business.

'So what do we do now?

'What can we do? We can't report in that we've spotted their invasion force for two reasons. One, it might NOT be that. Two, we cannot under any circumstances give away our presence.'

Ten minutes later Astute was lying quite still on the sandy bottom of the South China Sea vitally protected from sonar detection by the new hi-tech anechoic tiles surmounted on her hull. McCandless announced to the crew that this was part of an exercise and that the 'John Paul Jones' was now conducting a search for them with its new Westinghouse sonar. Any loud bangs would be practice charges to indicate they had been discovered.'

Ramsay went to a vacant bunk for some well deserved sleep. Normally he would have to have found a 'hot bunk' but the deliberate reduction in crew numbers made this unnecessary. McCandless went to the galley for breakfast, or was it lunch? Already time was starting to become a little hazy.

On the other side of the world, across the Dateline on the Eastern Seaboard of the United States, things were beginning to hot up.

17

Fort Meade, Maryland

Peter Fitzgerald drew the last milligram of nicotine from his Marlborough Light. He stubbed out the butt into an eighth inch of cold coffee in the polystyrene dispensing cup. He was happy. On the other side of the world it was 2.00 am, tomorrow, in the South China Sea. The John Paul Jones had reported in that she had 'caught three mackerel' en route to Haiphong.

Secretary of State Pamela Martin sat across the room from him on an English leather Chesterfield sofa. Dressed in a snappy dark grey designer suit she looked the picture of executive success. At fifty-two her neatly groomed dark hair betrayed only the slightest flecks of grey.

A genuine Scottish American, her parents had emigrated from the Outer Hebrides to New England when she was only a year old. She spoke with that slightly irritating Maryland drawl beloved of D.C. political pundits but punctuated it with a multitude of 'wees' and 'ayes' inherited from her Gaelic family background. Outside of work she kept herself to herself. She had never married and was named the Scottish Iceberg by her male colleagues. Half the male staff who worked at the NSA thought she might be a dyke.

Fitzgerald cleared his throat. 'Pamela, I'm sorry this has all come late to you. You had to get clearance for the 'Paul

Jones to go to Haiphong to give it the excuse to transit the South China Sea without creating suspicion. Now you know the rest. Well mostly anyway.'

'On the contrary Peter, I know more than you. In fact I have done for over twenty years as opposed to the ten that I suspect limits your knowledge.'

Fitzgerald appeared slightly annoyed. 'I'm sorry but you can't possibly, Pam, I ...'

'It's Pamela. To you and everyone else' snapped Martin, betraying her Gaelic temper with a flash of teeth 'and right now it's time for me to put you fully in the picture *Mister* Fitzgerald.'

'My late father's brother, also deceased, was Major General Alan Martin, commanding officer the Black Watch, the senior Highland Regiment , British Army, from 1975 to 1979'

For the next fifteen minutes, Fitzgerald listened attentively to Pamela Martin. He did not interrupt her. He dare not.. She was obviously eager to educate him. She did that beyond any doubt.

When she had finished Fitzgerald rose from his chair and strode over to the window. He had always enjoyed the view from his office but right now he wasn't seeing anything. In his mind's eye the flat green Maryland countryside was the dark green waters of the South China Sea.

'Pam, sorry Pamela, the revenge aspect I can understand. Regimental honour and all that stuff has been going on for centuries. It's nothing new. But this! This is not supposed to happen. The Excelsior Accord was quite clear. Our sole objective is to close off the new airport at Chek Lap Kok and leave Jiang Zemin stranded. The establishment of the new Administration in Hong Kong by Guandong politicians is not our concern. Well not yet anyway. The NSA has not sanctioned the execution of senior Beijing Government people let alone their god damned President. Our remit is SIGINT. Get that? We will not become...'

Martin cut him short. 'You don't have to sanction or agree anything. It is an entirely private matter outwith the compass of your NSA, my State Department or for that matter the British Government. Prime Minister Bligh won't even know about this bit, only the Excelsior Accord.'

'Pamela, this could blow the whole thing up into World War Three. Beijing is bound to blame the U.S. within hours and might well launch pre-emptive missile strikes against Taiwan. I simply cannot allow the President as Commander in Chief of our armed forces to permit those launches. I intend calling him right now and bring him up to speed.....'

'Peter, you're forgetting something. They are not our submarines out there. The NSA and the guys in Guandong might have paid for them but they are Royal Navy boats. We couldn't stop them if we wanted to. Don't you see... that's why it was done this way.'

The enormity of what Pamela Martin had just said struck Fitzgerald like a sledgehammer. Five minutes later Fitzgerald called the President on his direct line to the White House. It was a tough call and Fitzgerald knew that Powell would take it badly. He also knew that the President would meet with his Chief of Staff Clark and Navy Sec. Mark Heitman at the earliest hour. Defence Secretary William Bean was absent for medical reasons but he hoped to shit that Heitman would be available. He would steady the ship. Literally. Fortunately Mark Heitman was there in D.C. and Fitzgerald breathed a sigh of relief when he got the news. He knew that Powell could 'go a bit wobbly' when the going got tough on foreign policy issues. He'd been a real greenhorn on that subject before his inauguration but that sort of thing could happen when you've spent the whole of your previous life raising cattle in the Texas Panhandle. Powell had learnt quick and did actually listen to his advisers.

Unfortunately, nothing could prepare either him or his advisers for what was unfolding on the southern tip of the world's only communist country nine thousand miles away.

18

St. Stephens Beach
Stanley, Hong Kong
01.00 Hours

The two man crew of the big high speed inflatable cut the engines about a half mile out from the beach to avoid noise and rowed the last stretch.

'You have precisely fifteen minutes gentlemen. Then we go. Understand. This was not in the brochure or on the agenda and officially hasn't happened. Just go!.

Two Scotsmen in their early twenties jumped into the waist deep water and started to run up the beach and into the darkness.

The entrance to Stanley Military Cemetery was only four hundred yards from the beach. Immaculately preserved by the Commonwealth War Graves Commission since 1945 it was the last resting place for over a thousand British and Commonwealth troops killed defending Hong Kong against Japan in 1941. The bulk of the casualties were British and Canadian. The Middlesex Regiment and the Winnipeg Rifles had suffered the most. Almost both battalions had been wiped out in the last ditch effort to keep the Stanley peninsula secure. Eventually a lack of water and ammunition caused the Governor to order a surrender on Christmas Day.

Thus most of the graves were dated December 25 1941 but many reflected the fact that scores of others died of malnutrition and disease in the Prisoner of War camp the Japanese set up at Stanley.

Two graves were dated July 1st 1997. Their names were Iain MacLeod and Angus McLaren. Both white headstones bore the engraved unmistakable eight pronged insignia of the Black Watch and their names. Nothing else.

A week earlier Major General Alan Ferguson had driven to the county of Clackmananshire some fifty miles from Regimental Headquarters.

The Scottish countryside looked at its best and the yellow gorse flowers the brightest he could ever remember. Driving down through the village of Saline he came to the crossroads in the centre of the little town of Dollar. Turning right at the First World War memorial gardens he drove gently uphill and out of town to the tiny village of Pitgober less than a mile away.

Devonbanks Cottage was the last house at the end of the lane. It was a sprawling old property that had obviously been extended at both ends several times over its two hundred year old history. Ferguson got out of his green army Ford sedan and knocked at the old black door with a heavy heart.

He had been to see Mrs Moira MacLeod. When he left her in tears an hour later he had in his briefcase a gold cygnet ring. It was to have been a 21st birthday present to her son when he came home on leave in 1977. He never came home again.

On leaving Pitgober Ferguson drove to a farmhouse on the outskirts of Auchtermuchty, Fifeshire only thirty miles to the east. He realised he was only ten miles from the famous St Andrews Golf Club. How he wished he could have played golf today. The sign on the gateway leading to the property simply read "Finest Scotch Beef and home reared venison. Proprietor: Hamish McLaren."

Three hours later Ferguson was back at his desk at Regimental H.Q. in Perth.

Private Irvine knelt in front of Macleod's grave. Taking a sharp folding knife from his fatigues pocket he carved a six inch square of grass to a depth of about an inch a foot in front of the headstone. He peeled off the turf like lifting a green carpet tile. Unzipping a breast pocket he then unfolded the small white linen lady's handkerchief. It had a blue forget-me-not flower embroidered in one corner and in the opposite corner embroidered in pink were the initials MM.

Folding the handkerchief to exactly match the dimensions of the square he had cut out he laid it on the earth. Placing the cloth on the grass he then removed the gold ring from a secure pouch stitched to his leather belt. He touched the ring to his lips and spoke a dozen words so softly that even his partner, Private Campbell, only six feet away didn't hear. Reverently laying the unworn ring in the centre of the cloth he then replaced the square of grass and pressed it firmly back into place with the palms of his hands. The grave looked untouched.

Taking Irvine's knife Campbell removed a similar but larger patch of turf from McLaren's grave. He stood up and unzipped a small canvas holdall, removing a glass jar about six inches high and four inches across. He unscrewed the metal lid in an anti-clockwise direction. Holding up the jar several inches he gingerly poured the grey ashes as evenly as he could over the bare earth. He re-screwed the jar and put it back in his bag. Carefully restating the grass both men then stood, heads bowed, for one minute.

The eyes of a thousand dead men were upon them.

Mrs Fiona McLaren had died at home in Auchtermuchty aged eighty. Her body was cremated and her husband Hamish had kept her ashes for five years in the hope that one day Angus's body would be exhumed and returned to Scotland. Ferguson had told him that after today in all probability that would never be possible. Now at least they would be together.

Fourteen minutes later Irvine and Campbell scrambled back into the big inflatable. 'That', said the SBS officer, 'was cutting it a bit fine gentlemen.' They rowed the first half mile out into the bay and then started up the two outboards. The twin eighty horsepower Mercurys roared into life. In less than two minutes they were a mile to the southwest and the safety of darkness.

Luck was on their side. The giant Evergreen Lines container ship MV Ever Willing was in the Lamma Channel heading north west at about twelve knots towards the container port an hour away at Kwai Chung. The SBS helmsman steered his boat first into her wake and then gently under her port quarter on the ocean side. Ever Willing was the perfect screen until he could peel off south and head for the southern tip of Lantau Island another fifteen miles distant. They were on schedule.

19

The White House
Pennsylvania Avenue
Washington D.C.

Within thirty minutes of speaking with Fitzgerald a meeting was taking place in the Oval Office between the President, his Chief of Staff, the Navy Secretary and several aides within his inner wheel of confidants. Defence Secretary, W.L.Bean, was in hospital. Powell didn't care. Nor did Heitman.

Paul Powell had been the forty third President of the United States since January 2001 after the closest ever elections in American history. Economically he was having a smooth ride. The Dow Jones was still over 8000 points and the US still led the world in electronics, semi-conductor technology and aerospace. Boeing's newly announced Sonic Cruiser, half Concorde half Jumbo, was already proving a commercial winner and the spin off across the whole sector was acting like a new gold rush. It was like the 707 all over again. Sure, there were always problems to be solved but that was a President's job. The jobs of the people were important too. The U.S. was still the only Superpower in the world after the collapse of the old Soviet Union but industrially America had competitors that it could well do without. However, "free trade" was the name of the game and Uncle Sam was faster with a buck than most countries were with their euros, pesos or pesetas.

His first foreign policy problem had occurred on, of all days, April Fool's Day 2001 when a Navy Aries EP3 spy plane had been forced to land in Hainan Island while monitoring broadcasts off the southern Chinese coast. That it was only ten weeks into his Presidency was no coincidence. America was witnessing the emergence of a challenger for Superpower status. The Chinese, Zemin in particular, had wanted to test his mettle. He was not found wanting. The President had gained a reputation from the start for being cool, calm and collected. His critics were hoping that he would revert to type and come across as a Texas Ranger chasing varmints with a posse. They were disappointed.

The crisis had lasted for a week and a half but the President was a stronger leader for it at the end. It still wrankled with him though that Zemin had tried to embarrass him, big time. He would remember that, for sure, and if a chance ever came to get his own back without creating a war, he might just be tempted.

'Gentlemen, I cannot overemphasise the seriousness of the problem that faces us today,' the lingering Texas drawl accentuating the worried timbre of Powell's voice. Powell had been a novice in world affairs at his inauguration but surrounded by a good team he had quickly got to grips with international affairs. Aided of course by a well funded National Security Agency and CIA.

'I believe I am not exaggerating when I say that this is every bit as dangerous as the Cuban Missile Crisis forty five years ago. Put simply, very simply, the situation is this....'

It took the President eight minutes to complete the brief. He told them all about Operation Opium, the Excelsior Accord and the latest, most appalling development so recently expounded by Pamela Martin to Fitzgerald. He would deal with that red-necked Yankee bitch later. Nobody, but nobody, keeps information like that from him. But now was not the time. Besides he might need her – depending on developments over the next twenty four hours.

Navy Secretary Mark Heitman was the first to react. 'Do we hold any cards at all Mr. President?'

'Absolutely none, Mark. But I'm not sure if "holding cards" as you say is the right expression. After a few years ago we would have been real pleased if somebody, anybody, had acted as our mercenaries and blown the whole of Beijing to smithereens. When those gook assholes nearly walked into Taiwan in 2000 and half the Seventh Fleet was in refit at the same damned time we were powerless. The 'six hundred ship navy' that Reagan placed such importance on eventually dwindled to two hundred as you know. That was a major error. The Fleet Expansion Plan (FEP) after the Taiwan Crisis will take another coupla years to come on stream – ya know what those pissing liberal Congressmen are like with other people's dough. You know more than me on that score anyway I'm sure.'

Heitman looked a tad embarrassed. His ex wife Helen was now an opposition Ohio Senator and the divide between them had been a bitter affair fought out in the public eye. Powell had been under pressure to replace Heitman but why should he? It wasn't his fault that his wife had gotten caught up in that post Clinton gush of misplaced, sentimental claptrap. She might have had the decency to change her name back to the one she had before she had married. Maybe she didn't think that Helen Shwartz was as commercial as Helen Heitman. The double soliloquy and all that stuff. Bitch.

'Yeah, sure. The new carrier programme got well and truly goosed by those bearded, navel picking welfare "do gooders" who thought that by delaying the funds for the new CVN78 class they could help the poor people of Venus or someplace.'

'Mr President' interrupted Chief of Staff, Richard Clark, 'I think we should inform the Taiwan Government in Taipei without delay of the overall situation. Ling has always been up front with us and whilst we always have a standing naval force in the Formosa Strait to counter the ICBM threat I do think that anything we ...'

'I called President Ling while you guys were on the way over.'

'Guess what, Gentlemen? He already knew. I also called London. Bligh knows, their First Sea Lord knows, that smart ass ex-Governor knows, the Downing Street cat probably knows and in fact every sonofabitch this side of the Pacos probably knows. Jesus!'

Mark Heitman was one cool man under pressure. Of the three men in the room only he was thinking straight. He'd had plenty of practice.

'Mr. President. We can't influence events at all on this one – at least not yet . So let's not pretend we can. Best thing we can do is wait, Sir. In twelve hours or less we will know exactly what the score is. As you surmise the attempt to take out Zemin will almost certainly be made at Happy Valley Races following which the airport will be blasted to close it. Believe it or not Sir the Hong Kong Derby is being shown live on satellite TV.

President Powell gave a nervous laugh. 'Can you believe it? The end of the world might well be nigh and we're gonna watch it on TV!'

'Mark, I want a full report on this Commander Bedford guy as soon as you can get it. I can't believe that all this crap goes so far back. For the next few hours we may not be able to influence events but we need to know as much as we can about the background to this. I want Bedford picked up and questioned immediately and I want our consulate staff in the Hong Kong SAR to dig out what they can on this Jimmy Leung shipowner. Ten years is quite a time ago but we should be able to find out more. London may be able to help us with the latter particularly if his ships flew the Hong Kong Flag.'

'Sir, we've checked with Navy records already. Arthur Gordon Bedford died in Jacksonville, Florida on May 23 last year. He'd been retired for some time.'

'Hell! So that avenue's closed. Mr Heitman, before we go any damned further, can you or anybody else tell me? How can one of our own destroyers actually rendezvous clandestinely with three foreign subs in one of the most sensitive areas of the world without you or I knowing about it?'

'Well the problem is, Sir, since the Reagan, Thatcher, Weinberger era our two navies have gotten so close that they're practically doing each other's jobs on many occasions. Since Subic was lost and the Brits had to give back Hong Kong to the Chinese our combined presence in the area has been minimal to say the least. Pressure on budgets caused by the Son of Star Wars project doesn't help either, Sir.' Heitman was determined to get that one in. He had privately cautioned the President about the financial constraints this would put on the navy especially. In particular, operational time actually at sea, would necessarily decrease. Nobody had listened to him. Not even the President. The chickens were coming home to roost.

'With many of the Los Angeles class subs reaching the end of their service lives we rarely have major units in the South China Sea. The trip to Haiphong by the JPJ is a 'one off' as you now know and ...'

Heitman was interrupted by an aide knocking at the door. He had rushed down from the White House Signals Office.

He handed the President a small piece of computer generated printout. Powell swiftly took his eyeglasses from his shirt's breast pocket. He read it once to himself and then out loud to Clark and Heitman. 'It's from the 'Paul Jones' via San Diego.'

'Regret to report that an underwater explosion has partly disabled the ship. We have lost one screw and a rudder. There are no casualties. We think it was a mine. We can make ten knots only. Our position is ... etc etc ... We await instructions. Message ends.'

The President looked shell shocked. That's because he was. He didn't believe in co-incidences like this.

'Mark. This is looking like a set up. This is bad, bad news.

When the meeting closed Heitman made a very important secure call to Admiral Wayne Novak at CINCPAC, Pearl Harbour. He didn't think it necessary to tell the President. Not yet anyway.

Paul Powell also made a call on a encrypted line to James Bellringer, the head of the CIA at Langley, Virginia. Electronic Intelligence ELINT-was fine but it didn't beat a guy on the ground and in the know. It was not a long call.

'Hi, Jim. I guess that Fitz has already updated you. Jim, this is bad news for sure. I just cannot understand how in this day and age we can get caught with our pants down like this.'

Jim Bellringer was one of the new types. He had really been schooled in the post Cold War era and been concerned mostly with anti-American commercial espionage activity. To question him in this sector was like asking an Idaho potato farmer how to grow cotton in Alabama. Powell blamed himself. He should have had him replaced. If only he had the likes of Kissinger and Schlessinger around to advise him now. Even Nixon for Christ's sake.

But Bellringer did throw one interesting point into the ideas pot. He said that the CIA once had its own man in Government House, Hong Kong and that even the British Government didn't know. It was a long time ago – in the early Seventies. The Governor in question had previously been British Ambassador to South Vietnam when he had been recruited. Couldn't remember his name offhand. 'Sir Mac something. You know how tricky some of those Scottish names are.'

Bellringer promised to find out more. The continuing Scottish connection was making Powell feel more than a little uneasy. Maybe it was just nerves. One thing's for sure though. Pamela Martin is on her way out.

20

USS John Paul Jones
South China Sea
110° East 18° North

Captain James T. Bourke reviewed the situation with his Executive Officer.

'Boy. What a situation to be in. Can you believe all this? That must have been a mine.'

No warning, no nothing. Just a big bang and the fantail lifted up ten feet then crashed down again. A few buckled plates above the waterline but much, much worse below. A whole rudder and screw blown off on the port side. Divers would tell him more when it got light in just over three hours time. In the meantime the ship was making ten knots on a heading of 087 degrees away from Hainan Island towards the Luzon Straits and the open Pacific. The nearest dock was at Okinawa and he had his orders. The goodwill visit to Vietnam was out of the question.

If it was a mine then this was the second time that Bourke had experienced being hit. He was a junior officer on the USS Princeton back in the early Nineties when she had hit an Iraqi mine in the Persian Gulf. The entire keel of a billion dollar AEGIS cruiser had been twisted by a low tech five hundred buck aquatic firework. And here he was again.

With his left hand Executive Officer Michael Ramiros raised his dark blue baseball cap inscribed DDG53 John Paul Jones, scratched his thinning hair at the front and wiped the sweat from his brow with the back of his hand. The three nicotine stained middle fingers of his right hand drummed a steady repetitive beat on the desk top to imitate a horse at the gallop.

'Jesus, Number One, will you pack that in! We are in one hell of a mess and all you can think of is that horserace in Hong Kong today...'

'Captain, I wasn't thinking of...'

'I'm only joking. Anything to relieve the tension I guess. At first light we'll hove to and send over the divers. Was that a rogue mine do you think or is there a minefield there on the approaches to the Tonkin Gulf? Was it a Chinese or Vietnamese?'

'From what I've read Nixon ordered some mine laying back in '73 on the approaches to Haiphong to try and slow down the supply of materiel to the North by sea. '

Don't say we've hit one of our own mines over thirty years later. Is that possible? Can they stay active that long?'

'Number One, I don't know. I just don't know.'

Bourke suddenly had a thought as his mind flashed back to the mine incident in the Gulf.

'Number One, when we had that reconstructed duck shoot off the fantail last week to relieve the boredom of the trip – who won it?'

'It was a dead heat Sir between Seaman Sean Kelly and Seaman John Kitto. Why do you ask?'

'Listen, as soon as it's light I want the pair of them on the forecastle armed with the best and most powerful rifles we have on board and the best binoculars available OK. Their orders are to shoot at any mines they might see in the water.

Tell them to aim for the horns if they are not too close to the ship to detonate them. If a mine is seen close to the ship but it is obvious we are not going to hit it then don't shoot. We don't want a million bucks worth of collateral damage just because one of those guys gets a little trigger happy OK.'

'Yes, Sir, I'll see to it at first light.'

'And make sure you explain *exactly* what to do with Kentucky Kitto, you know what an asshole he can be. The only kind of horn he usually understands is the one in his pants when he's on shore leave in Honolulu.'

'Yes, Sir.' The Number One was smiling.

That was something that not every navy could do Ramiros mused to himself. A farm boy from the Bluegrass Country was gonna protect his ship with a fucking rifle. Ramiros tapped the glass of the commemorative barometer on the bulkhead. The needle dropped a fraction and he started to read the opening words of the inscription on the plaque on which the brass instrument was mounted. 'An American hero – the Legend lives on.' It told the story of the famous battle that John Paul Jones had fought on 23rd of September 1779 when his ship, the Bonhomme Richard, had fought off the supposedly superior English vessels the Serapis and the Countess of Scarborough.

Every time he looked at that barometer and tapped the glass he thought he had seen it someplace else apart from on the bridge of the John Paul Jones. Funnily enough, Bourke had once made a similar remark to him. Oh well.

They both decided to get some sleep.

Before he nodded off Bourke reflected that if only they'd had even a small helicopter on board they could spot ahead a few miles for these fucking mines and wouldn't have to go duck shooting … again. He did not sleep well. His mind kept harping back to when a sister ship, the USS Cole, had been hit by a suicide bomber in Aden on 12th October 2000 and seventeen men and women had died. It reminded him of the responsibility he had to his men and their families back home.

The John Paul Jones was typically manned. From the farms of Iowa, the industrial centres of the East Coast and the hick towns of Middle America, his ship was a microcosm of the whole of the United States. If the ship *was* lost with all hands then the whole of America would grieve. James Theodore Bourke would not let that happen. No Sir!

21

**Chi Ma Wan Inlet
Lantau Island, Hong Kong**
04.00 Hours

Blue One inflatable had laid low for the last two hours. After using the containership as cover she had peeled off and headed for Lantau at best speed.

After the rendezvous with Blue Two and Blue Three all three boats were now hidden in the dense vegetation that clung to the rugged coastline. The nearest buildings were the now disused Correction Centre half a mile away. In the last years of colonial rule the centre had been part of Her Majesty's Prisons Service and used mainly for low security prisoners. The Chinese hadn't used it since the Handover. They didn't have to.

In fact prison occupancy had fallen over 50% since 1997. Whilst corruption, or tea money was still rife, everyday crimes like theft and violent robbery had declined sharply. The strict Communist regime applied an almost Moslem attitude to crime. Police beatings were commonplace, kneecappings almost mandatory and of course the death penalty was reintroduced shortly after the Handover. There was not even an appeals procedure for the death penalty. Execution was by a single bullet in the back of the head within ten minutes of any guilty verdict. Relatives could not claim the body until the bullet had been paid for.

The almost derelict buildings of the Correction Centre had been the perfect place for local agents to hide the one hundred and twenty gallons of gasoline need by the three boats. They had topped up their main tanks and took the rest as reserve. Hopefully they wouldn't need it.

The three armourers, one in each boat, double checked the integrity of the two hand held Stinger anti-aircraft missiles allocated to each of them. There was little point in carrying more. At best they would have time only to squeeze off two rounds each. Each man also had one M16 carbine and a hundred rounds.

In one hour's time they would move out and start to get into position.

HMS Ambush
114° East 20° North
One hundred miles south of the Dan Gan Islands
04.00 Hours

For Richard Ribchester this was almost too much. He had known since first advised of Operation Opium in London last year that this was going to be the highlight of his career. But he wondered now if he, his boat and his crew were mere sacrificial pawns in a game of chess where the rules and prizes belonged to others whose only part in the game was to open the box.

For sure, he now knew that he and Sefton had not been picked at random. In their late forties they should by now be looking for that desk job in Plymouth or even Faslane, Scotland, their baseport. McCandless, Ribchester and Sefton had one thing in common. They had all served in Hong Kong before the Handover. Not on submarines but on minesweepers.

Not only were they familiar with the many islands that made up the former Colony, but from unpublicised sorties and deliberate skirmishes with Communist gunboats in the early nineties and right up to June 1997, they knew the geography of the main islands to the south. These islands had always been Chinese and outwith the Lease.

With the naked eye from Hong Kong Island, on a very clear day with no heat haze, you could just make out the mile-wide channel between the East and West Dan Gan Islands. They were uninhabited. The water in the channel was deep – five hundred feet – good submarine country.

Ambush had surfaced in the channel shortly after dark the previous evening to allow Blues One, Two and Three to set off north north west to Lantau Island. He didn't know that Blue One had been to Stanley or that the two other non Navy men were from the Black Watch. He didn't need to know.

He knew he had counted *eight* men out. He hoped to be counting *eight* men back later that night. The number *eight* seemed to following him round. There were *eight* Tomahawks down below soon to be launched. He knew from his time served in Hong Kong that the number *eight* was considered lucky in Chinese folklore. In a crazy kind of way he drew succour from it.

The boat cruised at periscope depth at a lazy twelve knots in a circular course to maintain a relative position.

HMS Artful
114° East 19° North
06.00 Hours

Sefton knew by now that Artful was the backup to Astute and Ambush. It was highly unlikely that she would be needed any more. Although his Tomahawks had been pre-programmed with the target data he was only to launch on receipt of another direct order to do so.

He had however played one other major part in The Operation. He cast his mind back two days and the rendezvous with the Cyprus registered freighter *Aphrodite*, two hundred miles south of Hong Kong.

They had made visual contact with the rusting hulk just after dawn. She had launched a seaboat and the two man crew had ferried its single passenger the half mile over to Ambush. Bearded, slim and about five seven he clambered onto the aft casing and barked orders in very loud Arabic to the two men. Arabic was obviously his mother tongue.

'Come on, quickly now. Get those three cases up here! He obviously didn't suffer fools gladly and his impatience and intolerance seemed to verge on the paranoid. Several of Artful's own crew had appeared on deck wearing the mandatory life-vests and man handled the three wooden cases each one about five feet long, below decks.

One Jack Tarr said to another 'What's a bloody foreigner doing on board. Looks like an Arab to me.' If only they knew.

Later that day, after nightfall, Sefton had taken his boat at high speed through the Dan Gan Channel and delivered his cargo of one man and three boxes to within three miles of Lantau Island. They were met by two Royal Marines in a high speed inflatable. Blue One.

For Jamil ibn Salim, the world's most notorious and expensive aviation terrorist, this was his first trip in a nuclear submarine. His fee was fifty million dollars U.S. – ten million up front, the other forty after the job had been done. He was believed to have been responsible for no less than six outrages involving civil airliners in as many years. In three weeks time he would be back home in Beirut and counting the money in his Zurich bank account. Allah u Akbar! God is good!

The stern voice of one of his Officers acted like the crisp click of a hypnotist's fingers and in milliseconds Sefton's brain reverted to real time.

'Sir, sonar is picking up a large surface unit about five miles to the north. Speed six knots and slowing. Course 087 degrees.'

'Planesman, bring the boat up to periscope depth.'

'Aye, aye, Sir'

'It was barely light and Sefton scanned the horizon through the full three hundred sixty degrees. It was a large warship for sure, the bristling array of antenae told him that. But what was it? Whose was it? Why had it come to a standstill near him? He felt uneasy, downed the scope and ordered a course to take the boat to a position four miles west of this visitor so he could get a better sight profile against the rising sun.

Fifteen minutes later Sefton had ascertained that the 'visitor' was the USS John Paul Jones. He called up the destroyer on VHF radio and spoke personally to the commanding officer, James T.Bourke.

Bourke told him about the mine and his orders to abort the trip to Haiphong. He told him about the damage below and he told him about the new orders to get to Okinawa.

'How could he and Ambush assist without compromising the Operation?'

Fifteen minutes later the divers gave Bourke even worse news. The starboard screw was also damaged and the ten knot run had further weakened the shaft. Engineering officers recommended a speed reduction to five knots on just one gas turbine. Bourke reported in to San Diego on a secure satellite channel and waited for fresh orders. He was pissed off. In three days time he would be spending July Fourth on a dry ship in the middle of nowhere. The shit will have hit the fan: Uncle Sam will be to blame and here he was a sitting god damned duck.

If any employees of the ship's builders back in New England had been on board, they would have told Bourke that he and his crew were lucky. They build 'em tough in Maine.

The signal from San Diego told him to head south to Singapore and that a civilian contracted tugboat, probably from the Dutch salvage experts Smit Tak, would assist as soon as possible.

Sefton told Bourke that he would stick with him indefinitely and the news was relayed to the destroyer's crew. They settled down to play cards and drink coffee for the next God knows how many days.

22

The White House, Washington DC

A full meeting of the National Security Council had been ordered by President Powell. If the daily routine of the National Security briefing bored him. then this *scared* him. He was not by nature a hawk nor was he a dove. Maybe he was a kind of a baby hawk. A sparrowhawk.

A Pentagon surveillance satellite had traversed the South China Sea in its elliptical orbit ninety minutes earlier. It was obvious that Chinese forces had invaded the Spratly Islands. There was clear evidence that major transport ships had carried troops and supplies sufficient to garrison the islands for some time. This was not a token flag raising exercise for photographic and propaganda purposes. This was real.

Among those present at the meeting were Fitzgerald, head of the NSA, Chief of White House Staff Clark, George Bowers (Air Force Secretary), Mark Heitman (Navy Secretary), and Pamela Martin, Secretary of State. Also present was General Walter Audsley, Chairman of the Joint Chiefs of Staff. who had just got back from a visit to Fort Bragg in North Carolina. He looked tired and jaded. But there again he always did.

Significantly, Defence Secretary William L.Bean was *not* there. He could not be there as he was still at Bethesda Naval Hospital ten miles away recovering from an operation to remove his tonsils. The operation had not been an immediate success and complications had set in. This suited the on-the-ball Heitman just fine. He had always regarded Bean as a bit of a fart and his guaranteed absence would give him some scope for a little personal initiative.

Was it LBJ or Nixon who had said 'if you can fly high with the eagles don't scratch around with the turkeys. Heitman considered Bean a *total* turkey. He always thought that if Powell's wife and Bean's wife had not been related somehow then Bean would still be growing apples in Vermont. Or beans.

'Gentlemen' commenced Powell, quite deliberately ignoring Pamela Martin's sex.

'You've heard the review of the satellite findings. The Spratlys invasion is fact albeit that China has not yet announced it to the world. That will undoubtedly come in Jiang's speech in Hong Kong tomorrow.'

'We also know that a second, smaller naval force is following twenty four hours behind. High definition satellite photographs reveal IRBM's as deck cargo on at least two transport ships escorted by several destroyer sized vessels.'

'This is looking like a Kruschev Cuba type scenario. The oil field and continental shelf argument was just an excuse. China now has a major military base in the southern South China Sea. Ever since we pulled out of the Philippines this has been waiting to happen!'

'Options please' the President almost coughed out the two simple words.

Air Force Secretary Bowers opened the batting. 'Short term our options are limited. We have one E-5 AWACS available from Naha, Okinawa. Two more are en route from Hawaii. Anything else will require major planning – three days at least for anything involving B1's or B2's. Since that volcano spewed ash all over Clark AFB in the Philippines in ninety ...'

'Thank you, George.' Powell cut him short. 'What you mean is that right now all we can do is watch. Don't take that the wrong way, George, but it's fact isn't it?

'Yeah but in a coupla days we can have some F117s in place in some friendly country, say Singapore. With the back-up kit on supporting C17's and a few Extender tankers we can be in business by say Tuesday. We still have a defence treaty with them and we can take out anything the Chinese assemble in the Spratlys with smart bombs. That is if the Navy isn't ready or fit....'

Powell cut in to stop any bitching between the two proponents – he was sick of the inter service rivalry and the constant lobbying for funds from Congress by both sides. It upset the overall fiscal strategy. He looked at the sole Army representative at the meeting. Quite what the Army could do for a problem like this he didn't know but Audsley was a real nice guy and he didn't want him to feel out of it. At sixty one Walt Audsley was looking forward to his imminent retirement, big pension and beach fishing for sea bass in his native Georgia. He hated these kind of meetings but he and Powell's father went back a long way and whilst he didn't want to be rude he didn't want to get too involved. Shit no.

'Your turn, Walt. Your recommendations if you please.'

Powell was right. Walter Audsley said it was a Navy problem. Well fuck him then.

He pointed his pen at the Navy Secretary to indicate it was his turn.'

Mark Heitman took a deep breath and sighed. Boy was this difficult. He alone at the meeting knew that he had already exercised his initiative. At CINCPAC, Wayne Novak had been most understanding. There was no way that he was going to allow a ship called John Paul Jones to fend for itself against overwhelming odds. Two Los Angeles class subs and one of the new Seawolf Class had already been sent. Fuck the President. This was a private Navy matter.

'Apart from the John Paul Jones itself, Sir, we have no major units within a thousand miles or more that can help. The AEGIS cruisers Valley Forge and Yorktown cannot be moved from the Formosa Straits. If anything, at times like this, they need supplementing not removing. Two more of the same class will be sent to that end without delay. They are the Bunker Hill and the Cowpens. All four ships are amongst the oldest of the class and I hate to say this but in the event of conflict they must be considered expendable.'

Powell swallowed hard. That last bit had upset him. Was Heitman already looking at battle losses? He must be. Jesus. Over three hundred crew on each, multiplied four times. Shit he's already discounting twelve hundred casualties and that's *outside* of the immediate theatre.

'The carriers Carl Vinson and Ronald Reagan are both at Pearl for the Fourth of July. John C.Stennis is at San Diego after having a minor shaft problem rectified. At this juncture in the proceedings we won't mention the time it had out of operational service thanks to that crazy movie premiere taking place on board at Pearl Harbor back in May.' The President looked more than a little embarrassed..

'Kitty Hawk decommissioned and was officially stricken only last week at Bremerton. The delay to the new carrier is regretted but we couldn't keep our oldest fossil fuelled ship going any longer. Forty five years service to the tax-payer was still good value. However we have the Wasp and the Bonhomme Richard, both loaded with choppers and marines in exercises with the Australian forces. Realistically they are at least a week away.'

He knew it wasn't really an option and bearing in mind what had already been sent he wasn't too concerned anyway. In any event to send in 4,000 grunts in a full frontal attack on the Spratlys would *guarantee* heavy casualties. Nobody ever actually admitted it but that's why in the 1991 Desert Storm operation the expected Marines attack on Kuwait City had been simply a feint. No U.S. President could withstand the political fallout from hundreds of body bags being returned to the States.

'So basically we have one damaged destroyer available and, diplomatic niceties permitting, a handful of F117's *maybe* in a few days time..' Powell was out of his depth and needed rescuing.

'I wouldn't put it quite like that, Sir. Within three days we can get at least two Los Angeles. class subs on the scene and possibly...' Heitman knew they had already been sent.

'We don't have three days, Mr Heitman, and "possibly" isn't good enough.' An air of gloom descended on the meeting.

Pamela Martin raised the forefinger of her right hand and looked directly at the President as if requesting permission to speak. Powell nodded somewhat reluctantly.

At six 'o' clock that evening, timed to coincide with early evening news bulletins the President of the United States and his Secretary of State made joint pronouncements on the security situation in South East Asia.

'...and accordingly, unless we receive verifiable information backed up by our own satellite intelligence that Chinese forces are withdrawing from the Spratly Islands by midnight tonight Eastern Daylight Time then the United States would convene an emergency meeting of the Security Council and expel the Chinese Ambassador to Washington...'

Inwardly Powell was seething. Three hours earlier Pamela Martin had made him look pretty stupid at the National Security Meeting. She had reminded him that they didn't require the military hardware to be in place. In twelve hours time the British would be launching their own attack as part of Operation Opium. The Chinese would think that the missiles were American and that Powell was talking tough.

Only one thing bugged him. What if the Chinese did withdraw? The U.S. still couldn't stop the British attack. This just wasn't fair. There was going to be a major military confrontation with the only communist state left in the world and it wasn't *his* fault. Darned good job he wouldn't be running for his second term for a long time.

Shit he hated that bitch. So much for tokenism. He, a Texan, had gone in for some blatant pro-feminist politics. Now look how much shit he was in! She knew he had no other options and she knew he was also exposed to that one fatal weakness. He also knew, deep down, that she hadn't told him everything. He was right.

With her Scottish and Black Watch credentials she already knew about Jamil. He didn't. That was probably just as well. He'd had enough surprises for one day.

23

Lantau Island, Hong Kong

05.30 Hours

It was still dark. Inky dark. Blues One, Two and Three left Chi Ma Wan at five minute intervals. They headed south west at twenty five knots out into the Pearl River Estuary where their engine noise would not attract undue attention. It was always busy. Every kind of vessel used the estuary from small fishing junks to giant container ships. In the dark they would go unnoticed. But dawn would come soon and with it the increased risk of discovery.

If all went according to plan, within the hour, the chartered China Southwest Airlines 737 carrying its VIP cargo would be in a thousand pieces at the bottom of the South China Sea, Jiang Zemin would be dead and Operation Opium could move on to the next phase.

It took just over forty minutes to cover the twelve sea miles to their pre-calculated positions. Skirting round the western edge of Lantau Island Blue One came close inland hugging the coastline before taking up position not far from the approach lights that guided incoming airplanes. Blue One was in the most dangerous and exposed situation. It was the one most likely to be spotted and challenged which was why she carried the two extra crew, Campbell and

Irvine. If any of the three boats were going to have to fight their way out of it then it was Blue One.

By six-fifteen all three Blues were positioned in a straight line with Blue One one mile west of a point midway between the main north and south runways. A mile further west lay Blue Two and Blue Three took up a position two miles west of Blue Two. Jamil bin Salim was in Blue Three. He would get in the first and best shots. There was a steady breeze from the south west and their sea anchors prevented drift.

Reports from Yip's agents had informed them that the Presidential 737 had stayed overnight in Macau, thirty miles to the west on the other side of the Pearl Estuary. This would guarantee the arrival time in Hong Kong and make security tighter.

The 737's flight time to Chek Lap Kok would be less than fifteen minutes. At five miles from touchdown Blue Three would fire the first two stingers. In the event of a miss then Blue Two would fire then Blue One as the final back up. The simulated attack carried out at Akrotiri, Cyprus several weeks earlier had proved more difficult than expected but on that occasion they were up against a top pilot who jinked on seeing the first two dummy missiles launched. The pilot of the Chinese 737 would not be expecting anything untoward. Needless to say Jamil had not attended the rehearshal. He didn't need any practice. It should be a straightforward turkey shoot. Jamil ibn Salim would not miss. He wanted his ten million dollars. And the rest. And Imogen.

It started to get light and with it the temperature rose. Unused to tropical climes the sweat poured from all eight Europeans soaking their light green combat fatigues a darker shade. Some of the men chewed gum. Jamil had lit up a Gauloise cigarette until Bryce had ripped it from his mouth with a string of expletives. 'No smoke or fire you Palestinian prick!' he yelled at the Arab. Jamil shrugged his shoulders. Who cares. The Englishman only earns a fraction in a year of what I will earn in a few days!

At six miles out the Chinese 737 banked to the right and lined itself up on the glide path to Chek Lap Kok. Airspeed one hundred eighty five knots. Altitude sixteen hundred feet and decreasing. At five miles out the crew of Blue Three could see the red and white colours of the fuselage glinting in the early morning sun.

Stinger One leapt from its launch tube with a whoosh followed six seconds later by Stinger Two. Flight time to impact was approximately fifteen seconds. The sea anchor was pulled aboard and the Mercurys started up. Blue Three revved up to a maximum forty knots and zoomed off to the southwest. Two miles to the east Blue Two watched. Three miles to the east Blue One waited.

The technology worked perfectly. Stinger One buried itself into the starboard Pratt and Whitney turbofan and exploded. It took the entire starboard wing fully loaded with fuel with it. The plane dived to the left as kinetic forces overcame natural lift. Stinger Two slammed into the starboard cabin just behind the wing roots and exploded.

It was academic. In less than twenty seconds since the first detonation the plane was in the sea hitting the surface at two hundred knots and breaking into many pieces. Burning fuel and debris covered the surface for several hundred yards. By the time the broken off tailplane had slipped beneath the waves Blues Two and One were also doing forty knots in the wake of Blue Three. This was now one serious place to get the hell out of.

Kwangzhou
Guandong Province, China

Seventy seven year old Cheung Chi-doi had just completed his Tai-Chi exercises in the park as he always did just after dawn. He sat down on one of the ornate green timber seats that edged the pathways through the park. He was at peace with himself and the world. The sun was getting up and already the temperature was heading for the upper twenties Celsius. He shielded his eyes with the back of his hand and glanced a mere six feet into the ancient banyan tree that had seen a hundred thousand sunrises. His favourite bird, 'SingSing' a miniature linnet, was singing in her cage like she had never sung before.

He instantly knew that all the Gods of Tai Mo Shan were on his side.

Dew lay lo mo! Zemin was a jerk. He'd tried to copy Mao's swim in the Yangtze by being photographed swimming in the Dead Sea in Israel in the year 2000. Now he was in his own Dead Sea except 'dead' meant deceased and not a geographical location.

His mind wandered back to that meeting at the Kam Sang Restaurant in Hong Kong all those years ago. He must meet Jimmy Leung again soon. In Hong Kong. Yes, why not Hong Kong? The hated Zemin was dead. The Guys in Guandong would have their own man in Beijing within hours. After all Li Shau King was a southerner. One of them. His parents had migrated north in the Fifties and he had seen the failings of all the old ways. Today was *his* day as well.

Yes, he would go by train to Hong Kong and see Jimmy on his own patch. He would take the new all electric KCR all the way to Kowloon and have lunch in that place where the Japanese had set up their HQ in 1941. He spat onto the grass. He had hated them too.

Standing slowly he reached up to retrieve SingSing's cage from the banyan tree and ambled slowly towards the park's exit. It was time for a celebratory breakfast.

24

The White House, Washington D.C.

21.00 Hours EDT

The President had just finished a working supper with his Chief of Staff Richard Clark. Heitman and Bowers had left for the Pentagon twenty minutes drive away in separate cars. Fitzgerald was headed back to Fort Meade and Pamela Martin was back in her office at the State Department.

Powell and Clark were deep in very personal conversation when an aide entered the room.

'Sir! CNN has just reported a major airplane crash at Hong Kong International Airport within the last hour. If you...'

He didn't finish the sentence. Clark leapt up and grabbed the remote control of the huge sixty inch monitor that dominated one whole corner of the room. The screen came to life in less than a second.

Many of the more prominent international news reporters were already in Hong Kong to cover the Anniversary of the Handover. When the word went out that Zemin was going to use the event to make a "major patriotic announcement" it seemed that every news magazine in the world wanted to be there.

Hank Jason was head of news for CNN Far East. In Hong Kong parlance he was an Old China Hand. There weren't many left. Membership of the Hong Kong Foreign Correspondent's Club had dwindled since 1997 and every time he visited Hong Kong he looked up old friends and acquaintances at the Club to see fewer and fewer familiar faces. At sixty-five he had covered major events in Hong Kong since he was a fresh faced reporter from Newsweek in the late sixties. He had seen it all. The communist inspired riots in 1967, the Queen Elizabeth liner burnt out in 1972, Margaret Thatcher's disastrous trip to Peking in 1982, Patten's appointment as Governor in 1992 and of course the Handover in 1997. But he hadn't seen anything quite like this.

The T.V. screen in the White House office kept fading as if there was a loose electrical connection someplace. Finally the picture steadied and a serious faced Hank Jason, microphone in one hand and a newspaper in the other, spoke to the hastily assembled camera.

'This is Hank Jason CNN Hong Kong. The news here is just unbelievable! Just over an hour ago a China Southwest airliner, a two year old Boeing 737, crashed into the sea on final approach to Chek Lap Kok Airport. Although I'm a mile or more from the scene I can still smell burning aviation fuel. There were no survivors. Eye witness accounts from a high speed hydrofoil en route from Hong Kong to Macau say there was a massive explosion under a wing followed by a second smaller explosion seconds later.'

'Immediate reports suggest that this was not a scheduled flight but a flight chartered to bring Jiang Zemin to Hongkong for today's celebrations. The Chinese President is missing presumed dead. I have here a rushed first edition of the China Mail evening newspaper. I quote "Chinese dissidents are blamed for the explosions which are believed to have been caused by devices planted on the airplane in

Macau overnight. Suspects are currently being arrested at Macau Airport and...."

The line went dead and CNN returned to their New York anchorwoman Nancy Tyler.

President Powell looked terminally ill. 'Richard, get me that bitch Martin. I want her back here as soon as possible.'

'I'm sorry, Mr President, Pamela Martin has commenced her annual summer vacation. To Scotland as usual I believe.'

'Oh my God, Richard. What the shit is happening?'

President Paul Powell, the forty third President of the United States of America, would have had to have been a fly on the wall of the Kam Sang Restaurant in Kennedy Town, Hong Kong on December 10th 1982 to even remotely understand the answer to his perfectly straightforward question. But even the fly didn't know everything.

25

Hong Kong

12:00 Noon

The scene at the airport was one of utter turmoil. The north runway was closed to all but Chinese and emergency traffic connected with the accident. Unlike the old airport at Kai Tak there was no public viewing gallery and the authorities were able to shield everything to do with the morning's events from the rest of the world.

All scheduled flights were coming in and out on the south runway. Hong Kong was now one of the busiest airports in the world, almost as busy as JFK New York and London Heathrow.

At any given time the airplanes of a dozen airlines could always be seen on the ground at Chek Lap Kok – Cathay Pacific, Korean Airlines, All Nippon, United, China Airlines, Dragonair, Qantas you name it. Right now it was pandemonium. There were ten planes boarded and queueing up to take off. Up in the sky it was worse.

With half the runway capacity off limits, the controllers were having nightmares trying to co-ordinate all movements. Some fights were diverted to Manila in the Philippines and those without ample fuel reserves were stacking up waiting for their turn to land.

Captain Keith Griffin was in command of the Cathay Pacific Boeing 747. He had been with the airline for almost twenty years and was coming up for retirement soon. His previous job was flying RAF F4J's in 74 Squadron. The Tiger Squadron. It still took him all his concentration not to waggle the wings on final approach. He would save that till his last day!

One of his passengers on Cathay Pacific CX250 due into Chek Lap Kok at 11:00 was Pat Corcoran, successful jockey and the most amiable of Irishmen. He was lucky. His flight was only sixty minutes late and with the special immigration facilities laid on for the incoming VIP's he was soon into the waiting limousine to take him first to his hotel in Causeway Bay – the New Sunning House – and later to Happy Valley.

He was riding the highly fancied Sherillius in the Hong Kong Derby that afternoon and he wanted to make it a special day for its owner, insurance magnate John Ross. He was after all Chairman of Sportsurance International, one of the race's major sponsors!

The Hong Kong Derby now ranked in the top six horse races in the world. It was right up there with the English Derby, the Kentucky Derby, the Melbourne Cup, the Dubai Gold Cup and the Prix de L'Arc de Triomphe. First prize was a million dollars U.S. – tax free! At twenty eight he had won four of these world classics. Only the Hong Kong Derby and the Melbourne Cup had thus far eluded him.

It had already been an extraordinary month for Corcoran. He had come second in the English Derby two weeks earlier, ridden two firsts at Royal Ascot and then got the call to ride in Hong Kong. He had ridden for John Ross before coming such a close second last year on "Hollywood Plaza" – named after Ross's offices in the Territory.

His non-stop flight from London had been very restful thanks to the comforts of First Class. He wondered how on earth people managed years ago when it took a Pan Am 707 or a BOAC VC10 twenty four hours to do the same journey with five stops. The long range Boeings and Airbuses had been a boon to jockeys of international repute. It was possible to race in three continents in one week. Corcoran was making a fortune.

Once at the hotel an hour's sleep in his suite and a shower would suffice. Then, into the car provided to take him the one mile to Happy Valley. He slept like a baby only to be woken by a telephone call just before 4 p.m. It was John Ross.

'Hello, Patrick. Welcome back to Hong Kong – how was your flight?' Ross's accent was a hybrid of Oxford English and Transpacific Australian but Corcoran never lost his soft Irish lilt.

'Hi der, John. Nice to hear your voice again it is. The flight was fine but a little late what wit' all the goings on, security and the like. T'is unbelievable!'

'After the accident here I was worried that you might be diverted and unable to ride for me. I know how much in demand your services are – you were riding at York yesterday I believe?'

'Yes I was. You're well informed. My schedule was always going to be a bit tight. You know – what with getting t' Heathrow and all but here I am! It's always a pleasure to come to Hong Kong and to ride for you, you know that. Here's hoping we can win today. Do we have a good chance?'

'Our trainer, Graeme Turner, is as confident as he can be. "Sherillius" has been here for a month out at Sha Tin getting acclimatised. If she wins today we'll put her in for the Melbourne Cup in November. It goes without saying you'll be my first choice jockey, Pat.'

'That's great but one step at a time! Your trainer's reports emailed to me on Friday read very well. Are we certain that the race is going ahead after the assassination – if that's what it was?'

'Oh yes. There's far too much money involved anyway. The world-wide T.V. rights are worth at least a hundred million U.S. Nobody is going to forego that sort of money just because a President has been bumped off. There's political expediency, Pat, and there's money! Check the South China Morning Post on Monday. I'll bet you that most shares are up and the Hang Seng's riding high. 'Scuse the pun.'

Corcoran laughed. This was only his third trip to ride in Hong Kong but already he realised two things. Firstly, that money transcended politics. Secondly that everything and everybody could be bought at a price.

They wished each other luck and promised to meet at Happy Valley a half hour before the race in the owners' lounge. He took one more call before leaving his hotel an hour before the race.

Just before five o'clock his Toyota Crown limmo nudged its way out of Hysan Avenue and into Leighton Road for the one mile journey to Happy Valley racecourse. The car followed the tramlines past the old Lee cinema on the right at the top of Percival Street. Normally there would be long crocodile lines of people waiting to see the latest movie at the five o'clock show but today was Derby Day and everybody who had a ticket would be at the races. The other six million without a ticket would be watching the race on TV. Such was the pull of the imported 'Sport of Kings.'

On the left he spotted the Pine and Bamboo, a restaurant renowned for its ginger prawns and onion cakes and where he had dined the last time he was here with John Ross.

They were dining there tonight at a private party John was laying on for close friends and a handful of other guests. The normal punishing diet a jockey endured could be overlooked just this once. In any case he'd probably lose ten pounds in perspiration in this climate!

The road curved around to the left for the next half mile past a seemingly infinite number of shoe shops and into Happy Valley itself. On the right were the remnants of the old Craigengower Cricket Club, a green oasis in a desert of tall featureless office buildings. On the left was Harcourt Place – three apartment blocks previously used by the Royal Navy to house the families of sailors posted to Hong Kong. They were now used as quarters for senior civil servants of the SAR.

The Toyota's driver indicated to right turn into Sports Road and the Jockey Club. As he did so Corcoran tapped him on the shoulder and asked him to go straight on and do a full lap of the racecourse itself on the road that paralleled the course. The driver was not amused as he altered course suddenly and swerved in front of a moving tram. The tram driver clanged his bell in angry response.

The limmo driver grimaced sharply into the rear view mirror. *'A-hee-yah! Dew- lay- lo- mo! Gweilo!!* This was the worst and most disparaging of Chinese insults.

Corcoran's knowledge of Cantonese was almost nil but he realised the driver had taken his name in vain, probably questioned the validity of his parents' marriage and his nationality. Quite apart from anything else, he didn't care.

A half mile later as the car past St.Mary's Roman Catholic Church on the left, Corcoran's eyes misted over and he crossed himself in silent prayer. Thirty years earlier this Church had seen the Requiem Mass for the late Father Patrick Corcoran – a Salesian priest, teacher and missionary. Hong Kong's Mother Theresa.

It had been the biggest funeral in Hong Kong since the kung-fu movie star Bruce Lee's. Adored and mourned by the thousands of his former students, for the most part desperately poor people, they had come to say their goodbyes. Pat had seen the black and white photos dated November 1971 in the family albums back in Cork. The massed crowds almost obscured the funeral cortege – the trams at a standstill, unable to move forward on their buried silver rails.

Eight years later Father Patrick's youngest brother Harry, a railway engine driver in Cork, had named his youngest son after him. His damp eyes dried only slowly in the high humidity of Hong Kong's tropical summer. Today he would be riding "Sherillius" not just for John Ross but for his Uncle Pat.

In Hong Kong all jockeys had private changing facilities and a private telephone line. He had changed into his racing strip of white vest with the fast green "Sportsurance" logo embroidered across his chest surmounted with a small red Maltese Cross, a personal touch of owner Ross, a Queenslander. The State Flag of Queensland contained a Maltese Cross.

An hour later all the riders were mounted and ready to go into the stalls. There were ten runners – the smallest field for years. Normally run in October, the race had been brought forward to July 1st to coincide with Handover Day and the drenching humidity of July did not suit any unacclimatised horse. Several owners had withdrawn their entries.

Handover Day, the day the colonial British had to give up their former territory, had replaced Liberation Day commemorating the Japanese surrender in 1945 as a national holiday. Admiral Harcourt's triumphant arrival in Hong Kong harbour in the aircraft carrier HMS Indefatigable on

30th of August 1945 now meant something only to Hong Kong's oldest residents. The thousands who daily thronged Harcourt Road in the busy commercial district didn't even know who Harcourt was.

The announcer on the Tannoy methodically called out the runners, riders and owners from One to Ten, firstly in Cantonese and then in English.

Number One was "Dragons Teeth" owned and trained by an unknown Mainland Chinese entrepreneur. Number Two – "Jimmy's Jade" owned by Jimmy Wong, a renowned gold and jewellery dealer, Number Three was "Ever Sprinter" owned by the Evergreen Corporation of Taipei and so on...

After Number Seven the crowd hushed to near silence followed by a tumultuous roar as the lucky Number Eight was allocated.

'Num Eigh' said the announcer, switching into Chinglish... "Sherirrious!"

Within two minutes all the horses bar one were safely ensconced in their stalls. Only Number Seven, Tai Tam Tiger, seemed reluctant to race. A hood was placed over its head and a stable hand walked the horse round and round in several circles before leading it into the empty stall. The horse looked startled as the hood was removed.

The Jockey Club Steward called the jockeys to order. They were mere seconds away from the "off" and Corcoran glanced first to Numbers Nine and Ten to his right then to One to Seven on his left.

A final command from the Steward and the stalls opened. The Hong Kong Derby was under way bang on time at six o'clock. All horses leapt from the starting stalls in an instinctive reaction. All, that is, except one.

26

The White House
05:30 Hours EDT

President Powell and his Chief of Staff Richard Clark were alone watching CNN. Washington was exactly twelve hours behind Hong Kong at this time of year which made it easy to calculate.

There was still no word from the Chinese Ambassador. They knew that Jiang Zemin was missing presumed dead. The fact that this was being blamed on internal Chinese dissidents was an extraordinary turn up for the books and extremely fortunate. Clark could not hide his amusement.

'You've gotta laugh, Mr President. Scottish soldiers have blown Jiang away in the type of operation that most special forces would be proud of and they think their own people did it!'

'Yeah, but we still don't know if that is it as far the Scots are concerned. You're forgetting we still have the little difficulty of the fact that sixteen or more Tomahawks are scheduled to hit the airport within hours. Ambassador Chan has been as quiet as a mouse and we still have half the Chinese navy at sea ready for combat. They have not withdrawn and we have one of our own ships almost totally disabled in …'

Clark interjected. ' Sir, I'm not trying to diminish or downgrade the situation but surely as things stand we can't either lose or be seen to be the losers.'

'Richard, I appointed you as my Chief of Staff for your ability to organise our human resources here in Washington and your ability to throw new light on difficult problems but only you could say that we can't lose!'

'Sir, consider this. Whatever Secretary of State Martin did or didn't know about Operation Opium doesn't really matter now. Zemin is almost certainly dead. We have not been blamed. China has invaded the Spratly Islands either for the oil or for political reasons – which doesn't matter. But only us and the Chinese know! We have given them a deadline to get out failing which we hit them at thus far undisclosed targets.'

'Richard, you are driving me insane. I fail to see...'

'Sir, just consider this. What if we tell China that we have decided to hit the new airport at Hong Kong and supporting infrastructure with cruise missiles as a reprisal. After today's assassination they can also blame this on the dissidents or irregular units of the PLA. They will think that we've done it, as promised, when in fact the Brits will have done it albeit with our technology and at least some of our money. They can use it as a massive excuse for a big political crackdown internally and save face all round.'

'On top of that they will have to withdraw from the Spratlys or face another attack from 'us' and nothing will get public about our involvement at all.'

President Powell sat down and pondered the complex simplicity of what his Chief of Staff had just said. Five minutes later he picked up the black telephone handset and spoke to the Whitehouse exchange operator. 'Get me Ambassador Chan please.'

Such was the orthodoxy of the Global Village that ten minutes later both men settled down to watch the Hong Kong Derby on live T.V.

27

Happy Valley, Hong Kong

6:00 p.m.

Tai Tam Tiger was dead. The three year old gelding had a massive heart attack just as the stall had opened, slumping forward and throwing its Taiwanese jockey to the ground onto the sandy all-weather surface. The crowd was stunned. A thousand punters who had put money on the horse tore up their betting slips in disgust. The horse was apparently fit and had ran a brilliant race at Shatin a week before to win the annual Plover Cove Plate and a prize of a hundred thousand dollars.

The three laps of the track at Happy Valley made it the most arduous of Hong Kong's races. Tai Tam Tiger's collapse at the start in the adjacent stall had unnerved both Corcoran and Sherillius. It had cost them at least two lengths and more as the jockey let the horse regain its composure over the first lap. He didn't want to push it too far. Ahead were four jockeys' hats. He was lying fifth.

Horse Number Six, Repulse Bay, had also been upset by the horse next door's collapse and was trailing badly in the field four to five lengths behind the rest. After just one lap, effectively there were only eight runners left.

After the race Corcoran would remember nothing of lap two. It was a total blur on the senses.

Lying third with one lap left Corcoran was relatively happy. So was Sherillius. Purchased by Ross from an Arab syndicate a year before for a quarter of a million dollars, the black mare was his most promising horse for many a year.

A considerable gap had opened up between the first three and the remaining five. There was little doubt that the huge prize moneys were going to be divided between Number Four "Fizzgin", Number Ten "Tai Mo Shan" and Number Eight "Sherillius".

With a million dollars for the winner, a half million for second and a quarter million for third the stakes were high. At the very least it looked as if Ross would recoup his investment.

Passing the main grandstand for the last time before the finish the noise was indescribable. Fifty thousand people were on their feet to cheer on the leading pack. Corcoran gingerly nosed Sherillius to the inside of the left handed track and away from the distraction of the massive thronging crowd. Fizzgin, in the lead by a length for the last lap, was starting to tire on the outside.

It's Australian jockey, Ronnie McKenzie, started using the whip but it was to no avail and his horse visibly started to fade. He made no further effort to stir the horse. At ten percent of the purse twenty five thousand bucks plus expenses was good value for a weekend's trip from Melbourne. No point in killing the horse. He would console the owner later when collecting his cheque. No worries mate! Two horses left.

"Tai Mo Shan" was owned by Mr Kelvin Kai-wing Kwan, a local Hong Kong Chinese businessmen and well liked amongst the local and expatriate communities. Educated at Strathallan, Edinburgh in the Sixties he now assumed responsibility for running one of the biggest bus companies in the Special Administrative Region of Hong Kong. Established by his late father, the Cathay Motor Bus Company with its unique franchise from the old colonial Government, had been a licence to print money in the three decades before the Handover. Kelvin Kwan, "Wing" to his friends, was a multi-millionaire.

Kelvin had named the latest addition to his stables "Tai Mo Shan" after the highest peak in Hong Kong. Dominating the geography of the former New Territories at an altitude of over three thousand feet, from the summit you could see most of Hong Kong to the south and deep into China to the north. Its 'feng-shui' was impeccable, hence the chosen name for the horse.

Rounding the bend at the south end of the course "Sherillius" and "Tai Mo Shan" were just about neck and neck. Corcoran knew he had the slight advantage of being on the inside. Every foot was precious. Towards the end of the bend just before the long straight he glanced up to see the white roof of St.Mary's Church shimmering in the evening sunshine. Ahead lay three hundred yards of straight track before the final bend to the left and the run in to the winning post.

He had chosen not to wear goggles finding them uncomfortable in the humidity from previous experience. Not so the New Zealander riding the competition. He looked like he was using a welding torch, his eyes deeply hidden behind the tinted glass lenses. With his largely black riding vest and black cap he resembled a parasitic insect on the back of an unsuspecting animal.

At the end of the long straight both jockeys were directly facing the Jockey Club Headquarters, a six storey office type building that belied the luxury within enjoyed by its Members and guests. Corcoran was only minimally aware of spectators on the Members Gallery. He saw everyone but nobody, such was the onslaught on the senses from the noise of the hooves, the bright lights of the prematurely switched-on floodlighting and the gallons of sweat that seemed to be erupting from every pore in his body.

Once again they went into the bend neck and neck. The advantage Corcoran had gained from being on the inside had slowly but surely been eroded on the straight. As they turned left for the last time the insect seemed to lose his concentration and "Tai Mo Shan" veered out slightly to the right as its jockey momentarily used one hand to prise the goggles up onto his forehead. Now at least he could see where he and his horse were heading, such had been the effect of the fog within goggles.

But sensing his moment, Corcoran had taken the whip twice to Sherillius and hugging the rails as close as he dare he rounded the bend and rode for home. With two hundred yards left there was not enough left in "Tai Mo Shan"s tank to make up the shortfall. "Sherillius" had won the Hong Kong Derby by a length and a half.

Seven thousand miles away in Cork, Ireland, twenty three members of the Corcoran family gathered around one large wide screen T.V. burst into tears and applause.

A thousand miles to the south the Master at Arms of the USS John Paul Jones swore and threw his sweepstake ticket into the nearest gash bin.

In the main saloon bar of the Tilted Wig pub in Cumberland Street, Edinburgh the landlord smiled down at his Dual Forecast entry "Tai Mo Shan" and "Sherillius" and poured himself a large Glenfiddich. Thank God for InternetBet.com. He raised his glass to Kelvin Kwan's health. He hadn't seen him for some time. He owed him one.

In the Members Bar on the fifth floor of the Jockey Club, John Ross and Kelvin Kwan clinked their gin glasses together. 'Three quarters of a million bucks each – not bad, Kelvin.'

'Not bad, John, not bad. Cheers.'

'Cheers my friend. See you about ten later.' Kelvin Kwan departed.

The White House

6:00 a.m. EDT

The President and Richard Clark had both watched the race on satellite T.V. After the plane crash earlier they had figured that the chances of a 'follow up hit' at the race meeting were slim. They were right. The hit on Zemin was a one-off.

Neither of them were betting men so the result made no difference to either of them. It was too late to go to bed. They ate breakfast from the buffet which was already serving the early shift staff.

28

Pine and Bamboo Restaurant
Leighton Road, Hong Kong

10:00pm

The Pine and Bamboo Restaurant is not exactly on the tourist trail. Any visitors seeking local culinary expertise have invariably been recommended by other frequent diners. Non Chinese faces are a rarity but are politely greeted by the genial proprietor, Mr. Lee, who quickly ushers them upstairs to the huge two hundred cover open plan room.

Downstairs it was a different story. The whole of the ground floor was subdivided by highly ornate partitioning of intricately carved teak and rosewood panels. Strictly private parties only were catered for.

John McMillan Ross, at sixty one, was an international insurance magnate and a guru in his own field. He was to insurance what Bill Gates was to computers. He also had the Midas touch and every company he owned or controlled kept making money,

Apart from Sportsurance International which he owned outright, he also owned McMillan Rand, Scottish Rand and Hong Kong Rand as well as substantial holdings in a string of other companies across the Asia Pacific belt.

John was a shade under six feet and with his dark brown hair, gold rimmed spectacles and permanent broad grin had often been mistaken for the Northern Irish politician David Trimble. Anne had told him that if he could manage only a passable Ulster accent he could have made a few bucks on TV shows! Anne obviously didn't know how much money John was worth and that was how he wanted it kept. Imogen Ireland knew to the penny! Oodles of it! Imogen Ireland knew things about Ross's businesses that would make Yul Bryner's hair curl. However she was a model of discretion. She was to Ross what Fawn Hall was to Colonel Oliver North.

The circular table was set for eight diners. John Ross was accompanied by his wife, Anne, a genteel Melburnian lady who said 'yiss' every time she was spoken to. On her left sat her eldest daughter Suzanne from a previously dissolved marriage. John Ross's personal assistant, Imogen Ireland, was also on the guest list. She was seated on Ross's right. Imogen was left handed.

Long divorced from her oil executive husband she travelled the world with Ross helping him to run his companies, including the mysterious McMillan Rand , established in 1890. Anne Ross had thought sometimes that John was playing around with the super attractive Imogen but dismissed it from her mind as fanciful. She was thirty six, he was sixty one and she could seduce lots of younger men if she wanted pure sex.

Pat Corcoran sat next to Imogen Ireland. They got on well, both having been born in the Irish Republic. On previous trips to Hong Kong Corcoran had been 'entertained' by innumerable Chinese young ladies. How ironic, he thought, if he laid an Irish girl in the Orient. But it was Suzanne who was giving him more than a willing gaze. To ride a mare and a filly in one day wouldn't be bad!

Kelvin Kwan and his 'wife' Alice chatted animatedly to Anne and Suzanne about the prospects of a trip to

Melbourne in November. Anne liked Alice. Of Kelvin's several 'wives' she was the most Westernised and they often shopped and lunched together while the two men discussed business. Both women knew that Kelvin and Alice were not really married but it was never mentioned by either. The centuries old Chinese custom of keeping concubines continued.

When Kelvin Kwan went to the mens' rest room Suzanne nudged her mother's arm and whispered 'I've just remembered who Kelvin reminds me of. Do you remember the ludicrous Mr Chow Mein in the early Benny Hill Shows?'

Anne giggled softly hoping that Alice had not heard. He did look like Mr Chow Mein with his black suit, black rimmed eye glasses, brylcreamed black hair and thick Chinese accent that no amount of tuition would ever remove.

'He's even eating chicken tonight as well!' laughed Suzanne. 'Mr Chicken Chow Mein!'

Only one seat at the table was empty.

At five minutes after ten a green chauffeured Rolls Royce Phantom drew up outside the front door of the restaurant. Two of Mr Lee's senior waiters immediately rushed forward, one to open the huge glass door that insulated the air conditioned interior from the outside hell, the other to open the rear kerbside car door.

'Good evening, Sir. A great honour for us to receive you again.' spoke Mr Lee as he bowed his head with just a modicum of deference and steered his customer to his private table and the other seven diners. Now there were eight.

Jimmy Kam-fai Leung was back in town.

Operation Opium was going according to plan.

29

Carmel Heights Stanley, Hong Kong

After the superb dinner at the Pine and Bamboo Jimmy Leung invited the entire party to his villa for Sunday lunch the next day. He perhaps only spent several weeks a year in Hong Kong (usually to coincide with major horse races) but his magnificent house was kept staffed all the year round with three house servants, a gardener and a chauffeur for his beloved Rolls Royce sedan. He invariably had house guests whenever he was in town but very occasionally friends and business associates also used the house in his absence.

Carmel Heights was a delightful location. It was a complex of large privately owned villas built on the site of a former convent and retreat called Mary Knoll. It had been redeveloped in the Eighties and Jimmy's was by far the best and most expensive. Thank God he hadn't had to pay for it!

The 'feng-shui' was excellent with the high green mountain of Stanley Mound behind it and the delights of the emerald South China Sea to the south. The views were exquisite. On a clear day you could see twenty miles to the south and the Dan Gan Islands looked so close you could almost touch them. They had always been Chinese, even during colonial days, and were strictly 'off limits' then and even now.

After lunch of dim-sum, roast pork, fresh vegetables and ice cream, which cook had arranged to suit local and western palates, Jimmy took Pat Corcoran to one side and steered him to a secluded part of the house's garden. They had not met before this weekend and Jimmy wanted to speak privately.

A slightly puzzled Corcoran followed him to an ornate park type seat made from bamboo and another more European looking lumber. He thought it looked slightly familiar. It suddenly dawned on him – it was an exact copy of one he had seen the previous night in the entrance to the restaurant. Of course – it was made from pine and bamboo. The Pine & Bamboo Restaurant!

A houseboy brought two ice-cold San Miguel beers poured them into spotless crystal glasses and discreetly left them alone. Over the next thirty minutes, under the shade of a 'flame of the forest' in its full bloom crimson splendour, Jimmy told Pat everything he thought he ought to know.

He started by reminiscing about the year 1966 when Leung Shipping was a junior player. Life was pretty tough for new-comers but Jimmy's business was well established and he could just afford to live in a good area and send his two sons, Peter and Simon, to the Salesian Secondary School for Boys and Girls in Shau Kei Wan on Hong Kong Island. Funded by the Catholic organisation which gave it its name it charged fees to those parents who could pay and nothing to those who couldn't.

The school itself was a marvel of civil engineering built as it was on a thirty degree hillside on no less than seven levels. No space was wasted. Every mezzanine floor seemed to hide another classroom packed with desks covered in books, pens and inkpots. Basketball courts seemed to be around every corner you turned and everywhere was the sound of 'ping-pong' as every student aspired to be Asian Table Tennis Champion within a year. Principal of the School was Father Clementi Cavalin. The vice-principal was Father Patrick Corcoran.

Jimmy had been lucky. You could say he had the luck of the Irish if he wasn't Chinese!

It was August 1966 and Father Corcoran was returning from leave in Ireland, as always by cargo-liner. His normal practice was to take the ferry to Liverpool and take one of the regular sailings on the Blue Funnel Line to Hong Kong via the Suez Canal and Aden – a journey of some twenty eight days. However the longest British Seaman's strike in history had just ended and all the scheduled services were in chaos as ships sailed half empty or loaded to the gunwales as they endeavoured to bring order to the maritime freight chaos. Britain still had the world's largest merchant navy and the knock-on effect was felt right around the world.

Father Corcoran disliked flying intensely but rather than wait for the next delayed Blue Funnel sailing he opted for the last available cabin on the 's.s. Bendoran' sailing from London Victoria Docks on July 23rd. A fast sixteen knot cargo liner of the Leith Registered Ben Line, the 'Bendoran' was no slouch. Although delayed in the Canal for nearly two days she made most of it up en-route. After bunkering in Aden and discharging much needed munitions for the Argyll and Sutherland Highlanders she sailed at her top speed to Singapore. Taking on stores and more cargo she arrived in Hong Kong at midnight on the 30th of August. It had been a good trip. The other seven passengers comprised a British Civil Servant called Victor McCandless and his wife and two small children and three girls in their twenties – all secretaries bound for the British Consulates in Rangoon, Kuala Lumpur and Singapore.

After clearing quarantine the MV Bendoran crept slowly toward her owners berth, the Number Three Kowloon Dock. It was taken. An Alfred Holt owned Blue Funnel liner, Neleus, was already berthed there as Holt's Wharf was already full, such were the repercussions of the strike. The Bendoran eventually berthed at Number Four Dock owned by Leung Shipping. Out in Kowloon Bay other ships belonging to these two British companies were unloading cargo onto lighters. Benledi, the fastest ship in the fleet at twenty seven knots was racing to load her cargo of textiles bound for England and the loadmasters were working around the clock. The Scottish Ben Line and the English Blue Funnel Line regarded themselves as the cream of the British Merchant Marine. In the Far East they reigned supreme for decades and their Masters were almost regarded as Gods by oriental sailors.

As a token of thanks Captain Sinclair personally invited Jimmy Leung aboard the Bendoran for drinks and introduced him to the remaining five passengers. Thus began a long, long friendship between Jimmy and Father Patrick. The offer of the ship's berth and a simple but polite reciprocation would one day have implications for the whole of China. One day.

The houseboy brought two more ice cold beers.

Jimmy told Pat all about how his own two sons came to be educated at the Salesian School and how Leung Shipping became one of the biggest private donors to the school. He told him how his Uncle Pat had literally rescued thousands of young boys from illiteracy on the back streets of Hong Kong and how they had received a first class education at the school and subsequently become not just good citizens but in many cases very influential and rich businessmen in their own right.

He told Pat about their concerns in the Sixties, Seventies and Eighties for the future of Hong Kong after the Lease expired.

He told him how a vast war chest of money had been built up to 'preserve' Hong Kong if after 1997 things did not go well with their new masters in Beijing.

He told him about how, after Margaret Thatcher's disastrous meeting with Deng Xiao Ping in the Great Hall of the People in 1982, the writing was on the wall.

He told him how his Uncle Pat had used his enormous influence with his wealthy business connections to help the cause.

He told him how, over more than thirty years, truly staggering sums of money had accumulated in foreign bank accounts that would one day, if necessary, be used to revert Hong Kong to the successful status quo that would once again make it the richest jewel in the East.

He told him about the longed for Pearl Delta Republic.

He told him about Gordon Bedford and the NSA's compliance.

He told him about Bruce McCandless.

Lastly, he told him about Operation Opium.

Retiring to his hotel bed that night Pat Corcoran reflected on what a truly wonderful person his Uncle Pat must have been. He felt so proud to be a member of the same family and decided that if ever 'The Cause' needed his help he would give it. Freely and voluntarily.

He dreamed that he won the Melbourne Cup in November.

He also dreamed about Suzanne.

30

HMS Astute
South China Sea
115.4° East, 14.7° North

2ⁿᵈ July – 20:00 Hours

It was 16:00 pm local time. In two hours time the launch process would begin. One Tomahawk missile every two minutes. Four tubes twice. They had rehearsed it a dozen times over.

Bruce McCandless glanced somewhat nervously at the stainless steel Roamer Vanguard on his left wrist. It was an old watch – the kind you had to wind up. It gained two minutes a day but he hadn't the heart to replace it. Ironically his father had bought it for him in Hong Kong in 1967 a year after he took up his first three year Government appointment in the Territory.

Despite the passage of time McCandless had never forgotten arriving in Hong Kong harbour that hot August night with his parents and sister. What was the name of that Irish priest on the ship? He could never remember. It was a long, long time ago.

He summoned the Officer of the Watch and the Principal Warfare Officer to his day room.

The final countdown to the 'time of launch' had begun. T.O.L. one hundred and twenty minutes. He knew they would get it right. A state of excitement started to grow over the boat. This was the first time most of the crew had been involved in live firings of Tomahawk

The drills had all gone like clockwork. Ignoring the accurate atomic clock on the bulkhead his own Roamer told him that the time had almost come. An hour before launch he ordered all the Tomahawks to be got ready. However sophisticated a weapon there was always something according to McCandless's tidy mind, that was incredibly puerile about them.

On a five inch naval gun it might be something like the words *'point other way'* painted in red at the base of the barrel. Did the manufacturer in Leeds, Newcastle or Minneapolis really think they were going to shoot off the bridge with it? Maybe it was just some kind of a joke. Likewise the yellow circle painted on the deck around the main gun. Would anybody in their right mind walk close to the gun while it was being fired?

On the million dollar Tomahawk missile the joke read *'this plate must be removed before launch'* engraved on a metal sleeve about the size of a dinner plate at the base of the giant cigar tin that contained the missile itself. What amused McCandless was that the cigar tin probably wouldn't get into the torpedo tube at all unless you took the fucking thing off anyway. Maybe it was a misprint. Perhaps it should read 'remove before lunch.' That at least would make sense.

In the event all eight dinner plates were removed and the first four missiles put into Tubes One, Two, Three and Four. There's another thing. After loading the tubes the Principal Warfare Officer stuck a two inch by one inch brass tag into a little slot on the tube doors that read *'Tube Loaded'*. Can you believe it? A piece of brass costing about ten cents tells you that a million dollar missile has been inserted into a torpedo tube of a billion dollar submarine.

A qualified mathematician would probably confirm that there was some order and logic to this progression. To McCandless it was bullshit. Maybe his seniors at Dartmouth had got it right. Maybe he was a touch too flippant sometimes.

No matter. All was ready. The launch sequence began. McCandless reached for the Tannoy mike.

'T.O.L. fifteen minutes.'

McCandless ordered the planesman to take the boat to periscope depth. Active and passive sonars confirmed there were no surface vessels anywhere in the vicinity. A quick viewing through the main periscope confirmed their isolation. Good. In half an hour they would be out of here.

'T.O.L. ten minutes'

In the torpedo room the weapons' handlers had prepared the second batch of four missiles. In many respects they were re-enacting old fashioned gunnery in the number of rounds they were going to expend in such a short time. It was physically demanding and brought back fond memories of the field gun competitions of bygone years at the Royal Military Tattoos at Earls Court. That competition had itself re enacted the feat during the Boer War in 1900 when four inch guns had been dismantled from the cruiser HMS Devastation in Durban Harbour and dragged, yes dragged, overland by men and ropes to relieve the besieged town of Ladysmith over a hundred miles away. How times had changed. Or had they? Was not Astute about to relieve Hong Kong of its *political* siege?

'T.O.L. five minutes.'

McCandless started to give the orders for the firing. Ten years of hope and expectation was about to give birth to a new country. His hand on the trigger could change the world. And all with eight little rockets costing only a million dollars each. That was cheap. He started to feel that overbearing sense of responsibility that was shared by all nuclear submarine commanders. Was he, McCandless, about to change the destiny of the most populous country on earth? It had been done before. By Genghis Khan. By Kublai Khan. By Mao Tse Tung. But never ever before by a Gweilo, a Foreign Devil.

He started to concentrate on the job in hand.

'T.O.L. sixty seconds.'

'Thirty seconds. Planesman, keep the bow *down.*'

'Aye aye, Sir.'

'Fifteen seconds.'

'Ten seconds. Planesman, start to bring up the bow....... now!'

'Aye aye, Sir,'

'Five seconds.'

With a stopwatch in his right hand McCandless moved his left hand towards the firing button on the control panel. The button itself was flashing, illuminating the word FIRE in red on LED's in the middle of the button. The red letters reflected backwards like an ambulance sign onto the clear face of his Roamer. It was almost surreal.

The next five seconds were the longest in McCandless's life. He thought of his childhood in Hong Kong as a schoolboy. His mother and father at Dartmouth for the passing out parade. His father's pride at another naval generation in the family. His first appointment as a junior officer on the Leander class frigate Apollo. The endless weeks at sea and the separation from friends and family. The submariners' Perisher Course to prove suitability to command submarines. The meeting at the Excelsior Hotel in 1997 which was to change his life forever. The secrets he had to bear alone for years thereafter. The 'holidays' in

Maryland to cover for the meetings at Fort Meade. The endless preparations for the operation. The tearful farewell with his father before departing the United Kingdom in case things went wrong. Memories of the loss of the Russian submarine Kursk on August 12th 2000 were still strong in the minds of all submariners. He thought of the thousands of people whose efforts had made even the attempt at today's operation possible. And he had thought about this a hundred times – was he doing the right thing? Did it morally stack up? Deep, deep down in his heart he *knew* it did.

'Three. Two. One. Execute!' His thumb pressed the button and the letters stopped flashing. Forward, in the torpedo room there was a huge rush of air as massive compressed forces ejected the missile from the tube in less than two seconds. Four seconds from 'execute' the missile broke the surface and the outer casing fell away as small explosive charges rid the weapon of its cigar case overcoat and the torpedo turned into a missile. At an altitude of only ten feet the ramjet ignited turning it into a rocket as the water beneath it turned instantly to superheated steam.

Back in the conning tower McCandless squinted through the 'scope. 'Missile seen to fly. Missile seen to fly!' A cheer erupted from the crew. Seconds later McCandless could see that the missile's ramjet had successfully burnt out and separated. The Tomahawk's tiny wings popped out and it slowed down to its cruising speed of five hundred knots. Twenty silver cylindrical feet arched into the sky as the setting sun in the west glowed onto the Royal Navy logo and White Ensign motif adorning the missile's side. It was the first time this weapon had been fired in anger since the Kosovo conflict. It was also the first time that the United Kingdom had ever attacked one of its former Colonies in anger.

McCandless reflected again momentarily on the irony and morality of what he had just done. The second inspection through the 'scope returned his mind to the job in hand.

'Transition to Cruise C. Launch successful. Down scope. One down, seven to go. T.O.L. two minutes!'

Northwood were just four minutes too late. Seconds before Tomahawk Two was due to be launched the coded signal came in from London.

'*Abort launches. Proceed south to rejoin Ocean Wave. Message ends*'.

Thanks to a Captain's sentiment for an old watch which gained two minutes a day, Tomahawk One was already on the way. But Bruce McCandless was gutted and confused. What the hell was happening in London? Has the P.M. been got at? Immune from all communication from the outside world for almost twenty four hours, McCandless had no idea of the events that were unfolding on the surface.

McCandless cursed under his breath. 'Navigating Officer, set a course for where those tossers at Northwood want us to go! If I'm wanted I'm in my cabin!'

'Aye aye, Sir.'

McCandless mused to himself that at least one of the Tomahawks had got away. Suck that you bastards! He obeyed the order to rejoin Ocean Wave to the letter. He didn't bother to tell Northwood that Tomahawk One had already left the tube. Fuck 'em.

Two hundred miles to the north at precisely the same time, Richard Ribchester had taken HMS Ambush through the exact same pre-launch procedures.

Five minutes prior to launch, at periscope depth, their message came in from London.

'Abort launches. Rendezvous with civilian pleasure craft Sino Lusitano at position 15 degrees north 115 degrees east precisely at dawn July 4th. Recover nine passengers. Sink craft and rejoin Ocean Wave. Message ends.'

Ribchester was not amused. What the fuck was going on now? What do we do for the next two days. Go fishing?

HMS Artful
116.5° East, 13.6° North

Graham Sefton checked the time. Sixteen hundred hours Zulu.

In the absence of orders from Northwood he instructed the Officer of the Watch to set a course of '185', speed 40 knots. For him and his boat Operation Opium was over. In just over a day's sailing they would join exercise Ocean Wave a thousand miles to the south. After delivering Jamil their services had not been needed. He did wonder how many others knew about Jamil. Perhaps it was better not to wonder at all.

Lantau Island
21:45 Hours

Passengers on an outlying islands ferry from Hong Kong Island to Discovery Bay were quite used to seeing lights in the sky at night. Since the opening of Chek Lap Kok airport in 1998 four hundred aircraft a day either flew into or out of this huge man-made island on the northern side of Lantau. At a cost approaching twenty billion U.S., in its day it had been the biggest civil engineering project in history. But somehow this plane looked different. In fact there were no lights at all. Usually the red and green navigation lights were clearly visible together with a strobe light on the tail or landing lights if they were on the way in.

This was a very small airplane. An orange pink glow like a passing firework announcing its arrival into Lantau airspace. It had taken about eighty minutes for the Tomahawk to get this far at its normal cruising speed. The on-board navigation computer knew exactly where it was. It had received its final positional fix from a satellite and was now comparing its pre-programmed data with the information it was collating from its own terrain radar. Had this been a passengers plane the Captain would now be about to give the order to fasten seatbelts for landing.

On the northern slopes of Lantau facing the Chinese Motherland is the biggest statue of Buddha in the world. Completed before the Handover, it sought to remind the people of Hong Kong of the massive political changes to come. Its builders at the time could not possibly have foreseen the role it was about to play. Tomahawk One was flying almost due west at an altitude of two hundred feet. Ahead lay the airport. To the left was Buddha. The navigation computer took its last fix from the artefact itself and programmed the last phase of its flight. Climbing to just over a thousand feet it levelled out. The computer transformed the passenger plane into a Kamikaze bomb and the Tomahawk dived earthwards to its explosive destiny.

At 21:50 hours precisely, Hong Kong Summer Time, Tomahawk One slammed into the southern runway of Chek Lap Kok Airport at its western end exactly as programmed. The one thousand pounds of high explosive left a crater a hundred feet across and fifty feet deep. Collateral blast affected three aircraft taxiing to take off on the slipway. Nobody was killed or even injured. The three planes returned to their departure gates for damage inspection. It was dark and the real cause of the explosion was unknown.

The airport authorities announced that a violent electrical storm *'had ignited a fuel bowser and that, purely as a precaution, the airport was to be closed until further notice.'*

The second major incident at this international airport was beginning to cause major panic in some quarters. The news of this latest development reached Beijing in less than sixty seconds. It made one old man very happy.

Hay Ling Chau Island
Ten miles southeast of Lantau Island
Saturday July 1st – 22:00 Hours

Sergeant Tony Bryce, Royal Marines, was in charge. A veteran of several campaigns, mostly illicit, he had a wealth of experience in tight situations. A year earlier he had been lucky to escape with his life when a night-time operation in Sierra Leone had gone wrong. Again, in an inflatable, he had been up a long river estuary directing medium calibre naval gunfire support from the frigate Chatham onto guerrilla positions when he came under fire himself.

A lucky shot had hit the fuel line in his boat. The explosion threw him into the water and he was picked up by a support boat. The burn scars on his left forearm were the only visible reminder of just how close he had come.

At least Sierra Leone had been a U.N. backed operation. Bryce half laughed to himself – Jesus could you just imagine those gooks at the U.N. knowing anything about this one! China would quite rightly demand the expulsion of the U.S. and Britain from the Permanent Security Council if not the UN itself. Of course Bryce knew nothing about the Spratlys. Yet.

Things had gone tits up on the way back from the airport. How one job could go so well and then an hour later things go so wrong he just couldn't figure. Half way back to Chi Ma Wan inlet Blue One's engines petered out. Both of them. One was bad luck but two? He suspected fuel contamination – probably water. Sabotage? Quite possibly. The thought scared him shitless. As a precaution they did not salvage any of the fuel from Blue One. He was left with two boats and nine men – four in Blue Two and five in Blue Three.

He had decided not to return to Chi Ma Wan in view of developments. If it was sabotage there might have been a reception committee awaiting them.

Two days earlier Commander Ribchester had told him about using Hay Ling Chau Island as a possible backup. Ribchester was a mine of information with regard to Hong Kong waters. Hay Ling Chau was not on any maps printed in the last fifty years. But it was on very old Admiralty charts that Ribchester had loaned Bryce. 'You never know' he had said when he passed them over.

The reason that Hay Ling Chau was omitted from new maps was twofold. In the Fifties and Sixties it had been used as one of the world's newest leper colonies and the British colonial government had wisely decided to keep it off the tourist routes. In the Seventies it had been used as a refugee camp for displaced migrants, mostly from North Vietnam. The so-called Boat People. Another reason to keep it quiet. The authorities didn't want it known as a sort of Holiday Inn of political sanctuary.

According to Ribchester it had been closed and unused for some years. However it possessed two things he needed most right now – sanctuary and fresh water in abundance thanks to its natural spring.

The island measured less than a half mile square – less than a quarter of a square mile in total. It had a small sandy beach on the south side facing the open sea and a long concrete jetty to tie up at. A narrow metalled road led up from it to what was once a small but well equipped hospital and several small single storey buildings probably used to house staff all those years ago.

After secreting the two boats amongst the trees that extended almost down to the water's edge they had set up camp inside the old hospital administration office. It had obviously not been used for years but still smelt of xylene and tincture like all medical centres.

The nine men laid up all day and got some rest. After dusk they prepared to move out and meet Ambush in the Dan Gan Channel. They had got almost half way when the shit hit the fan.

Blue Three, speeding at 35 knots a quarter mile ahead of Blue Two, had almost run straight into a PLA patrol boat. Missing it by a hundred yards or less they veered off just in time hoping they had not been seen. Their hopes were dashed when a loud hailer addressed them in Cantonese and a searchlight swept the surface in wide arcs towards them. For a second Blue Three was illuminated. Had they been seen?

The answer came seconds later with the deafening sound of a medium calibre cannon and the water only feet in front of the bow boiled like a volcanic geyser.

Blue Two saw what had happened and had already turned thru' one hundred and eighty degrees at full speed. A lucky Blue Three followed them.

Twenty minutes later both boats and all nine men were back at Hay Ling Chau. They had not returned fire and hopefully had preserved anonymity.

Bryce took stock of the situation. Service manuals didn't cover this depth of shit. It seemed to him that the Chinese knew they were coming. But how? They had only seen one patrol boat but it could have been one of several. Or even many. There could conceivably be a whole bloody gauntlet of them out there. He didn't want to be on Chinese TV tomorrow trussed up in chains. The other problem was Jamil. He had orders in this respect that only he knew about. If there was any chance of capture by communist Chinese then Jamil was to be shot and thrown to the sharks.

The best course of action was to do nothing except stay put. At least they had water, some rations and a small but welcome supply of papaya fruits he had spotted on the island. In its heyday as a leper colony it had been almost self sufficient.

He knew that Ambush could not wait for him beyond dawn tomorrow.

HMS Ambush
Dan Gan Islands
South China Sea

Commander Richard Ribchester was a very worried man. The intended rendezvous with Blues One, Two and Three had failed to materialise. If the first one failed the plan was to repeat the exercise every two hours. There were no contingency plans for this.

When the scheduled time had come for him to fire his Tomahawks he wanted to be at least a hundred miles to the south and heading even further that way.

As a last ditch effort to locate the missing craft and their crew he decided to surface and launch their own inflatable to scour the channel and the immediate proximity of the nearest coastline. It was to head south and meet the sub one hour after dawn ten miles to the south come what may with or without the others.

Two of his crew volunteered and armed only with highly unreliable SA80 rifles and powerful flashlights they headed off into the darkness. It was a fruitless if well intended gesture.

Just under two hours later they were back on board.

Nothing. Absolutely nothing.

With great sadness and reluctance Ribchester ordered his boat to head south.

31

The White House
05:00 Hours EDT

President Powell had decided to call the British Prime Minister, Ben Bligh, direct. After the usual pleasantries they got straight down to business. Well acquainted by now they were always on first name terms.

'You know, Ben, you and I were still in short pants in 1968 but if we don't look out this could turn into a Pueblo type crisis for the U.S.' Powell recalled the emergency of one of the Seventh Fleet's intelligence gathering ships being seized by lowly North Korea and the crew being held for months as hostages.

'The John Paul Jones is totally on her own. We now know that the Chinese fleet that invaded the Spratlys is on its way home. We leant hard on Ambassador Chan and it seems the message went home. It seems like the mere threat was enough. We really didn't think they would withdraw at all but they have! The fact that Zemin's plane crashed is still being blamed on internal dissidents is good news all round. My guess is that they are genuinely scared and do not want another front on their hands over the Spratlys. How do you read it?'

'Paul, I concur. But we now have reason to believe that at least one Tomahawk was launched by HMS Astute and hit the target. Our signal to abort was a fraction too late and...'

'What!? Jeezuz. How the fuck did that…'

'Well it happened. Maybe it did convince the Chinese that you were speaking the truth and that they are expecting more. Hence the fleet turning back.. But we have a new problem Paul. The guys that shot down the 'plane are missing. The submarine Ambush was due to pick them up hours ago but they didn't show. They may have been captured and the Chinese are biding their time releasing the news to maximise the propaganda value.'

'We understand you have a third sub out there, Ben. Is she still primed for launch?'

'Thankfully no. Artful's heading south out of it as far as…'

'Can Artful protect the John Paul Jones because, if you can't help, she's at great risk. Whatever the orders from Swatow or Beijing it only takes one recalcitrant Chinese naval officer to take a pot shot at her out of sheer spite and she's a gonner. In her present state she could not defend herself against so many vessels.'

'Consider it done. I'll have a signal sent immediately. In the meantime we still have the problem of the eight missing guys.' Nine actually. Bligh didn't know about Jamil.

They agreed to speak again in an hour. It was at times like this that Powell wished he hadn't gone for President. Bligh called Northwood. Powell called Clark.

32

Pacific Place, Hong Kong

John Ross stepped onto the balcony of his serviced apartment in Pacific Place overlooking the western approaches to the harbour. With a glass of ice cold Australian Wolf Blass chardonnay in one hand and his cellphone in the other he gazed knowingly towards Lantau Island and the airport at Chek Lap Kok.

Within an hour he knew that the airport would be hit and closed. He also knew following his last trip to Edinburgh with Jimmy Leung and Kelvin Kwan that it wasn't dissidents that had taken out that plane yesterday.

Purely as a precaution he had booked Anne and Suzanne onto the late afternoon Qantas flight to Melbourne Tullamarine. Pat Corcoran had gone with them as he was riding at Flemington on Wednesday anyway. He wanted to get his first look at the course where he hoped to make a good effort in the Melbourne Cup in November. Apart from that he had taken a real shine to Suzanne. If there was any chance of getting into her pants he was going to take it.

'John, there's still time for some fun you know' said the soft Irish female voice from inside the apartment.

Ross went back inside and grinned as Imogen Ireland, still naked and wet from a shower, sauntered towards him with a smile and the rest of the chardonnay.

His wife Anne was a very attractive lady. Problem was that John had spent too much time in the East and, as they say, when in Rome do as the Romans. Imogen understood this and had learnt all of his little quirks. It saved him time and money buying it someplace else.

Still standing up, the gorgeous Imogen twined one arm around his neck and one leg around his buttocks. Her blond hair was thick even when wet and he felt and smelt the perfume of the shampoo as the dregs of the water started running down his neck as she pressed his lips to hers. What would he do without his personal secretary?

When they had finished he called Kelvin Kwan on his cellphone. There was no reply and his voice-mail didn't seem to be operative. That was unusual, particularly today of all days.

The unflappable Imogen called him back to the bedroom. He wasn't interested. Nor was his equipment. It was almost six thirty and the silence was deafening. He turned on TV Pearl, the English speaking station, for the 6:30 news summary.

The news anchorwoman was the gorgeous Geraldine Green, a stunning Eurasian who spoke beautiful Queen's English. Just the occasional vowel, it was always thirty "wonn" degrees Celsius not "wun",..betrayed her Mother's Yorkshire upbringing.

Nothing startling today. Some goon from Beijing was reporting on the crackdown on dissidents. More arrests had been made in connection with the airplane crash and suspected assassination of Zemin. The authorities were 'fairly close' to the truth apparently but they would say that even if they hadn't got a clue.

There were shots of the previous day's Derby winner, Sherillius, appearing at a charity gala for the Sandy Bay

Children's Home at Chung Hom Kok. Perhaps that was where Kelvin had gone as Patron of the charity. His eyes strained at the TV screen but he couldn't see Kelvin, just hundreds of kids all wanting to stroke the horse and feed it yet another carrot. It's crap would be bright orange the next day!

The newsreader's voice was just perceptibly winding down towards the inevitable weather report and the 'thirty wonn Celsius' when her eyes seemed to rise up to the autocue and she stammered:

'The Marine Police Department has just announced that earlier today it had engaged and beaten off suspected terrorists acting on behalf of unpatriotic forces in a heroic sea battle twenty miles southeast of Lantau Island. All enemies of the state were believed to have been killed.'

Ross's mind was instantly racing. It had to be connected to Operation Opium. But why had it been publicly announced? This was very, very unusual. Anything like this was hushed up normally. It could be they were really frightened.

He had time to think no more. The bell to the apartment was ringing. Imogen Ireland opened it wearing an almost diaphanous silk housecoat. A sealed brown envelope was passed over for which she had to sign a chit. The young bell boy found it hard to take his oriental eyes off her ample top half and she smiled to herself as she thanked him and closed the door.

Ross broke the seal on the envelope instantly recognising the Chinese characters on the 'chop' in the green wax. It was from a known associate of undoubted integrity. The message was short and to the point:

'Eight Caucasian and one olive leopards require immediate assistance and safe passage at midnight tonight. Acknowledge.'

'Leopards' gave away the location of Hay Ling Chau. Eight false British passports would be simple but the code-name 'olive' told him that a Mid East passport would also be needed. Not quite so easy. It would cost a few thousand bucks to his friend Ahmed at the Saudi Consulate!

Ross grabbed his cellphone, dialled a string of digits, waited for the tone and speaking clearly, acknowledged with the words 'Nine leopards understood.'

Leaving the frustrated Imogen only half satisfied he changed quickly into clean casual clothes and took the elevator to the lobby. Within five minutes he was in a red and silver cab heading south through the Aberdeen tunnel to his company's boathouse. He hoped to hell that his senior coxswain Mr. Ah-Hoy (Ross's nickname for him) was not either away in some gambling den or getting laid in some third rate Aberdeen whorehouse as was his wont on a Sunday night.

He paid off the cab and walked into the semi-lit boathouse. He was in luck. Ah-Hoy and three of the boat boys were playing mahjong on a small pine table surrounded by tool boxes and wooden packing cases. They had recently replaced the main engines on one of the boats and the sturdy Volvo Penta packing cases were useful stools.

'Dew lay lo mo, you lot!' barked Ross.

Mahjong pieces, coins, banknotes, ash trays and glasses of green tea flew everywhere as one of the men accidentally knocked over the flimsy table in his rush to appear otherwise occupied.

They needn't have worried. Ross didn't mind. He was just thankful they were there at all.

He owned two identical boats both called 'Sino Lusitano'. One was registered in Hongkong the other in Macau, the former Portugese territory forty miles to the west. It was often useful to appear to be in two different places at the same time. They were big comfortable eight berth pleasure cruisers with a speed of thirty eight knots on the contra rotating Volvos or, if range was the paramount concern, fourteen knots on the Caterpillar diesels. At ten knots on the Caterpillars both boats had a range of nearly five hundred miles. Enough to get to Taiwan if the shit hit the fan.

Ross drew Ah Hoy to one side and into the small office where the boats' papers were kept along with spare charts, almanacs etc.

Ah-Hoy had been employed by Ross's companies for almost twenty years. One of Father Patrick's former students he had transferred to the Hongkong Sea School at Stanley and after graduating had joined Leung Shipping as a junior deck officer. His present job paid one hell of a lot more. Today he had to earn his corn.

Twenty minutes later one of the Sino Lusitanos slipped into the darkness of Aberdeen Harbor, her tanks full of high octane gasoline. She was optimised for speed. With Ah Hoy at the helm once clear of the harbour entrance the boat skimmed at full speed around Ap Li Chau Island then due south into the darkness. The three boat boys called Ah-Hoy every name under the sun as they headed seemingly into the open void of the South China Sea. It must be that cheap opium he was always shooting up! Off his head!

Hay Ling Chau Island
Sunday – 20:00 Hours

Tony Bryce had had to make a decision. He knew that the mission had been compromised somewhere along the line. The polluted gas in Blue One's tank. The reception committee of the patrol boat halfway to meet Ambush. He could not rely on Ambush coming back at all. He could not expect it.

This was a tough one. He calculated that if they had pooled Blue Two and Three's fuel and left in one boat they might, just might, get about eighty to a hundred miles south. But south to what? Starvation and dehydration on the open sea? What would that achieve?

No. They had to stay put. Ribchester had told him about Hay Ling Chau – even given him an old chart. Ribchester must guess that's where they are now. Rations were low but with ample water and those papayas they could conceivably stay many days yet.

He explained his thinking to the rest of the men. Without exception they backed his judgement. They mentally prepared themselves for a long stay.

On the bridge of the Hong Kong registered Sino Lusitano Ah Hoy scanned the horizon with his Pentax night vision binoculars. Ayeee ah! He knew that pox ridden Colonial leper colony was somewhere at this latitude. The boat had all the latest GPS navigation system but that was useless if the place you are trying to find wasn't on the chart. He had the three boat boys scouring the horizons port, starboard and astern. His days at the Sea School had not been wasted and he decided that the island had to be within ten miles from a certain position on the chart. It just had to be. Assuming a circular search pattern he started at the centre of the circle in a clockwise direction with each lap increasing the radius of search. Two hours later there was an ecstatic shout on the port side as land was spotted a mile away in the dim moonlight. This had to be it.

Sino Lusitano circumnavigated the island twice to be on the safe side. Ah Hoy was not taking any chances. Ross would shoot him if he lost a boat. On the third time round he nosed Sino into the beach and cut the engines – alive but in neutral ready to reverse at maximum power at the first sign of trouble.

Irvine, on lookout, had alerted Bryce and the others as soon as he heard the big powerful engines. They saw it coming in from a half mile out and assumed defensive positions in the trees, M16 carbines at the ready.

When Bryce realised there was only one real adult and three boatboys barely out of high school he knew this was friend not foe. He emerged slowly from the vegetation and walked towards the water's edge, his carbine cocked but not threatening. Bryce's keen eyes surveyed the boat. What a beauty. This was no patrol boat. Ah-Hoy jumped into the knee deep water and knees shaking walked up the sand. He passed Bryce an envelope which he quickly opened and read.

'All aboard, boys. We're going on vacation to Hong Kong.'

Sino Lusitano powered its way back to Aberdeen at its full thirty eight knots. Less than an hour later all nine men were safely secreted in Ross's boatyard. The eight carbines and ammunition (and four unused Stingers) were laying somewhere on the bottom of the South China Sea. They were now civilians. Jamil had gone crazy when Bryce had thrown the Stingers over the side. He had vented his spleen about the cost of them at $50,000 each even to him via a source in Islamabad. As a consolation Bryce had let him chain smoke his beloved Gauloises all the way back to Aberdeen.

It was eight in the evening in London. Prime Minister Bligh was informed that all eight missing men were safe and in hiding. He heaved a sigh of relief and decided to call Powell with the good news. He still didn't know about Jamil. It was hoped that neither Powell nor Bligh would ever know about Jamil.

33

Pacific Place, Hong Kong

Ross was mightily perplexed. He had heard only one explosion from the west and the airport sometime earlier. It could even have been thunder. Surely the first Tomahawks must have been launched by now. Perhaps he had been given the wrong information. Had he got the time wrong? Had he got the date wrong? Surely not.

He tried calling Kelvin Kwan – still no reply.

He tried calling Jimmy Leung at Carmel Heights. A houseboy told him in broken English that Mr Leung would be 'back soon out for dinner.' After seventeen years in Hong Kong Ross had never ceased to be amazed at what he called the *noodle fix*. Ninety five per cent of the population seemed unable to go three hours without food. His waistline had also paid the price over the years for the ongoing gluttony. Every time he went on leave to Australia he tried to lose weight but like his wife said….'more of him came back than went.'

Imogen Ireland had said he should try and screw some weight off. He didn't argue with that! She had read somewhere that the average male loses three ounces of weight per coital act. That's a lot of pussy to the pound!

Fuck it. He had got the leopards evacuated safely and into his old 'safe house' at Oaklands Path. For the time being he had done more than his bit for the Operation.

He would await some further news and in the interim go and lose some more weight.

34

James Bellringer had invited his opposite number from the NSA, Peter Fitzgerald, over for a meeting. The CIA and the NSA were in theory on the same side but it didn't always quite work out like that sometimes. The Freedom of Information Bill had been a thorn in the side of both organisations for some time and it bothered Bellringer the most. Those pissing Liberals again! Wanting to know this. Wanting to know that.

Fitzgerald was a little more fortunate in that his department was clouded in a little more mystery than the CIA and its budget was never questioned. Not even by a pissing Liberal. Quite simply they couldn't find out enough to query anything. Powell was not informed of their meeting by either man. It wasn't that they deliberately kept him in the dark but, well, sometimes it was best not to bother him with the humdrum of everyday intelligence matters. After all that's what *they* were paid to do.

With enough coffee on the table to see them through without being disturbed Bellringer started to probe Fitzgerald's thinking.

'Peter, we both know that since the end of the Cold War the CIA's job has been diluted somewhat. Not exactly downgraded, just watered down a little. But the President is asking me things I just can't answer. You guys can listen in to any broadcast, cellphone or faxline anywhere in the whole world! I'm still relying on people, *hopefully* friendly, giving me information which we *hope* is correct. That means that we have to do deals with real people not switch on satellite links. Are you reading me?'

Fitzgerald frowned. 'Go on.'

'Well what I'm trying to say, Peter, is that much of the input from our end has to be verified before we believe it by more than one source. Sometimes that's not possible and we have to take a gamble on the integrity of the provider of the information. Sometimes we get suckered but mostly we get by surprisingly well in the circumstances. I want to talk with you specifically about Hong Kong.' Bellringer shuffled somewhat uncomfortably in his seat. 'You may not be aware of this but at the end of World War Two after the Japanese surrender in August 1945, the liberation of previously Jap occupied territories was a close run thing. Hong Kong was essentially up for grabs. The only reason that the Brits got it back was because the British Pacific Fleet was closer to Hong Kong than anybody elses. Some Admiral Harcourt guy steamed his carrier in, the King's flag went up and that was it. Now as it happened that was probably not a bad thing in the long run because nobody then knew that Mao Tse Tung's Communist Party would take over China. When that happened we decided to maintain more agents in the field in Hong Kong as our window on China. We had agents inside our Consulate who were known to our Consulate staff and we had others who were clandestine agents. Believe it or not a former Governor of Hong Kong was also one of us. He was a former British Ambassador to South Vietnam, as it was then, and his advice was invaluable. As you might expect. Since the Handover life has been tough – in fact almost impossible.

Fitzgerald let him talk. The NSA had funded all the British electronic intelligence gathering since 1965 but Bellringer didn't need to know that.

'Anyway, bottom line is that since the Handover we have had to, shall we say 'forge new links and make new friends' sometimes with people who not so long ago were regarded as more than a little unsavoury. Unlike you guys we have to talk to people, yah know?' What I'm getting at is that in the common interest we have gotten into bed with factions that would have been deemed unthinkable only say five years ago. What do you know about the Triads?'

Fitzgerald's jaw dropped about two inches. 'You can't be serious! Triads? The U.S. is in bed with Triads? Do you know what those mothers are like?! They virtually control all the Far East drugs trade don't they? Contract killing, vice…you name it.'

'Look, Peter, this is *realpolitik* OK. Some of our longest serving agents in Asia recently passed information to us about the attack on Jiang Zemin. We not only knew it was gonna happen. We assisted with the finance for it. Fifty million from the slush fund is what it cost.' He paused to let that sink in.

'But the Triads didn't actually do it. They hired the world's best aviation terrorist. Jamil ibn Salim. He did it – with more than a little help from ourselves and allies. Off the record of course.'

A low whistle came from Fitzgerald's lips. 'Wow. That's dynamite. If that ever came out..'

'It won't! But there's an added complication which we can do without. Ya know that with the Middle East boiling over again that I was called to visit the Palestinians over the 'intifada uprising' problem recently? Well part of the price that those guys have to pay, unconditionally, is that the senior terrorists, who seem to be beholden to nobody except themselves, have to be taken out. It's the only way to guarantee Israel's security, and the integrity of the Gaza Strip and the West bank. The Palestinian High Command have already acted, fearful of direct Israeli attack, if they didn't act quickly. Over twenty have already been killed. The PR guys just said they had died on martyrs' suicide missions. In fact they were shot by their own people. The big problem is Jamil. He's top of the 'take out' list. In theory he's attending a cancer clinic in Switzerland. In reality he's on a chartered rust bucket called the Aphrodite somewhere in the South China Sea between Hong Kong and Singapore. Exactly where we don't know. We don't have agents at sea! Can you help?'

Fitzgerald nodded silently, still staggered by what he had just learnt. 'I take it that the President doesn't know about this bit. All things being equal we can probably track down the Aphrodite from their radio broadcasts. With their mission over they almost certainly aren't maintaining radio silence. I'll have the boys onto it immediately. Give me twenty four hours.

Fitzgerald knew with a fair degree of certainty that the ongoing spy flights from Okinawa would be immensely useful and that satellite intelligence would also assist to a certain extent once its rough position had been ascertained.

'Yeah. Good boy. That's right. When the moment is right we'll tell him of course. Now there's something else my friend that you and I need to think very seriously about. Son of Star Wars.' Bellringer poured them both some more coffee.

Peter Fitzgerald had heard quite enough for one day but when he left Langley two hours later he was as concerned as Bellringer was. About his job and his pension. Jesus, he had no idea the position was so serious. If what he had been told was only half correct, or even a quarter correct, then the whole of the NSA's future was at risk. Bellringer had told him that inside sources on Capitol Hill had informed him that Son of Star Wars had become totally, totally unfundable. It had got out of fiscal control beyond anybody's wildest imaginations. Technically development of the project was on schedule. Fiscally, it was over budget by a hundred billion and the Federal Reserve Bank had privately advised the President to consider three options. Option one was to cancel. Option two was to increase taxes thirty percent across the board. Option three was to wind down the NSA and the CIA so as to effectively save enough money over the next twenty years to pay for it. Options one and two were both non runners for political reasons. Powell would want to go for another term for sure. Option three was his only way out. Both men knew it. What could they do to stop him?

35

At his desk next morning in Fort Meade, 'Crypto City' to the people who worked there, Fitzgerald was not his normal cheerful self. He had the air of a man who had been given a ninety day redundancy notice. Over at Langley, Bellringer was in exactly the same frame of mind. He scanned the front page of the Washington Post for the tenth time that morning.

'President gains further support from allies: Son of Star Wars forges ahead.' Yeah sure, he thought, but at what price? His job? The twenty thousand staff at the NSA? No Sir, that was not gonna happen. If the American public only knew that the country could head for financial disaster because of a President's obsession there could be major civil unrest. Wall Street would go through the floor if all this came out. The guy most likely to get Son of Star Wars stopped was Jiang Zemin – and he was dead. The CIA must be bitterly regretting their part in that operation, however tenuous. Shit, what a conundrum.

He was still waiting for the initial reports to come in from the South East Asia desk on the Aphrodite situation and had promised to keep Bellringer updated every few hours. Between them they both knew that they had to pull off something spectacular to save their own necks and jobs. If they could save the President's position as well so much the better. He would owe them both major favours, right up until the end of his second term. If he got re-elected.

His mind wandered again to the previous day's discussion on the Palestinian problem. The word 'problem' was a gross understatement! Fitzgerald believed that to look forward you also had to look back to the mistakes that had been made by others. The whole Middle East situation had been Armageddon waiting to happen since the Israeli State was constituted in 1948 after the UN Partition had failed the previous year. In the 1949 War Israel had lost the Gaza Strip and the West Bank and here we are over fifty years later with the situation still unresolved. There had been a multitude of Wars and conflicts in the interim. The Anglo-French invasion of the Canal Zone in 1956. The Six Day War in 1967. The Yom Kippur War in 1973. The Lebanon battles in which America paid heavily in human lives. The Iran hostage crisis that essentially doomed Jimmy Carter's presidency. The Iran Iraq War that lasted for eight years. Desert Storm in 1991. Terrorists operating from South Yemen. More dead Americans. Bin Laden. It was a long, long litany of tragedy and sadness for millions and millions of people. Mostly good honest folk who just wanted to lead peaceful lives, no more no less. Few peoples in the world are more hospitable and humble than Arabs and Jews and yet the never ending animosity between them, in the centre of the world's biggest oil reserves, posed endless problems for the whole world. Peace and stability in the Middle East was a bigger prize than even accord between China and Taiwan.

Fitzgerald pondered just how much effort had gone into solving, or trying to solve, the Asian and Chinese situations. Look at Vietnam. Americas biggest disaster, socially, militarily and politically. Yet the biggest trophy was still the Middle East and the Palestinian problem. He turned on the local radio station for the mid morning news which he often did if he was alone in the office. He listened to banal ads for diet colas and a new mega burger from a fast food chain. Then, on the hour, the newsreader gave a sixty second summary of news and events before the sponsoring company's repetitive little jingle reminded you of the new burger. There were usually four news stories lasting fifteen seconds each. That's news coverage for you. News item number one was about traffic build up on the main routes south to the resorts for the July 4th holiday. Number two was about a Right Wing Congressman who had been caught 'in flagrente' with his personal secretary by his wife who was now suing for divorce. Shit, nothing changes! Number three was an item about the price of gas being increased by some gas stations by twenty cents a gallon over the holiday period in a bid to extort motorists driving away for the holiday. News item number four was not a domestic story and took all the station's listeners unawares. By its very nature it was an announcement that would only come once every four years. The newsreader cleared her throat.

'And finally, news just in. The International Olympic Committee meeting in Moscow have just announced that the 2008 Olympic Games will be hosted by the City of Beijing. That's it. Tune in again at twelve noon for more news. This is Radio City on 96.2!' The burger jingle faded back in.

Jesus, what kind of society do we have these days, thought Fitzgerald as he lamented the lack of real news on the bulletin. Zemin's death was now ancient history. All most folks were concerned with right now was a two day holiday, a few beers, fireworks and the Bar-B-Q. That last item was interesting though. The decision as to where to hold the 2008 Olympics had been a long drawn out saga.

Several other countries apart from China had lobbied hard to find favour with the Committee. France. Canada. Turkey. Japan. There were the usual allegations of money changing hands, corrupt officials, unsolicited gifts to politicians. All the usual guff. Beijing had tried the hardest. Zemin had been dumb enough to really believe that the Olympics could have been held in a country where, on average, sixty people every week still got shot in the back of the head in football stadiums on a Saturday afternoon. Asshole. But hellfire, it's happened! Maybe things will be different in China by 2008. As sure as eggs are eggs they'll have to be. ' OK folks, we'll take a commercial break while a drug trafficker and a prostitution ringleader get shot in the long jump sandpit. Viewers wishing to watch the executions live can access via digital channel .....using your Visa or Mastercard.'

With the Palestinian situation still on his mind Fitzgerald walked out into the courtyard that was his little oasis from the ongoing hassles and tribulations of the office. There were not many staff about. People were taking advantage of the flexi-hours system and leaving early for the holiday. Critical ops rooms would still be manned twenty four hours a day though for sure. Not just here at Fort Meade but around the globe.

He thought about the Olympics announcement on the radio news and his mind interdigitated the story with the Palestinian massacre of athletes at the Munich Olympics in 1972. God forbid if that ever happened again. There would never be peace. Just imagine if some guy like Bin Laden or Jamil ibn Salim pulled off a major terrorist attack in Beijing. The situation was too horrific to even contemplate.

Suddenly Fitzgerald's mind clicked. That's it! That's it! A Munich-style Olympic massacre would be too ghastly to contemplate.. But there isn't going to be one. So let's invent the possibility. He rushed back to his office and called Bellringer on the encrypted line.

He had seen the latest CNN report from Moscow and was up to speed. Bellringer could not believe the news either that the IOC had been dumb enough to select Beijing as the 2008 venue because *anything* could happen in China in the next few months. Anything. They knew that better than most. Fitzgerald cut him short. 'Listen James, this is our big solution OK. The Olympics. The Beijing Olympics. Just listen to me please for two minutes.'

He reminded him of the Munich disaster. The shame on the host nation for the lack of security. The political fallout which had stirred up the Arab-Israeli hatred which was followed by a full scale war the next year. Imagine what would happen if say Jamil shot down a plane carrying the whole of the US Olympic team en route to the next Olympics in China. The President would never recover from it would he? Would he?'

'I guess not. Never. But it's not gonna happen...'

'So tell him that's what's *gonna* happen. He won't know any different! Tell him that during your recent meetings in Cairo with the Palestinian hierarchy that you were given highly sensitive information as regards Jamil's future intentions. That's why Jamil is top of their secret hit list to be taken out. Lie to him. Tell him you've done a deal. Tell him that Jamil's plans are well advanced. Tell him that the Palestinians have guaranteed that if Jamil is taken out by us then they'll take care of the rest. Tell him they guarantee peace with Israel for generations. Tell him! When you've done that we'll tell him that with the Mid East stabilised, and Iraq and Iran effectively neutered that the whole ethos behind Son of Star Wars will diminish. He'll go down in history as the American President who finally solved the problem of lasting peace in the Middle East, saved Uncle Sam countless billions and that without the need for Son of Star Wars money can be spent on welfare. Jesus, not only will he win a second term, if the Constitution allowed it he'd win a third!'

'All you have to do then is go back to Cairo and tell the ragheads that the deal is done. Powell will buy it for sure!' Jesus it's so simple but we don't have a lot of time. Firstly you have to do the deal with the President today. You must do it today OK? In fact you must do the deal with Powell within a few hours.'

'Why the rush, can't we think this one over for a few.....'

'No we can't, James. We can't because I have been passed information within the last fifteen minutes on the whereabouts of the Cyprus vessel, the Aphrodite, on which Jamil is sailing to Singapore. The Australians at DSD in Melbourne have come up trumps. Their listening post at Geraldton on the coast of Western Australia has been monitoring all the Aphrodite's radio transmissions for the last two hours. We have narrowed its geographical location down to a certain sector in the South China Sea and I am about to impart this information to San Diego and then to McCandless on the...'

'Mac who?' Bellringer didn't need to know.

'Our allies. Powell will ask the Brits to help hunt down Jamil. They have major naval units on exercise in the area including modern subs.'

'But that means that by conning Powell we con the Brits as well.'

'Who gives a shit? They've let us down badly over the undermining of NATO by accepting the European Army ideal. Its probably only a matter of time before they're out of the frame on our Intelligence Treaty anyway and UKUSA will be history. Trust me, James. Trust me.'

Just do the deal with Powell. He *will* buy it. If he looks like he won't move on Son of Star Wars then tell him we both know about the underfunding and that if he doesn't go along with all this we'll fuck him up good and proper. Start acting like J. Edgar Hoover. He didn't take any crap from anyone, Presidents included. You and I are gonna have to act real smart over the coming weeks and months James. Call me in two hours.'

'Check.'

36

After John Ross had lost another nine ounces shagging Imogen Ireland for the third time that Sunday, another message came by courier. This one was different. It was Government. British Government.

Would you bloody believe it? He'd managed to get the "leopards" off Hay Ling Chau and out of the Emerald Soup (his knickname for the South China Sea) and into his old flat and now some Gummunt Tossers wanted them back *in* the bloody soup.

Early next morning he drove down to the boathouse at Aberdeen. Ah-Hoy was just finishing his breakfast of congee and tea followed by six 555 State Express cigarettes. Ross didn't enquire where the cases of American cigarettes came from in the boathouse. Smuggling contraband tobacco and booze was just one of Ah-Hoy's little sidelines using one of the two fast boats. He thought he would wait a while before breaking the news that after today he would only have one boat to play with.

Ross told Ah-Hoy of the new orders and that the boat would have to sail out that night straight after dusk if it was to meet the rendezvous. He instructed Ah Hoy to remove the new Volvo Pentas and install extra tanks for diesel fuel only.

'*Dew lay lo mo* I've only just put the new fornicating engines in' said the exasperated Ah- Hoy.

'Yes I know. Just be grateful that you don't have to sail out into the Emerald Soup to rendezvous with something you can't see over three hundred miles away while all the time some guys with big cannons might well be trying to find you and blow you out of the water!'

Ah Hoy looked inscrutable as always and pondered why Mr Ross always talked about food.

He set to work on the Volvos.

At just after seven in the evening the nine men arrived in four taxis at about two minute intervals. Bryce arrived in the first cab and looked over the Sino Lusitano allocated to him. He checked the engines and the fuel load. The Caterpillars should easy take him the three hundred and twenty nautical miles to the anticipated rendezvous with Ambush, *ceteris paribus* – all other things being equal. He also checked the water and food that had been stored. If Ambush failed to show he didn't want to starve to death or die of thirst on the open sea.

Just before eight o'clock Ah-Hoy sailed Sino One out of the boathouse and into the inner harbour. A fisherman mending a net on a nearby junk gave him a friendly wave. With good joss he would bring him back a carton of Lucky Strike as a token of appreciation for his silence!

A minute later Sino Two followed in the wake of Sino One.

The fisherman waved again and…'*Dew lay lo mo*, what the fuck is this? Another Ah-Hoy?' Another boat? Oh well his last whiff of opium must have been a better quality then he thought. He went on fixing his nets.

Two miles south of Aplichau Island Sino One peeled off to the east in a sharp turn to port and the green luminescent waters boiled in its wake. Sino Two was on its own.

Ah-Hoy called Ross on his cellphone. The timing could not have been worse. He was just in the process of ejaculating the last ten percent of the next three ounces.

He was however glad of the news and made a mental note to send a bill for the boat to….shit…who *was* going to pay for it? He would speak to Jimmy about that. He rolled off Imogen and walked to the fridge for some more Wolff Blass.

This girl just couldn't get enough. Of cock or chardonnay.

37

McCandless had been gutted at the way the Tomahawk attack had been cancelled. He sure would like to have a private chat with Fitzgerald right now. All the planning and expectation was wasted. Just wasted. He did not know of course just what effect that *one* Tomahawk had had on the overall proceedings.

Dispirited to say the least he spent most of his time in his cabin. Astute was proceeding south towards Exercise Ocean Wave as ordered by Northwood but he had that nagging suspicion that the story might not be over just yet. He didn't know exactly *why*, he just felt it. Many submariners had a sixth sense like that. He always considered himself to be a very perceptive person but this extra sense gave him an awareness that sometimes bordered on the uncanny. He could not properly share his feelings with any of the officers or crew. He was the only one aboard who knew the full story of the Guys from Guandong and the NSA's involvement in attempting to bring a 'brave new world' to the most populous country on the face of the planet. He tried not to let his dejection show to the others and encouraged them to look forward to the rest of the deployment followed by the trip home and the reunions with their loved ones. But who would be waiting for him? In all probability nobody. When they eventually reached their Faslane baseport it would be three weeks leave. He might take a vacation. Just the mere thought seemed crazy. He would have just circumnavigated the entire globe and the first thing he was contemplating doing was taking a vacation. It would be early to mid August when they got home. Maybe he would visit some old friends from his school days in Hong Kong who had settled in the Isle of Lewis. A spot of fishing maybe. Then on to Edinburgh for the Festival and the delightful company of the delicious Irish girl that could earn a fortune as a Corrs lookalike if only she could sing! If McCandless had ever met John Ross he would have known about the 'singing and fucking' joke. He hadn't.

For the first real time in his life McCandless took stock of his life and his future. He could leave the Navy in October if he wanted to. His commission was coming to an end and the thought of a few more years behind a desk was anathema to him. No thank you. Maybe it was time to say goodbye to the Andrew and quit. His nose wasn't brown enough to get any higher up the tree anyway and only his close association with Lister, the First Sea Lord, had saved his bacon on more than one occasion. The Navy had changed immeasurably over the last twenty years or more and he did not like what he saw. The main problem was that too many good men were chasing too few commands as the numbers of destroyers and frigates in the Fleet had halved. On the other hand some things had changed for the better. For a start there were women on most ships and whilst the rules had said 'No shagging allowed' it should have read 'No shagging aloud!' He had recently read in the Telegraph that no less than nine female crew of one frigate, the Sheffield, had got pregnant. The Wrens were obviously spending too much time on the nest! He thought it would have made a great cartoon for the Navy News if only someone had the balls to do it. That was the problem. There just wasn't any fun in the Navy anymore. Unless you were on the Sheffield.

Lying on his bunk and contemplating teaching the Irish girl to sing and do what else the Italians did well, he was awaiting the call for dinner when a knock at the cabin door brought an encrypted message. It was from Crypto City. Fitzgerald had been working hard. It snapped him back into reality. Thoughts of Edinburgh were quickly replaced by mentally planning the possibility of military action in the next few days. That's more like it. Whammo!

38

John Ross was quite frantic by now. Although Jimmy Leung had got back home from his third noodle fix that day he still hadn't got a hold of Kelvin Kwan. He gave Jimmy the latest news and left the apartment, kissing the half dressed Imogen almost as an afterthought.

The cab got Ross to Number One Kennedy Road in about six minutes. He pushed the brass bell button and heard deep resonant chimes within. An amah came to the door dressed in the typical black trousers and white top, the uniform of her profession. Instantly she recognised Ross.

'Come in please. Missy here. Miss Alice . Please wait.'

He had been here for dinner many times. It was the favourite of the three houses that Kelvin owned in Hong Kong. Years before, in Colonial Rule, it had been the Masonic Hall or what the locals referred to as the White Man's Triad. He had kept the name – Zetland Hall.

When he had bought it in 1998 Kelvin had intended to extend it up another three levels to get a better view of Victoria Harbour. His plans turned into sand when he discovered that the previous owners had sold the *airspace* above it to the owners of the apartment block immediately behind it to preserve their good harbour views and therefore sky high rents. Had he ever joined the Freemasons he would have known that. Ross had laughed when Kelvin had told him. It was the only time to his knowledge that Kelvin had been caught out in a business deal.

Suddenly, Alice appeared from one of the two drawing rooms.

'Hello, John. It's always nice to see you but you do know that Kelvin's gone on a business trip don't you? He'll be away three days he said.'

John Ross was stunned. At a time like this?

'Do you know where he's gone, Alice.'

'Sure. He's gone to Scotrand. Back Thursday. Can I get you a beer?'

He drank several beers. That last bit of news was as welcome as the spring thaw after a New England winter.

Mentally he started to unwind and thought about the flight to Melbourne tomorrow afternoon. The internationally acclaimed win of Sherillius in the Derby only forty eight hours earlier had proved a massive publicity boost for one of his companies, Sportsurance International. He had received a call from a senior Australian financier who wanted to buy it. The company not the horse. Sherillius was too precious now as a brood mare, particularly if she won the Melbourne Cup in the coming November.

He thanked Alice for her hospitality and went back to Pacific Place. The adorable Imogen had run out of Wolff Blass but not energy. What a girl. Another six ounces!

39

South China Sea
16° North, 115° East

Bryce had trimmed the twin Caterpillar diesels to use as little fuel as possible. Thirty hours earlier on leaving Hong Kong waters he had skirted Sino Lusitano around the Dan Gan Islands rather than risk going through the Channel.

The fracas with that patrol boat several days before had interfered with the pattern in his underwear and he didn't want to take the risk. If they had been betrayed that was where they would be waiting to jump them. And now they were totally unarmed having previously ditched the carbines and ammo. With twenty twenty hindsight that had been a mistake. Too bloody late now.

The detour to the west had added over fifty sea miles to the trip but at least by daylight the next day they were out in the open ocean. It was now pure arithmetic. Miles to run divided by the fuel consumption…shit, why were the fuel gauges on the extra tanks detailed in litres? He asked Irvine how many litres there were in a gallon. Irvine asked him if he meant Imperial gallons or US gallons. Smart ass! Mutual discussion between all eight of them decided that there were approximately four litres to a US gallon and five litres to an Imperial gallon.

That gave him a possible error factor of twenty percent. Enough for some further interference in his nether regions which he could well do without. At least the boat had well equipped heads!

Out in the Emerald Soup the waters were now more than a little choppy. The two landlubber Jocks started to throw up. Bryce was quite pleased because the stiff northerly wind was assisting their progress. But probably not by twenty percent. More like ten.

The readout from the state of the art GPS system was updated by satellite every two and a half minutes. In fact the system on this Sino Lusitano was the very latest. Thank fuck Ah-Hoy had not swapped those over. Bryce could picture Ah-Hoy's face when it dawned on him in a few days time. *Dew lay lo mo!*

As the Officer in Command Bryce had control of all navigational matters. He had decided his best course of action much earlier. He had brought the boat to exactly 115 degrees east as confirmed by the GPS. He then headed 180 degrees magnetic exactly. His thinking was that if they ran out of fuel then Ribchester would second guess what he had done. If Ambush couldn't find him at 15 degrees north surely a sailor's instinct would make him search on that same vector to the north. He sincerely hoped it would not be necessary.

One thing did slightly bug him. They were now three hundred plus nautical miles south of Hong Kong and there was no danger of any Chinese patrol craft but they were however in the main recognised shipping lanes for sea traffic going to and from the huge container terminal in Hong Kong. It had overtaken Rotterdam as the world's biggest back in the Nineties and a million tons of shipping a day headed towards it on just about the reverse of his own heading.

He had already recognised the aquamarine blue colours of a fifty thousand tonner belonging to Maersk Line some dozen miles to the west heading north. They had probably not been spotted at that range being low in the water but it would be just their luck if they ran straight into some Long March Line vessel that reported their position. Also he did not want Ambush compromised if he could avoid it.

They headed due south all day. It was fiercely hot and all the men were glad of the shaded cabin space and ample water supply. Even Jamil who was used to the heat. Years of air conditioned offices had softened him up.

They had a mild panic mid afternoon when they heard the noise of a large jet airplane fairly close. Binoculars revealed what looked like an old Ilyushin cargo plane heading roughly northeast. Recovered from his sickness Campbell quipped that it was probably the 'crayfish flight' from Ho Chi Minh City to Taipei! His attempt at humour relieved the tension all round. If only he'd known he was right.

Night came. Bryce had to decide whether to put the navigation lights on or not. He had seen two more big ships before dark. Do I put the lights on or not? They might just assist Ambush to find them but there again he didn't want to be seen by anyone else. He decided to leave them off for now and put them on next morning for the last hour of darkness as they approached the agreed rendezvous point.

He never got the chance. Just after four in the morning the last of the litres, US gallons or Imperial gallons of diesel fuel passed through the Caterpillars and the twin propellers fluttered to a stop. The silence woke everybody up. A thorough search of the boat for more fuel, however little, revealed seventeen cartons of Lucky Strike in a hollow compartment. Poor old Ah-Hoy. Here we go again – *dew lay lo mo!*

The GPS revealed they were a half a degree short of where they wanted to be. At this latitude that was about thirty nautical miles by Bryce's mental reckoning. He was about right.

He decided to switch on the port and starboard red and green lights. He recalled how he had been taught to remember which was which. A bottle of port is red and the ship left port. Another hour of drifting roughly south and he would start to hallucinate bottles of port!

They were lucky. Dead lucky. At dawn Ambush was already at the appointed place at the appointed time. A sort of ocean going date except the girl was late as always!

Ribchester had no idea of what 'civilian craft Sino Lusitano' was. A yacht? A motorised junk? A passenger liner? He would sure like to speak to the asshole that had sent a signal like that. If it had engines then Ambush's sensitive passive sonars would pick them up many miles out. If it was a sailboat then the sails would be visible for some distance – even through a periscope.

After twenty miles of trawling due north he decided to surface. The added height of the conning tower would give them about another five miles visual range depending on the size of the vessel they were looking for. Ambush was doing 35 knots even on the surface and she left a brilliant cream stream in her wake. Shortly after 6 am one of the three lookouts reported a craft in the water about three miles off the starboard bow. It was Sino Lusitano drifting sideways to the east. Fifteen minutes later with all nine men safely aboard, Richard Ribchester then considered the practical application of the second order on the signal 'sink the craft.'

This little issue caused him more of a problem than he first thought. Nuclear submarines don't carry medium calibre guns. Sino Lusitano was more than a rowing boat.

He ordered a 0.5 calibre heavy machine gun brought up on deck. Campbell asked if he could do the honors. With more than fifty of the sixty six crew topside to watch the spectacle Campbell opened fire at a range of no more than two hundred yards.

Two hundred and seventy five rounds of ammunition and two minutes later Sino Lusitano looked like a chef's kitchen colander. She was about a foot lower in the water but just looked like she was fully loaded but with holes. With no fuel left on board to catalyse an explosion this was going to be a bigger job than first thought.

The crew were in cheerful mood. 'Come on you bloody pongo, can't you shoot straight in the Army?' Campbell was a touch embarrassed.

Irvine took over.

Then Bryce.

Sino Lusitano did not want to sink. Ribchester half considered ordering another case of ammunition to be broken out.

'Why don't we just ram it, Commander?' suggested Bryce to Ribchester.

'Because I don't want some dockyard flunkey back at Faslane asking me dumb questions about where the red and white paint came from on the bow when we get back to Scotland. That's why bloody not. OK!?'

Suddenly he had an idea. He ordered the crew to 'action stations' and submerged. Fuck it. He'd been denied the big firework display for reasons still unknown. Now he was going to have some fun. After all, orders were orders. Two minutes later he ordered Tube Number One to be loaded with a torpedo.

Another two minutes and the little brass tag was in the slot. 'Tube loaded.'

The GEC Marconi Mark Two Spearfish torpedo was the most sophisticated and expensive torpedo deployed in the whole world. At almost two million dollars it was twice the price of a bloody Tomahawk. And it didn't even leave the water!

He would call it 'target practice' and explain his dilemma to the naval accountants when they got back home. At a range of three miles Sino Lusitano was a tiny target. The firing solution was calculated by the arming computers and Ribchester gave the order to 'fire Tube One.'

Three seconds later the sonar operator shouted out… 'torpedo in the water, torpedo in the water.'

At a speed of sixty two and a half knots the Spearfish hit home just under three minutes later.

The explosion was heard by all on board and was followed by cheering all round the boat. A two million dollar torpedo had just sunk a boat worth less than one per cent of itself and fifty percent of Ah-Hoy's tobacco trade turnover went down with it.

If any of the seventy four men had been on the surface at the time they would have caught more than a faint whiff of some of Virginia's finest. They had forgotten to take off the seventeen cartons of Lucky Strike.

Ribchester had a little chuckle to himself. He reminisced about a conversation he had had last year in the Officers' mess with Bruce McCandless. It concerned the ten cent brass tags on the torpedo tube doors.

McCandless would have wanted a twenty cent tag for a Spearfish!

He ordered the Number Two to set a course for Ocean Wave.

40

It was mid morning on the 3rd of July and a comparatively relaxed John Ross rose from his bed fairly late. He was only an early riser when Imogen demanded it.

They had watched a late movie on satellite TV after he had returned to Pacific Place from Kelvin's house, Zetland Hall, and they both retired well into the early hours. After tea and toast on the balcony John suggested to Imogen that she went over to Kowloon with him before he took the airport coach to Chek Lap Kok and his flight to Melbourne. Imogen would not be going with him on this occasion. For the next few days at least he would play happy families with Anne and her daughters and after the business meetings would try and relax for a few days.

He knew that Kelvin would be looking after everything in 'Scotrand'. He also knew, following his conversation with Jimmy, that Pat Corcoran could be relied upon. John made a mental note to have separate discussions with the young man later in the week in Melbourne.

Having packed his suitcase he took the lift to the lobby and walked the hundred yards to the airport's City Check In. That was one of the reasons he had chosen an apartment at Pacific Place. So useful. They would both take the Star Ferry to Kowloon and have tea at the Peninsula Hotel before he took the bus to the airport.

Disembarking from the ferry on the Kowloon side after the ten minute crossing he pondered for a second on what an English friend had once said to him at that spot. 'Do you realise John that from here you can, in theory, walk all the way to Calais and be only twenty two miles from home?' The thought had stuck with Ross for years as typical of a Pom still suffering from Dunkirk Syndrome. Maybe it was a Pommy genetic disorder he thought!

Ross bought a London Sunday Telegraph from a newspaper vendor outside the terminal and quickly scanned the front page. There was nothing relating to Hong Kong whatsoever. A small paragraph at the bottom read – 'New moderate leader appointed in China – see feature on page twenty three.' He would read it later, perhaps on the flight.

Walking away from the ferry concourse they walked past the magnificent Victorian clock tower that had once marked the terminus of the Kowloon Canton Railway before a new station had been built a mile away on reclaimed land almost thirty years ago. The clock tower now stood in splendid isolation surrounded by elaborate flower beds and waterfalls. Walking fairly briskly despite the heat and humidity they crossed over the road and up to the junction of Nathan Road and Salisbury Road where stood the majestic Peninsula Hotel. The Pen.

Hong Kong's Peninsula Hotel surely ranks as one of the world's finest. It is right up there with the Waldorf, the Savoy, Raffles, Reids and Shepheards of Cairo. It was Ross's favourite venue for a meeting on the Kowloon side of the harbour. As they walked past the ornate fountain and the hotel's gleaming green Rolls Royces parked near the front door, Ross exchanged a familiar smile and waive with the top hatted doorman resplendent in his long coat and white gloves. To Ross it was the only hotel in Hong Kong with *real* class.

As he walked into the lobby and towards the giant reception floor a string quintet high up on a wrought iron balcony struck up "Greensleeves" and he pondered to himself that nowhere else in the whole universe could lay on a show like this. Little wonder that after successfully invading Hong Kong in December 1941 General Tokunaga had chosen the Peninsula Hotel as the Headquarters for the occupying Japanese Imperial Army. You could not feel more imperious anywhere in the world than at The Pen. Two months later in February 1942 the Japs commandeered the Raffles Hotel in Singapore. They were starting to acquire taste.

Settling at a 'table for two"towards the rear of the cavernous lobby, Ross ordered Earl Grey tea and cakes for them both.

The Earl Grey arrived in a silver teapot and Ross poured some into his china teacup without using the little chamois glove to prevent his fingers being scalded. In fact he had secretly used the cuff of his shirt. It was a little trick he always used to impress Chinese waiters. And Chinese girls!

They relaxed in each others company but somehow Imogen suspected that a change was beginning to come over John. Women's intuition possibly but a change nonetheless.

Before parting company John Ross ate two of the dainty little cakes from Imogen's plate and made a mental note to lose another six ounces of weight on his return.

They kissed goodbye at the door and John Ross took advantage of the hotel's courtesy coach to the airport. On the coach he read the Sunday Telegraph's feature on the new leader in Beijing. Ross laughed and wondered whether Li Shau Kee would ever attend a Burns Supper and eat haggis in gratitude. Almost certainly not. He would head the Politburo until he died of old age like all the rest. He recalled that old joke 'Why are all the members of the Chinese Politburo in their eighties?' Answer: 'Because all the ninety year olds are dead!'

As the hotel coach passed over the first of the suspension bridges towards the airport Ross tried to imagine what they would be like today if the four scheduled Tomahawks had hit home. It would have looked like the Rivers Tigris and Euphrates in Iraq in early 1991 that's what!

Twenty minutes later Ross was in the Qantas First Class lounge and mentally attuned himself to being back in Oz. His thoughts started to turn to the deal in Melbourne.

OstenBank Privat S.A.
Sion, Switzerland
Same date – 10:00 Local time

It was a warm Monday morning in the middle of summer and Heidi Roth (nee Muller) had dropped the kids off at school on the way to work. Since getting married and starting a family she only worked one full day a week, Mondays, and the half day on the Saturday. She still worked in 'Inward Remittances' but was now responsible for looking after only about a dozen private clients accounts. They all had the suffix 2007. When she had set up the first such account ten years ago in 1997 she hadn't picked up on the fact that 2007 might be a year. In the Nineties you didn't think about the Noughts very much. What were they going to be called anyway?

The first working day in the month of July seemed to herald a whole plethora of inward credits to the '2007' accounts. Heidi logged up the latest credit received today, another ten million US, to LSK2007. That was the tenth consecutive annual credit in the same amount. With interest it now stood at just over one hundred and six million US.

Whoever LSK was, he or she was a very lucky person. She glanced at the computer screen to check the other accounts. BVM2007 five million. RRR2007 two million. GES2007 two million. FLL2007 four million.

GTL2007 four million. The last five accounts were in round sums. The Bank's Partners had fallen into line with most other banks and had stopped paying interest several years ago. These accounts had only been opened for a year.

Heidi was always mildly curious about her anonymous clients. Somewhere in the world there were some stories to be told. Of that she was sure.

41

The White House

President Powell and his Chief of Staff, Richard Clark, were alone in the President's personal suite. They were unwinding with a couple of whisky sodas. Navy Secretary Mark Heitman had left an hour before to join his family for the traditional Fourth of July party down the coast. The President was in a relaxed if reflective mood.

'Ya know Richard, Mark is one smart guy. So is Peter. Where is Fitz anyway?'

'Gone to Cape Cod for a coupla days. Back Friday I believe.'

'Well they both deserve a break. One thing I have learnt over the last four days Richard is that politicians come and go. In the end they have to go, that's democracy. Like me at the end of the term in four years. In theory I am Commander in Chief but its guys like Heitman and Fitzgerald who have to bear the ongoing responsibility for security matters. OK, so Heitman went behind my back when he contacted CINCPAC but he knew things I didn't. Also, when Walt Audsley said the whole issue was a navy problem Heitman already knew that.'

'Between you and I this whole, possibly explosive situation over the last few days has gotta cause us to rethink a few important issues. Walt's a real nice guy but, ya know, is there really any point in today's world with having an Army General as Chairman of the Joint Chiefs of Staff? Today's technology has almost guaranteed that there will never be another major land war ever again. George Bush was probably the last President to order tens of thousands of troops into action in the Gulf in 1991. We will never need another 'Stormy Norman' again. We need guys like Fitzgerald and Heitman who really understand what's going on in the world.'

'That still leaves us the problem of China as a whole. We were caught napping and this time we got lucky. But next time? Well next time it will be some other son of a bitch's problem because I will have retired. I hope. Dear old Ronald Reagan was right. Bless him. South East Asia will always be a problem. Inscrutable Orientals. Chinese whispers. Bamboo curtains. You name it. Next we'll have Chinese Olympics. Shit I *still* can't believe that is actually gonna happen.'

'Richard, if Winston Churchill was right when he described Russia as a *'mystery wrapped in an enigma'* what does that make China?'

'A deep fried spring roll I guess, with a bit of everything inside it!'

'That reminds me, Richard, lets go eat!'

'Love to, Sir, but before that do have we any feedback yet on the situation regarding Secretary of State Pamela Martin?'

'That little problem, my friend, is going to require a lot more thought, a lot more thought. Did you know that the Vice President's almost certainly decided to pick Martin as his running mate for the next Presidential Election? Yeah, Symington told me only last week – in confidence of course. For the sake of the Party I'm gonna try and talk him out of it. Look what tokenism did for me! There are plenty of young guys with potential coming on nicely. There's Jim Callaghan if you want to pick up the Irish vote. There's Bret Hartenstein Macleod, the smart Long Island lawyer if you want the Jewish vote. But if I was Symington I'd pick Cuthbert Nestor, the young black from Louisiana. He's got a background in the oil industry and hates lawyers as much as I do. The guy in the street can equate to him! A kinda black JR Ewing! I don't think that Joe Public is ready for a Hispanic VP yet.

Richard Clark would pretend he hadn't heard that last bit. His wife was of Mexican origin. His second wife anyway. The first was dubbed 'the Hurricane' in White House circles. When she finally blew off..... he'd lost the house, the car, the camper...

'One last thing Mr President, strictly between you and I. Do you think that the 'Pearl Delta Republic' will ever come about?'

'Yes, Richard. I do. I really do. But not in my Presidency. Possibly in Symington's, if he wins. Operation Opium was only a limited success but it did result in a new Chinese President.'

'The way I see it it's only a matter of time before there's another Operation Opium, or something similar. Even with a more liberal President in Beijing the guys in the south of the country are not gonna stand for any crap anymore. After all they generate half of China's GDP with only ten percent of the population. Shit, would you stand for that? If the State of California was worth half of the US GDP do you think they'd send two Senators to D.C.? Would they fuck. They'd figure a way to make the San Andreas fault a hundred miles wide.'

'Like I said it's only a matter of time. In the meantime we have to maintain our vigilance to protect Taiwan. If the ROC decided to become part of the Mainland of its own volition then that's different. Li Shau King might be a better guy than the previous ten sonsabitches but he's still a gook and they've still got 1.4 billion mouths to feed despite extreme population control. Taiwan might be the political problem but it's oil, or the lack of it, that's gonna become the economic problem. Ten years ago most of them rode bicycles but now they all seem to want a Buick. Shit, if only they could afford them!'

'Come on let's eat. Tomorrow's another day. I almost forgot that it's the Fourth of July in two hours time. With all that's gone on in the last few days I think we deserve a break.'

'Yes, Sir.'

42

The Fourth of July 2007 brought different news for different people.

In San Diego it brought Commander Don Ramsey USN a headache. Assisted by crossing the Dateline from west to east he made all the flight connections from Darwin to Sydney and then to LA and finally home. He had a headache because he arrived on the night of the Third and drank too much Schlitz and bourbon *before* he started drinking on the Fourth. In his dreams! In reality he was still stuck on HMS Astute. However there were compensations. Her Majesty's vessels were not dry. He was given a bottle of Bells by the canteen manager. Ding dong!

In Washington DC it brought President Powell some mental peace and tranquillity after the absolute turmoil of the last five days. Although the Presidential Sikorsky helicopter was always on call to take him and the family anyplace within range, he decided to spend the holiday in Washington for a change. In a departure from tradition the President and his First Lady served the White House skeleton staff with T-bone steaks, Caesar salad and enough Budweiser to float the new CVN78 – if it ever got built. The story did not make the papers. Powell wasn't like that. In any case he wasn't running again for a long time yet.

It brought the hapless crew of the dry *John Paul Jones* another day of being towed at six knots. At least they were safe.

It brought Mark Heitman a very pleasant day indeed as he enjoyed an excellent Hog Roast with his family at their condo on Chesapeake Bay. Helen Heitman was in Columbus, Ohio with her feminist friends eating organic carrots and drinking distilled well water. Mark and his beautiful wife, Consuella, consumed an entire bottle of the best tequila money can buy. After watching an excellent fireworks display across the Bay they retired early. He was real tired. But not *too* tired.

Designed to create maximum embarrassment to the United States on its day of national celebration, a giant chartered Ilyushin cargo plane brought the U.S. Navy Aries spy-plane back to the U.S. in several large pieces. It was reminiscent of the way in which a Soviet Mig fighter whose pilot had defected to Japan had been returned to its rightful owners in 1979. Except that this time the boot was on the other foot. However, *because* it was a Holiday, few noticed.

In Tampa Bay, Florida, Pete Schaefer celebrated the Fourth of July by opening the 25th Farting Horse Motel in the chain. It was so successful it had almost reached cult status. He was real sorry that Gordon Bedford wasn't there to share it with him. Boy, now that would have been a session!

In Melbourne, Australia John Ross celebrated the sale of Sportsurance International to Bancasurance Australia PTY by losing another nine ounces, this time with the assistance of his long suffering wife and not his secretary. However, more of him still came back than went.

Peter Fitzgerald and James Bellringer did nothing of any consequence over the holiday period. They didn't need to. For the time being they were in the hands of others.

At River Road Apartments, Jacksonville, Florida it brought a ring at the doorbell for Betty Bedford just after nine in the morning. She was midway through making a Yorkshire pudding mix! She thought it was odd. There was never any US Mail on the Fourth of July. It was a FedEx courier on a motorbike. She signed the delivery note and shut the door. Puzzled, she took a sharp vegetable knife from the rack and sliced open the manila brown envelope. Inside was a smaller white envelope with a green wax seal at the join. She opened this too. Inside was a slip of pink paper that looked almost like a banknote. It was a cashiers check for six hundred and fifty five thousand seven hundred and seventy pounds sterling drawn on the Head Office of the Bank of Scotland at The Mound, Edinburgh. A million dollars negotiated at a rate of one dollar fifty five cents to the pound. Yesterday's official rate. Betty Bedford knew what it was. Gordon had been right. The 'Guys in Guandong' had kept their promise. Arthur Gordon Bedford was not *'such an asshole'* after all.

Betty cried like Niagara Falls.

43

10 Downing Street, London

The regular Thursday morning meeting of the J.I.C. – the Joint Intelligence Committee – had been brought forward seventy two hours at the request of the Americans.

As always, the meeting was chaired by the Prime Minister. Bligh was more than a little anxious at Peter Fitzgerald's personal call from his holiday home in Cape Cod the day before. On Independence Day as well for God's sake. Hadn't he got anything better to do?

Bligh glanced around the table before formally opening the meeting. They were certainly a mixed bunch, no denying that. To his immediate right was Admiral Sir George Lister, the First Sea Lord who was looking a little too smug for Bligh's liking. To *his* right, and he so wished it was anybody but Leadley, was Air Marshall Sir Paul Leadley, Chief of the Defence Staff, and on *his* right was Arthur Jones, the Director General of GCHQ in Cheltenham. At the end of the table sat Sir Lindsay McDougall, the Foreign Secretary and the Right Honourable Member of Parliament for Greenock and Inverclyde. At sixty nine he was the oldest member of the J.I.C.. In fact he was the oldest member of the Cabinet. Bligh had not been slow in realising that the Party was losing Scottish parliamentary seats to the Liberals and the Scottish Nationalists and that McDougall was hugely popular north of the border. As an Islander from Jura he was immune to the constant tribal warfare between the posh Edinburgh set and the more down to earth Glaswegians. If his pancreas held up with the whisky intake he would still be standing at the next election and could well pull in a few more seats in Scotland for the party. Bligh rather liked McDougall's slow thoughtful style and often called upon him for a resumé of complex situations. He was also ideal for sending on those tricky diplomatic missions overseas, mainly because the hybrid accent of his mother Gaelic and his adopted Greenock made him largely unintelligible to foreigners. On the other side of the table were the two Americans: Terry Moncrief was representing the NSA at Fort Meade and Herb Towse was representing the CIA. The NSA was regularly represented at JIC meetings but this was the first time in over forty years, at the height of the Cold War, that a CIA delegate had been present. His presence was the gist of Fitzgerald's call the previous day. Chief of the General Staff (Army) Sir Frank Lunn was absent on 'a golfing vacation' in Thailand. He always seemed to be on vacation in Thailand. He had been divorced for some years. Rumours of liaisons with nubile Thai hostesses were the source of constant gossip in Whitehall and Bligh was always under pressure to replace him but Bligh was his own man and Lunn was a bloody good soldier who knew the Far East like the back of his hand. He had served in Singapore as a boy soldier, Hong Kong, Brunei and the Jungle Training School in Malaya. Not for him the parochial idea of a Euro Army. The future was in Asia. His eventual successor would be some superannuated self important tosser who had strutted his stuff in the British Army of the Rhine. Bligh could always call on Lunn to back him up and he was real sorry he was 'golfing' again. Lucky bastard. He'd heard on the grape vine that in full flow Lunn made James Bond look like a woofter.

Just after nine 'o' clock the Prime Minister opened the meeting in his customary way by banging his black and red HB pencil against the side of his coffee cup. He often wondered why pencils were always supplied for these type of meetings and not pens. Maybe some office supplier had a little scam going. No matter. Bligh cleared his throat.

'Good morning, Gentlemen. Thank you for attending this meeting at such short notice. As you are almost certainly aware the events in the Far East over the last few days have dominated world headlines and all of us here today are privy to *most* of the facts.' He stressed the word most and as he did so Lister shuffled uncomfortably in his chair. So did Moncrief.

'As you know, the shooting down of the Chinese airliner which killed Zemin has resulted in the appointment of his successor Li Shau Kee who has already started to make positive overtures to the West. This is good news for us all and the expectation is that this will improve the prospects for Hong Kong, not to mention Taiwan. However what will never become public knowledge is the fact that a British Army Regiment was at least partly responsible for this.'

'However, there is apparently another twist to the scenario to which I am not yet privy, certainly, and this is why our two American colleagues are with us today. Welcome.' Bligh nodded towards them and they acknowledged with polite but silent smiles. 'Mr Moncrief, would you like to speak at this juncture please.'

'Thank you, Prime Minister.' Terry Moncrief lent his considerable frame forward but kept both elbows on the comfortable arms of the polished yew chairs. 'If I may, Gentlemen, I would like to give a resumé of the whole situation going back to even before the Handover. As you all now know, the NSA actually funded the United Kingdom's entire intelligence operation in Hong Kong from about 1965 onwards.' To McDougall this came as a shock but his impassive and pleasant red face, which was always red, kept staring straight ahead. What prompted this of course was the detonation of the first Chinese atomic bomb in Sinkiang Province in 1964. That was just the first Chinese mushroom. Three years later when they exploded their first hydrogen bomb in 1967 we all knew we had a problem. Things were moving so fast over there that to keep pace we, by *we* I mean the Western Alliance, had to have permanent listening facilities on the very edge of China itself. I'm sure that Mr Jones would testify to the huge success of the Hong Kong stations at Little Sai Wan, Tai Mo Shan and Kong Wei in the Sixties, Seventies and Eighties. And also at Chung Hom Kok in the Nineties almost right up until the Handover.' Moncrief paused momentarily to allow Arthur Jones to speak if he so wished.

Jones nodded in agreement. 'Yes Mr Moncrief, that is absolutely correct. Such an ongoing operation for over three decades was enormously expensive and without the NSA's funding would have been a non-runner.' He rather enjoyed his equine analogy which was lost on all of them except McDougall who had backed Sherillius in the Hong Kong Derby four days earlier. Scottish Foreign Secretaries seemed to have a yen for horses. He and his Labour predecessor, a fellow Scot, often met for lunch to discuss matters of the turf.

Jones continued. 'As a D.O. in Hong Kong in the early Nineties I can testify to the value of information gathered.' He finished abruptly. He was dying for a cigarette. He knew how much the Prime Minister disliked smoking and was secretly hoping that one of the Americans asked if was OK to light up. Bligh would not be impolite to a visitor. Jones removed a pack of Silk Cut from his suit pocket, placed in on the table in front of him and doodled with his stainless steel zippo lighter depicting the 'artful monkey' in the ship's crest of HMS Artful. His nephew had given it to him as birthday present before going off on Exercise Ocean Wave around the world. What a great experience for the young man at only twenty two. Jones hadn't known the full story. He was about to find out. Unfortunately, neither Moncrief nor Towse took the bait with the cigarette pack. Jones looked furtively to his immediate left. Surely to God, Leadley couldn't last much longer without a fag. He was right. The reason that Bligh had been appalled to find Leadley sitting next to him was that he positively reeked of tobacco and lit up incessantly. The sight of Jones's pack on the table had sent Leadley over the edge and he turned towards Bligh. 'Prime Minister, would you mind awfully if we had a two minute break to allow the weak willed amongst us to...'

He didn't finish the sentence. Bligh pushed a button for an aide who was duly instructed to bring in an ashtray that Jones and Leadley could share between them. At least the smoke would be limited to one section of the gathering. Leadley lit up a Lambert and Butler accepting the offer of a light from Jones's zippo. Bligh was appalled to notice that before returning the pack into the pocket of his Air Force Blue uniform he had placed five more cigarettes on the leather place mat in front of him.

'To continue, Gentlemen.' Moncrief's already attentive voice pitched up a few decibels. 'I can also inform you that our NSA made substantial contributions to the cost of the three new Astute Class submarines. The remainder came from inside China itself. Stunned silence all round. Lister smiled. Bligh noticed. Fuck him. He knew already!

'The plan 'Operation Opium' was in fact the general code name for the overall operation to unsettle the Chinese

Government in Beijing at the appropriate moment.' He told them about the Guys in Guandong and the meeting at the Excelsior Hotel in 1997 just before the Handover. The Excelsior Accord. 'Certain people were also on the NSA payroll at that. time. Some *still* are. The US Navy's Purchasing Officer in Hong Kong one Commander Bedford, was also responsible to Fort Meade as well as being a serving Naval Officer. I can also tell you with full authority that the Royal Navy's Captain Bruce McCandless and Commanders Ribchester and Sefton are also on the NSA's payroll.' Lister smiled inwardly. So was he, but he knew that Moncrief would have the good grace not to mention that. Not yet anyway. At the mere mention of the name of Artful's commanding officer, Jones stiffened up and he gripped the zippo suddenly realising that his nephew was under the command of an officer being remunerated by two countries. He hoped to shit there wasn't going to be a conflict of interest here. His fears were groundless.

'However, Gentlemen, apart from putting you in the picture with regard to the background to today's situation I would now like to introduce Mr Herb Towse, my colleague from Langley, Virginia. Herb.'

'Thank you ,Terry.'

Towse hailed from Mystic, Connecticut, and spent all his vacations restoring old paddle steamers back home at the Mystic Seaport maritime museum. He was a straight up sort of guy and what you saw is what you got. This was his first trip outside of the States but he addressed the meeting like he had done it every week. Bellringer had briefed him well and he knew his job and thousands of others were on the line at Langley and Crypto City. He and Ralph had rehearsed this mornings events like they were about to shoot the closing scenes in a Humphrey Bogart movie. The props meant nothing. It was dialogue, pure dialogue and it had to be the best. He pushed his silver Zeiss spectacle frames to the top of his nose and took a slow deep breath. He drew the forefinger of his right hand from left to right across his light brown moustache and deliberately looked in turn into the eyes of all five Brits before speaking. His voice had the timbre of a clergyman delivering the eulogy of the deceased to a mourning family.

'With full authority from Langley I can inform you that there is another fact of which you have to be made aware.' He spoke crisply and cleanly with no gaps between the sentences for reaction. It was like he was reading a mission statement.

'The person who actually shot down Zemin's airplane was Jamil ibn Salim.' He paused as others present drew in gasps. Bligh looked shocked.

'He was hired indirectly by agents in Hong Kong acting through known associates in the Gulf. The CIA effectively brokered the whole deal. Jamil had been on our wanted list for years but we could never pin enough on him to prove to the world that he was responsible for so much carnage. You must remember that to the outside world he is a philanthropist to the Palestinian cause and you all know how clever their PR is. Always has been. Our problem now is this. Jamil has done the job and as we speak is aboard the Cyprus registered cargo ship Aphrodite, heading for Singapore and...'

Leadley had just expired his own mushroom cloud of blue grey smoke towards the ceiling and interrupted Towse. 'How can you be so sure about this Mr Towse...'

'Let's just say, Sir, that in this life only two things really motivate men. If it isn't money it's pussy. Or what you guys call fanny I believe. Take my word for it, the Aphrodite is heading for Singapore. I'm sorry, Prime Minister, if this comes as a shock to you but if it's any consolation, Sir, President Powell was also only informed recently about Jamil's participation. That is why he asked for me to attend today, Sir. There is no question at all of sensitive information being withheld from our only real military ally in this world. But we now have another problem which has to be sorted. We at the CIA are almost one hundred percent certain that Jamil's cover at a hospital in Switzerland has not been blown. The world believes he is near Lake Geneva being treated for a rare lymph cancer. We know this because he is getting more than a hundred 'get well' cards a day from well wishers. The problem is that his next mission has already been planned and, if executed, will be the most terrible aviation disaster in history. He is planning to shoot down one of the new Airbus A380's as it takes six hundred competitors to the next European Games. Unfortunately we don't yet know where he intends to do it or any other details. There is only one way to ensure that it doesn't happen. We have to take him out now whilst he's a sitting duck on the South China Sea. The President has given it his blessing. It's the only way, Gentlemen. That's why I'm here.'

Stunned silence.

The silence was broken by the metallic crack of Leadley's brass zippo lighter going off. The weak chested Bligh coughed softly, almost not wanting to add to the noise. He made a mental note to place Leadley at the far end of the table at the next JIC meeting. The sound of Jones's zippo followed a few seconds later. Towse continued. He laid it on thick.

'Bottom line is, we badly need your help. Satellite intelligence isn't helping much. It's taking time to shift orbits and the South China Sea is positively heaving with traffic these days. We have one Los Angeles class sub in the region. You have three subs. Can you help us? There will never be any glory in this for anybody because nobody will ever know. If we succeed then we suspect that an announcement will be made that he died quietly in Switzerland while undergoing treatment. Gentlemen, may I suggest that Mr Moncrief and I retire from the room for a short time while you discuss this amongst yourselves? Only you can decide. I pray that you make the right decision and that God is with us all. Thank you.'

Towse and Moncrief retired to the rest rooms. As soon as an aide had closed the door all five remaining men started to talk at once. Bligh tapped the coffee cup with his pencil. Silence again.

'Gentlemen – please.' Fifteen minutes discussion followed. Bligh was against the idea. If it ever got out then with the Saudi crew going down along with Jamil the UK could kiss the ass goodbye to a few billion pounds worth of trade deals with Saudi Air. How the shit could he justify that to thousands of workers in the aircraft and construction industries? In any event he'd already promised his Euro Cronies at Airbus and in Brussels that a colossal deal for A380's was in the bag. If that went west his Euro-credentials would be wiped out. No, he was firmly against it. But if nothing else Bligh was a democrat. It would go to the vote. With only five men present there would be a decision immediately. Fuck it, Lunn wasn't there! He was already a vote short.

One by one, the other four men gave their view. Leadley, who had lit yet another Lambert and Butler, said to go with it. 'Sink the bastards!' Leadley knew that the RAF would not be involved at all so his yes vote was perfunctory. Bligh was inwardly seething – at the decision and the latest smoke bomb. Fuck him. Leadley was definitely going on gardening leave – real soon. One each. Three to go.

Arthur Jones was a career Civil Servant and not particularly military minded. He was a good egg and a nice man but he had spent a long time getting to the top of the tortuous GCHQ tree and he wasn't going to blow it now. He'd worked for his job. It hadn't been handed to him on a plate because he was an Admiral's son or because his former career in the Life Guards had petered out. He wanted his gong when he retired next year – a KCMG at least. Yes, *Sir Arthur* it would be. ' I think the whole idea is far too risky Prime Minister. If we lost a submarine we also have the loss of life on our side to contend with. Please remember that I have a young nephew on the Artful as well. I vote no.' Bligh smiled the sickly sycophantic grin that had become his hallmark. Good boy 'Sir'Arthur. Two to one.

Bligh nodded to his right indicating that it was Lister's turn to speak and cast his vote. The First Sea Lord already knew that he was going to vote in favour of the sinking attempt but for purely cosmetic reasons he tried to give an honest opinion. There was no way he was going to jeopardise his second NSA 'pension' when he retired in two years time. No Sir! Fifty thousand US a year paid directly into his Jersey account would double his earnings in retirement. The strong dollar against sterling would also help enormously. He folded his hands together and placed them on the table, looking at the other faces as he delivered his analysis.

'From a naval point of view the position could not be clearer. One modern submarine would easily be able to dispatch the Aphrodite – if its position could be determined. With three, four if you add the US sub, the odds are overwhelmingly in our favour. But it must be a clean kill, no flotsam drifting onto tourist beaches in a few weeks time with Arab writing on it. I cannot speak for the commercial consequences of being discovered which the Prime Minister has quite rightly brought to our attention.' Bligh nodded appreciatively. 'There are risks however, potentially grave ones. If the Aphrodite is roughly where we think it is then it is heading at some speed into extremely shallow and largely uncharted waters. The country's investment in new hydrographic survey ships was too little too late, as always. For that we can all blame parsimonious former Chancellors. It is unfortunate that it is our three latest submarines that are involved. As you know since 2000 major problems have occurred with the remainder of the submarine fleet with possible radioactivity consequences. Remember the hassle with Gibraltar in 2000? That was a close one. To risk Astute, Artful and Ambush which are state of the art platforms for Tomahawk and the only subs in the fleet that are totally reliable, could be considered irresponsible in the extreme.'

Bligh beamed. Lister was edging his way.

'Additionally of course there is the humanitarian aspect. Those three boats each have sixty plus men aboard. If we lost just one there would be all sorts of explaining to do to the British public. The political backlash to you Prime Minister, could be electoral suicide.'

Bligh was overjoyed at the level of support Lister was giving him. An elevated Knighthood perhaps at the next New Year's Honours list as reward? The Order of the Bath? Even a peerage.

'However, at the end of the day I am not a politician. I am paid to oversee Her Majesty's Navy in its capacity to defend the Realm. In my opinion the Realm is being threatened. I vote in favour of the action.'

Bligh was gobsmacked. The bastard! There would be another senior 'has been' going on gardening leave very soon. Two each. All eyes turned to Honourable Member for Greenock and Inverclyde. His vote would decide the issue.

The Foreign and Commonwealth Secretary scratched his chin. He was not best pleased at having to attend this meeting at all. He had been due to attend a dinner function the previous evening at the Glasgow Rangers Supporters Club in Bouverie Street, Port Glasgow. As guest of honour, he had a delightful speech prepared for after dinner which had now been wasted. After receiving a call from Downing Street in the early evening, his wife Margaret had driven him from their modest home in Greenock into Glasgow Central where he had taken the new West Coast Sleeper service to London Euston. He never slept well on trains and was a little jaded this morning to say the least. However he would do his best to impartially view the situation and try not to let his displeasure colour his judgement.

'Well, as I …

Bligh started to fidget immediately. When McDougall started to talk with the word *well* he knew they were in for a long haul. He was right. McDougall leant back in his chair as far as possible and pushed it back from the table with both hands, the cuffs of his Harris tweed jacket riding up his arms as he did so.

'Well, as I read the position, Gentlemen, we find ourselves with a very difficult dilemma indeed. But there again perhaps not *too* difficult. We have listened to the information and news delivered by our two American colleagues and I do not use this word flippantly. Colleagues they most certainly are. When I visited Washington in the Spring I was taken to both Fort Meade and Langley for a very thorough update on both organisation's operations. I have to tell you that American national interests, often scorned in our tabloid press, do not always come first. I was free to speak and openly converse with staff wherever I went and it was perhaps the sheer diversity of ethnic and cultural backgrounds that impressed me and yet they all regarded themselves as Americans, but aspiring for a better and more secure world not just for America but for the *whole* world. You have only to consider the names of the people we are involved with. Powell. Fitzgerald. Heitman. Novak. Moncrief. There's five different national backgrounds to start with. At Fort Meade I must have met people from thirty national backgrounds.'

'As the First Sea Lord has said in defence of the Prime Minister's economic concern, any adverse reaction from the Saudi's could put thousands of UK jobs on the line. Particularly in aviation. But Gentlemen, the same is true in the US. At Boeing. At Lockheed Martin. At Chrysler. At Jeep. We are not alone. The Americans probably have five times as many jobs at risk as ourselves. The only beneficiaries would be the French and probably the Germans. We all know how hard they have lobbied to get into the lucrative Middle East contracts, in Riyadh especially. No, our decision must be made without selfish financial considerations. From a political viewpoint you must accept my assurances that if the operation goes ahead and is successful, then not all Arab leaders will be sorry to hear of Jamil's death, in Switzerland or anywhere else. At a meeting I had in Qatar only last month the Emir advised me, privately of course, that there would be no long term solution to the Palestinian problem whilst there was even the suspicion that supporters' funds were being raised illicitly by various factions. There have even been rumours in some circles that some leading pro western Arab heads of state have put a price on Jamil's head. The last plane load of tourists that was blown up while landing at Luxor was attributed to Jamil in several quarters.

Egypt's tourist industry, always tenuous to say the least, is now totally bankrupt. What I'm trying to say is that if the operation was bodged and either we or the Americans were blamed then not all the Arab World would hate us. The US and the UK are still earning points from the Gulf War in 1991 and the much smaller but just as dangerous repetition when Iran's fundamentalists spilt out into the smaller Gulf States. The permanent beefing up of the US Fifth Fleet has been an enormously expensive exercise even for the US. That is one of the reasons their Seventh Fleet is perhaps not as strong as they would like. We have no reason to question the CIA's long held suspicion that Jamil ibn Salim is yet another bin Laden character. Mr Towse spoke most decisively on the potential dangers in general, not just the predicted Olympic disaster next year. An even worse scenario would be the consequences of not acting now and it subsequently transpired, after the event, that the US and British Governments not only *knew* of the possibility but were in a position to *prevent* it. I could not live with myself if in July next year I saw on television the wreckage of the airliner and all the human misery that goes with it. Just remember what the terrorists did at the Munich Olympics in 1972. Was it six dead? Imagine six *hundred*. You can't can you? Gentlemen, this is not just a question of supporting allies in times of need. Like Mr Towse put it. There is no glory in this for us. Only the glory of knowing that we were right. In my Island home we ask God for support when we need Him. We all need Him today. I think I have said all I want to say. Thank you.'

Bligh looked glum but McDougall's arguments were sound and well delivered. McDougall had almost convinced him that he was wrong. Maybe he was. Oh well. As the late George Brown had once said 'The nature of democracy demands that democrats must democ.'

'Thank you Foreign Secretary. That settles the issue. I will ask for Messrs. Moncrief and Towse to be brought back into the Cabinet Room.'

He rang the bell and an aide appeared who was asked to bring in more coffee as well. When the aide remarked that the two Americans were out in the garden having a smoke Leadley laughed audibly. Even the Prime Minister laughed. With the reaching of a very difficult decision the tension had all gone and the meeting thenceforth assumed if not a happy, a certainly more convivial atmosphere. Maybe there was no need for certain people to take up gardening after all. Towse and Moncrief returned to their seats and accepted the offer of more coffee. Bligh grabbed the moment.

'Gentlemen, I am delighted to tell you that our decision was unanimous and unequivocal. You have our full support for action. The necessary orders will be given without delay.' Bligh didn't know that McCandless was already planning the attack. The two Americans smiled and leaned across the wide table to shake hands with the Prime Minister.

Politicians will always be politicians.

A week later, back at their respective desks in Langley and Crypto City, Towse and Moncrief opened identical packages about nine inches across that had each been delivered by the Armed Forces Courier Services. Inside were miniature Oscars inscribed 'best supporting actor' and a hand written note saying 'well done, P.F.' Fitzgerald's sense of humour rarely shone through his professional capacity but he hadn't been able to resist.

44

After the meeting at Downing Street in the morning Towse and Moncrief did some sight seeing in London and flew back to Washington Dulles on a civilian American Airlines flight that evening. Next day, their body clocks in ruins, they reported back to Bellringer and Fitzgerald respectively.

On the ninth floor of his Ops 1 Building Fitzgerald started to unwind. The day before he had sent Bellringer a message with the 'Double gamma' heading. In Cryto Cityspeak gamma was the highest security rating for any communication intended for either the head of the CIA, the Secretary of State or President of the United States himself. Double gamma meant that it had to he hand delivered.

Fitzgerald had chuckled when Moncrief told him about Towse's virtuoso performance and it was then that he decided on the Oscar's prank.

'That's great, Terry. Now listen. Now that Prime Minister Bligh and his Scottish Secretary of State or whatever they call him, the Foreign and Empire something…well anyway, now that he's got your confidence we may have to play the game again at some time. We know that McCandless now has the *official* OK from his masters to hunt down and sink Jamil ibn Salim but we can't guarantee that he will be successful. If he fails, for whatever reason, then the deal that James has done with the Palestinians in Cairo will fall down and Star Wars will still be on track.

'Bligh is the weak link because of his problems with the European Army, the Eurodollar – is that what they call it? And other matters. We may have to put pressure on him to stop Son of Star Wars from a different angle. There is already a nice little divide starting to erupt between Bligh and Powell and the President was so miffed recently about Bligh consulting Clinton about foreign affairs that he deliberately left England off his itinerary for the last trip to Europe. That suits us just fine at present.'

'The message I sent Bellringer confirms what we are all hoping for. He flies to Cairo again today and it's all looking good. The Aussies have done a great job locating Aphrodite but it's up to the British Navy now. McCandless is the best, believe me, but he still needs luck and plenty of it. We should all be with him in spirit right now.'

Fitzgerald's mind wandered back to his lunch meeting at the Royal Overseas League in London and all those wall plaques representing countries that, over centuries, became English speaking via the British Empire. Now, in the 21st century, the NSA was the nerve centre of the new Empire of English Speaking Peoples. In his heart Fitzgerald liked to think that it was the biggest and most powerful force for good that the world had ever seen. At Crypto City the unofficial motto was 'In God We Trust, All others we monitor.' It was a maxim, a tenet even, that bound the whole of this huge international organisation together. It had seen off politicians and even whole Governments before. It might have to do it again.

45

Fitzgerald had decided that a heart to heart with his Deputy Director was essential and he had asked him to his private office where they would not be disturbed. It would not be a short meeting – he had a lot he wanted to discuss. An awful lot of water had passed under the bridge in recent weeks to put it mildly and, mindful of his own predecessor's sudden demise so recently, he didn't want his deputy to be in a similar situation if, God forbid, anything happened to him. If anything *did* then his deputy would be sworn in within twenty four hours.

Edward Eagleburger Jr. had been promoted to Deputy entirely on merit only six month's earlier. A Major General in the USAF he had all the right credentials and, more importantly, all the right experience for this job. At fifty one he had served the last twenty years in SIGINT in the places that really mattered as far as the world situation demanded now. Kadena, Okinawa. Missawa, Japan. Pearce, Western Australia and Menwith Hill, England. The last posting was absolutely crucial.

'Ed, what do you know about Son of Star Wars' from a fiscal viewpoint?' For the next few minutes Fitzgerald told Eagleburger about the gross underfunding and his secret meeting with James Bellringer. He was genuinely appalled.

'But doesn't the President realise that with a strong NSA and CIA the US doesn't need 'Son of Star Wars' at all. Any real threats will be discovered months in advance giving the military plenty of time to react with the forces we already have. Hell, we've had a specialist department to deal with the missile threat for a long time. Hasn't the President heard of DEFSMAC?'

Fitzgerald sighed. 'Yeah, but it's politics again. And dough. Many years ago Eisenhower was far-sighted enough to warn against the military industrial establishment becoming too powerful. He could see the problem decades ahead. The fact is that you can't beat a war for making dough for a lot of people. Vietnam made fortunes for many. With the end of the Cold War the vast orders for materiel have dried up. Just look at how few aerospace companies are still left in business. They've had to merge to simply survive. The contracts for Son of Star Wars will be compensation to a lot of people.'

Eagleburger listened while he was told about the 'set up' on Powell and indirectly the British. He also asked for his impression of the guys at the top at GCHQ in England, NSA's UK partner within UKUSA. Was Jones, GCHQ's Director, any good? Could he be trusted to work with us if we had to set up Bligh directly?

'I would say he is a good man, Jones. But we know he's due to retire soon and he won't want to upset the apple-cart before then. You know how the Brits work that old system of time honoured patronage. He'll be looking for a Knighthood I guess. Thank shit we don't have that crap over here.'

'Amen to that. But who will replace Jones eventually? Can we somehow put 'our own man' in there soon do you think. Maybe we should give this some very serious thought, Ed. Some very serious thought.'

46

Melbourne, Australia

On the other side of the world the deal with BancAssurance Australia PTY (BAA) to sell Sportsurance International had gone through with amazing speed. Nobby Clarke, an old school friend of John Ross, had set the deal up with alacrity following the world-wide publicity of Sherillius's win in the Hong Kong Derby. Nobby was Chief Executive of BAA and had had his sights on Sportsurance for some months without telling John Ross as such. Clarke chided himself that if only he had made the bid before July 1st he might have been able to buy it for a lot less than the three hundred million Australian dollar price tag agreed. Never mind, it was still just a drop in the Pacific Ocean to BAA. He must remember though to make sure that Sportsurance was still the sponsor for Sherillius in the forthcoming Melbourne Cup in November.

After signing the deal the evening before in a late night session in BAA's plush Collins Street offices, John Ross had been met by Anne who drove them to their family home in Box Hill in Melbourne's eastern suburbs. He was absolutely knackered but after a hot bath and some supper he had started to unwind and relax. How could so much have happened in five days? A day earlier he had wondered how so much could happen in four days.

He had not expected to see Anne for some time after she and Suzanne left Hong Kong on Sunday and in a way he really felt sorry for her being alone so much. After all, she was his wife despite the attractions and distractions of the insatiable Imogen. Anne was still a very attractive lady and although her genteel Victorian and reserved nature was always omnipresent, she still had a twinkle in her eye for a bit of 'sport' of the bedroom variety. *She* didn't have a 'bit on the side' in Melbourne! After serving John his favourite corned beef hash washed down with a half bottle of Hunter Valley red, her libido took over.

By the time he settled down to sleep, John had already expended sufficient energy to account for the two cakes he had eaten from Imogen's plate at the Peninsula.

The next morning John rose feeling refreshed and after a light breakfast he took the commuter train back into the city. Anne was spending the day with her elderly mother and this suited John fine as he had two important meetings today that were not in any way connected to the family. He got off the train at the Flinders Street terminus and, crossing the road towards St.Paul's Cathedral, he walked past City Square and north up Swanston Street.

It was damned cold to John. Melbourne in July is cool anyway but flying direct from tropical Hong Kong he felt it particularly bracing. He had never been particularly keen on Victoria as a place to live and his native Queensland was much more amenable to his laid back nature. The problem with Melburnians is that the first question they invariably asked you was 'What school did you go to?' Who gives a stuff. Why didn't they ask you if you wanted a beer first?

Turning into La Trobe Street by the State Library he crossed over into Russell Street and could see his 'Melbourne Office' only a hundred yards away. The 'office' was a beautifully restored bluestone building dating from about 1860 and, as the name implies, was constructed of stone quarried from the Grampian Hills about a hundred and fifty miles to the west. If the early settlers of Scottish descent who built it had known at the time that it would one day house the offices of the McMillan Rand Investment Bank they would have smiled. It was only a stone's throw away from Old Melbourne Gaol where the infamous outlaw Ned Kelly was hanged in 1880. His last reputed words of 'Such is life' had virtually become Ross's own personal motto over the last twenty years and like most Australians he had a grudging admiration for a rebel. After all he was an arch rebel himself in many ways.

To read the polished brass plates at the lobby entrance one could be forgiven for thinking you were in Charlotte Square, Edinburgh at one of those grand old buildings that now housed some of the worlds most prominent names in finance. John always read them from the top down as if he was having a sort of reunion every time he came back to the office. McMillan Rand Investment Bank. Scot Rand. Hong Kong Rand. And so on until he came to Sportsurance International at the bottom which after yesterday's deal would soon have to be deleted from the list.

John Ross rode the ancient elevator to the third floor of the ancient building. He loved it here. He would hate to be up in the clouds in one of those new fifty storey monsters that dominated Melbourne's new skyline. In his opinion the inter city rivalry with Sydney had got out of hand and Melbourne's response to the 2000 Olympics of building ever taller glass and steel monoliths was erroneous. Besides, Russell Street was more suited to their low key, non public profile. The historical external appearance of the 'old bluestone' belied the actual reality of the secret nature of the companies within.

'The Office' was essentially the Bank for the entire financing of Operation Opium and had been so for over ten long years. That inter bank transfer to British Nuclear Shipbuilders plc on July 1st 1997 had been effected from here, not Guandong.

Bob Chung, a former Hong Kong citizen who had emigrated before the Handover, welcomed John Ross as he always did. Bob ran the Melbourne Office. He had full security clearance. He poured a pot of jasmine tea for two as always without the help of that little chamois. It was Bob who had taught John Ross the trick

The two men settled down to talk, sipping the delicious jasmine tea as they did so. It had been a while, three months or so, since John had been at 'Head Office' and they had a fair bit of catching up to do.

'Well, Bob, I got your message that you wanted a chat. I'm here until the weekend now. With the Sportsurance deal signed so quickly I actually have a few days to myself for a change.

'Actually, John, it's money I wanted to talk to you about. Since the final payments to the shipbuilders in Barrow, England, we did have something of a shortfall in what I refer to as the Operational Account. You know the one I mean. The Hong Kong Derby earned us one and a half million U.S. in winnings if we add yours and Kelvin's prize money together and then…'

'Oi! Just a bloody minute. Sherillius is *my horse* not the Bank's and Tai Mo Shan is Kelvin's. I paid good money to that Sheik Ali Baba or whatever his name is and I'll be buggered if….'

'Sorry, John, I'm only joking. I know you've got an expensive lifestyle to fund *and* an expensive Irish secretary I hear!' They both laughed. 'But don't you and Kelvin forget that we paid twenty five thousand at this end for Ronnie Mackenzie, Fizzgin's jockey, to have a bad day. Also, there is the outstanding vet's bill for Tai Tam Tiger's "heart attack" that came through on E Mail today!' They laughed again. Wasn't racing in Hong Kong wonderful?

'No, it's the sale proceeds of Sportsurance I wanted to talk to you about. The Nominee Transfers were completed this morning and the three hundred million is being transferred across from BancAssurance this afternoon. With a few other odds and sods, some shares in British Nuclear Shipbuilders plc that we sold at a huge profit and the three hundred mill today there is now almost four hundred million in the Operational Account. If you remember, the last time we spoke to Frank Millard over at Williamstown, he mentioned a figure of three hundred and twenty million to convert all six boats. Didn't he?'

After they had finished the discussions and John had promised to pay the vet's bill and Mackenzie's payola, Bob said he was hungry and set off the ten minute walk to his favourite food stall in Little Bourke Street in Chinatown. That bloody noodle fix again!

Bob Chung did not have to remind Ross of the previous meeting with Millard. It had been in January at the end of the Christmas Holiday period when John had taken a break from Hong Kong and the physical excesses of the impossibly demanding Imogen. Their last meeting had been over at Williamstown Naval Dockyard on the west side. A sod of a place to get to even via the West Gate Bridge over the Yarra River.

No, bugger it. He had bribed Millard with a lunch at Mietta's in Alfred Place. To class conscious Ross in egalitarian Australia, Mietta's, like The Pen, had a touch of imperiosity about it that belonged to an earlier age. It should do. It was formerly the Naval and Military Club but its present owners had maintained its splendour. The formal restaurant was upstairs in what was the former ballroom. He had reserved a table for two by the window and Vice Admiral Francis Millard, R.A.N., was already waiting for him.

They both ordered. Mietta's had a reputation for some of the most imaginative and formidable food in Australia but in line with the Naval and Military image they also tried to preserve the sort of fayre that suited the Ross's and Millard's of this world. Ross ordered a steak and kidney pudding (baby's head in navy parlance) and Millard beef Wellington. Some imagination.

The two men had been friends for years and their respective fathers had served together in the old 'V' Class destroyer Vendetta in the Sixties. They exchanged salty and ribald jokes for most of the meal and left the bones of the discussion for the deserts. Trifle for Millard and bread and butter pudding for Ross. Even less imagination.

Ross was driving Millard to distraction and enjoying keeping him waiting for the news he was hoping to hear. It wasn't that Millard didn't have a sense of humour. Far from it. Ross recalled the first time the two had met for 'operational reasons' in Hong Kong in November 1990 – a long time ago. The destroyer Perth and the frigate Swan were tied up alongside at HMS Tamar, the smaller Swan outboard of the Perth to save jetty space. The sewage plant on the Perth had broken down and someone with a sense of humour had placed a huge hand painted sign on the gangplank up to the Perth which read 'Do not shit on the Perth, shit on the Swan.' The next day an artistic matelot had done a brush and paint cartoon about six foot square of a sailor, cap at jaunty angle, strides down, squatting over what looked more like a duck than a swan. It had amused thousands of passengers on the nearby Star Ferry. Ross was one of only a handful of people who knew that it was Millard who had painted it!

Ross had reflected what a good job it was he hadn't mentioned it to the late Gordon Bedford. He'd heard about the Farting Horse Motel chain.

Pudding and trifle consumed, Ross finally gave Millard the news. 'By the way, Bob Chung says to go ahead and place the order.'

All things being equal, within twelve months, the Royal Australian Navy would become the third member of the Tomahawk Club.

'Shall I inform the guys over at DSD at Victoria Barracks?'

' No. They already know but we won't go into that.'

Ross had known for some time that there had been agreed correlation between the membership of the Tomahawk Club and the NSA's UKUSA Sigint Treaty. It had only been a matter of time before Australia joined up. They'd had to wait for the new Collins Class subs to prove their reliability in service and solve the noise problem with the shafts. After that it was only a matter of finding the money from outside the Australian defence budget. The tax payers might object. So might a future government. The problem of the Canadians, another Treaty member, was already half solved. The UK Government had been leaned on to sell off their four Upholder Class subs cheap and their conversion to accept Tomahawk was expected next year. If the NSA could raise the spare cash. The only Treaty Member that would not get Tomahawk was New Zealand. It could not afford expensive submarines but in any case when a Labour Government had declared the whole nation a 'nuclear free zone' it had ceased to be a fully fledged Member and was consulted on important issues only when absolutely necessary.

Ross also knew that the NSA was about to embark on a major build up of its facilities in Australia. From a technical point of view it was prime real estate. The antipodes had long been regarded as an excellent intercept zone and had effectively replaced Hong Kong as the main monitor of Asian radio traffic – spy flights excluded. Politically it was safe as well. Even a Labour Australian Government was about as right wing as Genghis Khan. If he did decide to quit Hong Kong then, even Sportsurance apart, there would be a slot for someone of his experience with DSD or its derivatives. For sure!

The next four days were very enjoyable for John Ross. He spent more time with Anne and the family than for some time and although the air was a little too chilly for his liking it was good to get a break from the stifling heat and humidity of Hong Kong's tropical summer.

On the Thursday he and Anne had lunch with Nobby Clarke and his wife out at their ranch-style house at Ballarat. It was a two hour drive but it was a sunny day and Ross enjoyed the open space and big sky. During the drive he realised how much he really missed Australia. Secretly, Anne hoped that this little holiday might just make John think that he was not getting any younger and with a solid bank balance and a nice house all paid for maybe, just maybe, he might consider giving up the high flying Directorships of all the 'Rand' companies and think about *them* for a change. The problem was that Anne had absolutely no idea whatsoever of John's other commitments to The Cause and his country. Let alone his weight reduction programme with the insatiable Imogen.

Lunch with the Clarkes was a light hearted affair. They were good company. Afterwards, whilst the girls talked about shopping and grandchildren, Nobby and John strolled around the ranch's immediate grounds discussing the world and business in general.

'You know, John, the majority of our Board thought we were mad paying three hundred mill for Sportsurance. I only just managed to swing the vote because two Directors owed me one from a deal last year. When we saw your horse, what's its bloody silly name again…Sherillius..win that big race with the name on your jockey's shirt I just knew we had to have it. I reckon that by the end of the year we'll have the Sportsurance logo over every major sports ground in Australia – starting with the Grand Final of the Australian Rules Football at the Melbourne Cricket Ground in September. It's all so exciting!'

Ross didn't doubt it for one moment. BancAssurance Australia would easily recoup its investment within two to three years in sports mad Australia. If only Nobby knew that the money was going to finance the R.A.N.'s Tomahawk Club subscriptions and to further the aspirations of the NSA.

'John, you and I have known each other for years now and I trust your judgement in the insurance market entirely. If you decide to pack in chasing deals all over the Far East for that crazy quasi-Scottish Investment Bank then let me know, OK. There's always a seat on the Board of Sportsurance PTY here in Oz for you whenever you want it. Just bear it in mind mate.'

'Nobby, that's very kind. Really. Can you keep that to yourself for the moment and I'll ponder over it for a month or so.' Instantly, Ross's mind started to whirr round. Maybe it *was* time to stick with Anne. After all she is still a 'looker' and likes her nooky now and again. And there's also the corned beef hash to take into consideration. He adored his Imogen but he thought in many ways that the Irish were a bit like the Italians. All they could really do well was sing and fuck. Jockeys excepted of course.

The drive back to Box Hill was peaceful and uneventful. Ross mulled over Clarke's offer.

Over the weekend John and Anne did all the things they used to do. Shopped at Myers department store. Strolled along the banks of the Yarra. Looked up some old friends and generally had a quiet, pleasantly relaxing time. They invited Pat Corcoran over for lunch on Sunday together with Suzanne. Seemed like they were getting on just fine. Despite Pat's best seductive efforts he had yet to 'ride the filly' as well as the mare. Anne had chuckled to herself when she saw the glint in her daughter's eye. When the two men withdrew to John's study to talk horses Anne had a quiet word in Suzanne's ear.

'Don't dilly dally with this one my girl. He's loaded and a really nice bloke. He's another Dettori you know! Why don't you take him up the Gold Coast for a few days and, you know,…well you know what I mean. Just get on with it. I'm sure he's a red blooded male and if you'd moved as fast on him as you did the last bloke you fancied half your eggs would be fertilised by now!'

'Mum! Honestly.'

However, she took the point. It was time to take the bull by the horns. Or in his case the stallion by the nuts. Twenty four hours later, at the Ross family condo near Surfers Paradise, several hundred thousand of Pat Corcoran's little horses were charging into the straight heading for the egg carton. He wouldn't know for some time whether he'd got a win, a place or a quarter of a million non-runners. Frankly, he didn't care. He was smitten. So was she.

Later that evening Anne packed John's case for the flight back to Hong Kong the next day. He would have an early start – it was the non stop daylight flight arriving in Hong Kong mid afternoon, local time. The two hour time difference working in his favour might just give him some time in the office later. Setting the alarm clock for 6:00 am they went to bed. Sometime between midnight and sparrowsfart (dawn in Oz slang) John lost another six ounces. Anne was deliriously happy. After breakfast Anne drove John northwest up the Tullamarine Highway to the airport. The Qantas A330 departed on time.

Brunch was served on the plane about an hour into the eight hour flight. The thoroughly modern aircraft had all the latest high tech entertainment including a staggering selection of no less than five hundred movies to choose from. He scanned once very quickly through the electronic movie menu from 'Apocalypse Now' to 'Zulu' to see if something caught his fancy. Then he did it again, more slowly this time, sweeping the cursor more deliberately and paying more attention to the titles. A's. B's. C's. D's. E's The Elephant Man. Entrapment. Equinox. Eyes wide shut. Firefox. The Faculty. The Getaway. Godzilla. The Good The Bad and the Ugly. The Grapes of Wrath. The Great Escape. Happy Days. Heaven Help Us. Hit man. Hotel. Human Traffic. The Hunt for Red October. *Yes! The Hunt for Red October.* His mind was already in submarine mode after the discussion with Frank Millard. He'd seen it before ten years ago but it would kill the next one hundred and nine minutes according to the menu.

After the stewardess had removed the meal tray he settled down to watch Sean Connery starring as a Soviet nuclear submarine commander wanting to defect to the West. About half way into the movie there was a scene of a meeting taking place in the Admiral's day room on an American aircraft carrier. On the bulkhead was displayed a large wall plaque surmounted by a brass ship's barometer. *'Surrender be damned, I have not yet begun to fight!'* read the illustrated caption. It was identical to the barometer on the USS John Paul Jones that Bourke and Ramiros had wondered where they had seen it before. It was in the movie –The Hunt for Red October! No wonder! Red October and Crimson Tide were big hits amongst navy men and Ramiros practically knew the dialogue backwards to both movies.

Despite its vintage Ross enjoyed the diversion of the Soviet Connery and after watching it from start to finish he reached into his flight bag for the paperback that Anne had bought him at Tullamarine. It was a raunchy novel called The Gold Miner's Daughter set in rural Victoria in the days of the goldrush when Melbourne was the richest per capita city in the Empire. He read the first two chapters before the stewardess brought afternoon tea. Blimey she had changed her tune! It was the sexiest book he had read for many years. Not quite the Gardening in Retirement he had expected when she handed him the book wrapped in the bookstall's own glossy packaging.

The last hour's flight was entirely over water – the South China Sea. As he looked down the thirty thousand feet to the Emerald Soup he was reminded to invoice Jimmy Leung for the replacement cost of one of the two Sino Lusitanos. Plus the seventeen hundred bucks that Ah -Hoy was claiming for the lost cartons of Lucky Strike!

This would be his last flight into Hong Kong. He had decided to go home.

47

South China Sea
110° East, 10.5° North

McCandless was now fully aware of the enormity of the job ahead. The signal from Northwood following the meeting at Downing Street was expected. He'd already decoded a message from Fitzgerald in Maryland. He now had to earn his other salary. Not that he regarded it just as a remunerated task. He had believed in the ethics of the Tomahawk attack on Hong Kong and it wasn't his fault it had got altered. No way. He had smarted from the cancellation of the remainder of the attack but now he had the opportunity to do his country and his cause some good.

He started to analyse the duty he owed to his Queen and Country as a Royal Naval officer and to balance it with the personal affiliations he had with the NSA. Fortunately there was no conflict of interest. Far from it. One day there might be, who knows? He sincerely hoped not because, like Fitzgerald, he regarded the NSA as the ultimate keepers of world peace that transcended national and international politics.

He studied the charts with his Executive Officer. This was going to be difficult at best and impossible at worst.

DSD in Melbourne had passed on Aphrodite's location and within eight hours Astute was in her wake, five miles astern. From course and speed McCandless calculated that there would be an optimum time and place to sink her. Ideally he wanted to sink her just about dusk and preferably in as deep water as possible. Like Lister at the London meeting, he was worried about evidence surfacing at a later date. He was looking for a depth of five hundred feet if he could get it, better still six. He'd read the files about the Pueblo case in 1968 and its commanding officer, Bucher, had orders to ditch all secret papers in leaded bags in six hundred feet of water if possible. Retrieval at that depth is almost impossible. Sadly Bucher had never got the chance to do it and the Koreans had seized his ship before the US Air Force in either Korea or Japan could get there to help him. That catastrophe had set back the NSA many years in esteem as well as intelligence. It wouldn't happen again.

It was just after twelve noon. The Cyprus registered Aphrodite was heading roughly southwest at fourteen knots towards Singapore. The Saudi crew were in high spirits. At first light that day they had rendezvoused with a huge black submarine and taken back on board their 'boss' Jamil. Ambush had spent only three minutes on the surface and Ribchester wasn't taking any chances in being spotted as they lay right in the middle of the main Singapore to Hong Kong shipping lanes.

Over lunch of lamb, rice and lentils washed down with bottles of Cyprus Keo beer they had found in the ship's stores, Jamil bragged to his Moslem brothers of the money he had just earned. True to his Faith and philosophy he had already donated more than half of the ten million deposit to the Palestinian cause. Mostly to alleviate social deprivation. But the extra forty million? Well, that was different. To each of the ten skeleton crew he would give a million dollars. No wonder they were celebrating. Jamil promised to open

Swiss accounts for all of them with the money. Apart from their silence being essential, he might need them again.

After lunch Jamil took a well earned rest and slept for several hours. In less than two days he would be in a luxury hotel in Singapore in the company of the luscious Imogen and all his other dreams would come true. At sundown the sound of several of the crew at prayer on the main deck awoke him. He decided to join them. Allah had been good to him. So far.

Two miles to the east on a parallel course of 211 Magnetic and also travelling at fourteen knots lay HMS Astute. The final cards in the life of Jamil ibn Salim were about to be played.

McCandless and his boat had tailed the Aphrodite for over a thousand miles. He knew Jamil had done his job for the Guys in Guandong and the Regiment. He could only assume that he was heading for Singapore and the promised sexual liaison with the Irish girl he had been told about. She must be quite a girl to have sold Jamil this one. Why didn't he ever meet women like that?

Only a handful of people knew that Jamil was not going to reach Singapore, or anywhere else for that matter. In the UK only McCandless and all those who had attended the meeting of the JIC knew. In the States Fitzgerald, Heitman and a few trusted staff in both their departments were aware of what was about to happen. So was Wayne Novak at CINCPAC at Pearl harbour. Powell and Bligh had eventually had to be told. Apart from protecting the USS John Paul Jones this was the other reason that following Heitman's advice, Novak had dispatched three U.S. submarines to the South China Sea at great haste.

The USS Sea Wolf had covered the exit to the Pacific north of the Philippines. She would not be needed. The USS

Toledo had covered the Sulu Sea in case the Aphrodite had headed for the comparative safety of the Moslem State of Sabah and possible diplomatic protection. But no, Jamil was following the route of a thousand warriors before him. After the victory the spoils. Imogen.

McCandless knew that the third US submarine, the City of Corpus Christi, was laying in wait for the Aphrodite twenty five miles to the southwest. He had updated CINCPAC direct every half hour. The plan was for both Astute and the American sub to attack Aphrodite with two torpedoes each at 7:15 pm local time. They could not safely leave it any later. By that time the Aphrodite would be midway between Ladd and Discovery Reefs on the edge of the Spratly archipeligo. The waters were getting shallower and shallower. The First Sea Lord's reservations about the dangers had been genuine. At the intended attack co-ordinates Aphrodite *should* sink in about eight hundred feet of water – beyond diving depth for any subsequent investigation if word got out.

As the brilliant orange sun set in the west towards Vietnam and the Mekong Delta, McCandless ordered his crew to action stations. He told his crew over the Tannoy that as part of Exercise Ocean Wave they were firing two live Spearfish at a former Malaysian frigate that had been listed for disposal and target practice. The crew believed every word. Under the Five Power Defence Agreement in South East Asia, Malaysian Navy participation was commonplace.

Just after 7:00 pm the Commanding Officer of the Corpus Christi, Captain John Leroy Bridges, a black from Woodhaven, New York City, ordered his crew to General Quarters. Tubes one and two were loaded with Mk 48 torpedoes and the boat was brought up to periscope depth. Boy, if only Mark Heitman could seen him now. They had both served in Naples together. Mark had gone into 'paperwork' and eventually become Navy Secretary but John had stayed with the sea. Both were happy. The conversation over their next beer together would be fascinating.

Suddenly, there was a problem that McCandless and Bridges spotted at the same time – a huge container ship heading north north east. Silhouetted against the orange sky in the west McCandless could see the huge white superstructure with a yellow funnel – almost certainly a ship of the OOCL, the Orient Overseas Container Line. These truly colossal skyscrapers of the seas had long since taken over the once dominant role of the classic Ben and Blue Funnel Line cargo liners that belonged to a gentler more leisurely age. They would have to wait for it to pass. They couldn't afford any witnesses to this little accident. Thirty minutes or more lapsed until the visitor was out of sight over the horizon. In the interim Aphrodite had travelled another ten miles at least. The waters were getting shallower and shallower. It was now or never.

Six miles away on Astute tubes one and two were loaded with Spearfish. At exactly 7:15 pm both commanders gave the order to fire tubes one and two. One hundred and eighty three seconds later the first Mk 48 struck Aphrodite's hull amidships on the starboard beam followed eight seconds later by the second which ripped into the steering gear and shaft. Spearfish One almost missed, such had been the sudden deceleration of the ship caused by the first two torpedoes but it blew the bows of Aphrodite clean off.. Spearfish Two exploded in the ship's fuel tanks. The resultant secondary and tertiary explosions were catastrophic. Within less than two minutes the namesake of the Greek Goddess of Love had sunk without trace.

It had taken seventy two days for Diana, the Goddess of Hunting, to get her man.

For over five years the CIA had been right about Jamil ibn Salim who died never knowing that he had been set up. But this was one example of the Special Relationship that would never become public knowledge. The world would also never know that it was a sixty-nine year old Scotsman who had ultimately decided his fate. The Honourable Member for Inverclyde had asked Him for His help. And got it.

In his own way Fitzgerald had asked Him for his help as well. He also asked somebody else – just in case. McCandless hadn't known that a third submarine, HMAS Collins, had been lurking just outside Singapore territorial waters. It was the final insurance policy. Fitzgerald's tentacles spread a long way.

At Crypto City, Fitzgerald got the news of the sinking via satellite within three minutes. After the Japanese attack on Pearl Harbour which brought America into the Second World War, Winston Churhill admitted that he had slept the sleep of the Blessed and the Saved. Fitzgerald felt like that too. It had been a close run thing. A close run thing.

48

Beirut, Lebanon

Seven days later, it was obvious to his trusted confidants at Al Aktar Aviation that Jamil was not coming back. The Aphrodite's Cyprus owners had filed a claim at Lloyds of London for the loss and the Lutine Bell had been rung in the time honoured way. They paid up, *In the Utmost Good Faith*, as always.

On Monday 17th July at 12:00 noon precisely, local time, Radio Television Beirut issued a special news flash.

'It is with the greatest sorrow and regret that we announce to all our Islamic brothers across the Arab World and in Enemy Occupied Palestine, that our dear Brother, Jamil ibn Salim, has died peacefully in Switzerland whilst receiving treatment for cancer. Peace be upon Him.'

TV screens depicted Jamil's portrait for the next twenty four hours in total silence. National radio played sombre music. The empty coffin returned from Geneva in one of Al Aktar's own private Dassault Falcon jets to be met at Beirut International Airport by a hundred thousand mourners.

In line with Islamic tradition Jamil was 'buried' the next day. It was the Middle East's biggest funeral since King Hussein of Jordan's in 1999. It was attended by as many Heads of State as possible. Particularly those States that were short of oil.

Powell was not there. Nor was Bligh. Nor Li Shau Kee.

49

An aide awoke the Prime Minister shortly before five in the morning to tell him that an urgent call would come in within a quarter of an hour from Peter Fitzgerald. He dressed and took the call in his private apartment at Downing Street.

The line, although encrypted, was as clear as a bell. 'I'm sorry to trouble you so early Prime Minister but we have to speak.' Fitzgerald lied. He wanted Bligh awake but not too alert.

'Firstly, I want to thank you for your unwavering support at the recent JIC meeting in London. Terry Moncrief told me that your support was solid.' He lied again. Lister had told him how all the Brits had voted.

'The mission was successful as you probably know already and for that we can all be truly thankful. But the main reason for this call today will have to remain confidential to the two of us Prime Minister.'

'On that you have my personal guarantee Peter.' Bligh always liked to use first names. In the UK it fitted in with his folksy image but in the States it was common practice anyway.

'OK Ben, great. Thank you.'

'Ben, do you have any inkling, any inkling at all, that the Son of Star Wars project is in deep financial trouble. Did you know that?'

'What!?'

'Yes it's true. The implications for us at the NSA are horrific. Confidential sources inform us that the President is considering winding down our operations across the board and reducing its status to that of the Boy Scouts. The knock on effect to your GCHQ will be catastrophic as you can imagine. You still have to find an extra three hundred million to complete your new GCHQ complex at Cheltenham don't you? The Donut Project.' Fitzgerald was referring to the new and enormously costly circular edifice that was running over budget to the tune of three hundred million sterling. The Public Audit Committee were already starting to ask too many questions about an organisation that was not supposed to be in the public eye.

It means that the UKUSA Treaty will be terminated.

Bligh started to take stock of the news. Hellfire. Without the intelligence that Britain's membership of UKUSA provided then the country's status within the new European Army would be severely curtailed. France and Germany would walk all over Bligh at the next summit. He might as well be Prime Minister of Luxemburg for all the credibility he would have. The mere thought caused him to consider handing over to a successor straight away. Quit while you are at the top. Go back to being a lawyer. However mediocre.

'However, Prime Minister' said Fitzgerald deliberately reverting to Bligh's current status, 'I think there might be a way. Tell me, Ben, when Arthur Jones retires this coming fall, did you have in mind a successor?'

Bligh swallowed hard. He had to think quickly.

'Actually yes, Peter. Richard Rogers is my first choice. An excellent man. Brigadier Rogers is coming to the end of his time as Commanding Officer of the Life Guards, Household Division and will prove a worthy successor to Jones I can assure…' Fitzgerald cut him short. Jesus, he just could not believe these guys. He cast his mind back to the CNN coverage of the Trooping of the Colour at the Queen's birthday parade, The Queen Mother's funeral and the Golden Jubilee parades. All those red tunics, bearskins and horses. Terribly impressive and only England could do that sort of thing but we do not need a brassoed dung creator to run NSA's main partner in the twenty first century. Period.

Fitzgerald went back to first names. 'Ben, I'm sure that Rogers is a good guy but listen. I'm sure that I don't have to tell you that You personally are not exactly flavour of the month with the President at the moment. This whole Euro Army with its own rapid reaction force has gotten right under the President's skin. Not because it might be wrong but because it looks to undermine NATO and his ultimate authority as Commander in Chief. You just would not believe how uptight all US Presidents get about that kind of thing. Lemee tell you, when a new President is sworn in and sits at his desk in the Oval Office with the Star Spangled Banner in the corner he kinda goes all gooey and thinks that he's Custer, Wyatt Earp and MacArthur all at the same time.'

'Listen, Ben. We are both in the shit, you more than I. But I think there might be a way. I think that Jones's successor should be one of us. You know what I mean. Somebody who already understands where we are and can defend our corner when it comes to dealing with Washington. I have somebody in mind. All I'm asking for is your agreement in principle. As regards the underfunding at your end I think we can take care of that from surplus funds we asked Congress for earlier this year. As you know until recently we could get any our hands on virtually any amount of dough. All we had to do was think of a half genuine reason for it and Congress coughed up. Those days are over for ever but we have enough to get your donut baked with even a little spare for the sugar and cream. What do you say? We will have to be fairly quick to ring-fence the money angle. Do we have a deal?'

Bligh was completely off guard. He hated with a vengeance the dreaded American style breakfast meetings. Breakfast was supposed to be civilised. Tea, toast and the Telegraph. Here he was being asked to make a major decision involving hundreds of millions of pounds three hours *before* breakfast. But he was in a trap and they both knew it. God, he'd already told Richard Rogers that his next sinecure was 'in the bag' and that nobody else was in the running. On the other hand he needed friends right now over the European problem. He still needed UKUSA. And the donut kneaded the dough! He laughed at his own little quip to himself. It was a nervous laugh.

'Peter, it does look rather as if we are in the same boat, I have to say. The embarrassment with Rogers I can overcome somehow. I'll think of something. Yes. I think we can agree on this one.'

'That's great, Ben'. Fitzgerald laid on the flannel. 'I knew that you and I would solve this. Terry Moncrief was most impressed with the manner in which you chaired that crucial JIC meeting I can tell you. Your grasp of world affairs is a refreshing change from some of the guys around the world that we have to deal with. So can you leave the issue of Jones's successor to me then? Thank you. He will of course of necessity have to be a British National but he will be one of us Ben. He will be one of us.'

Bligh still hadn't shaved. Five minutes later, his brain in a complete tailspin, the Gillette razor knicked the corner of his lip and in seconds his white shirt collar was spotted with red dots. Still, that's an awful lot better than blood on the carpet. Especially his blood.

50

Firth of Clyde, Scotland

August 12th

It had been a long and tedious voyage home after 'Ocean Wave' had effectively finished. The exercise held with the Australian and Malayasian Navies under the Five Power Defence Agreement spelt fun for the surface ships but mediocrity for the submarines. The only bright spot was transiting the Panama Canal. More than a few eyebrows were raised at the sight of three submarines all flying the White Ensign. In ten days they would be home.

It was a beautiful summer's morning. After parting company with the other ships on Exercise Ocean Wave south west of Ireland, Astute, Ambush and Artful proceeded submerged towards the cooler waters of their Scottish base. After rounding the tip of Northern Ireland by County Antrim they headed first east then north towards the Firth of Clyde.

Twenty miles from home and the safety of the loch that was their fortress, they all surfaced and proceeded north in line astern – Ambush in front followed by Astute with Artful at the rear. McCandless had insisted despite the fact that he was in command of the Squadron. The Islands of Arran and Bute seemed so close that they could almost smell the scent of the brilliant purple heather.

Passing Ailsa Craig they turned right into the mouth of the Clyde Estuary itself. McCandless was always left in awe at this sight as his mind's eye conjured visions of generations of ships, men of war and merchantmen, departing the Clyde as they ventured into the wider world of a growing Empire. It would be the last time he viewed this sight. Sometime during the six week voyage home without sight of land for nearly all that time, he had decided to quit the Navy. His twenty years was up at the end of August and he would not be renewing his Commission. It was time to start a new life. Somewhere.

He was on the conning tower in short sleeve order. It was hot. Twenty five Celsius and it was still only mid morning.

Led by Ambush, the three submarines slowed down to eight knots as they rounded left past the lovely town of Helensburgh. Passing yachtsmen were amazed to see three boats. One was a common sight but *three*. They entered the Gareloch. Faslane and home was only minutes away. The helmsman of a pleasure boat raised binoculars to his eyes as he picked out an unusual flag fluttering on Astute's aerials. It can't be. It was! It was the black and white skull and crossbones of the Jolly Roger. Not since HMS Conqueror had sunk the Argentine cruiser General Belgrano in 1982 had a British warship flown a Jolly Roger.

As the three boats rounded the last rocky promontory before entering the base itself, a Scottish piper standing almost at the water's edge played a rousing welcome of 'Ye Bonny Boys are Home Again.' He had ginger hair. It was Private McPherson.

They were almost home. The busy little tugboats nudged the three submarines into the three vacant berths and within minutes the hawsers had been secured and the gangplanks fitted. All three boats had their individual names on the navy blue and white sheeting that fitted down the sides of the handrails of the gangplanks.

The three commanders disembarked first to be met with a welcoming handshake by what looked like a very senior Army Officer. The dockyard flunkey attaching the last hawser to Artful raised an eyebrow and wondered what the hell this was all about. Who was he? It was of course Major General Alan Ferguson.

Five minutes later McCandless, Ribchester and Sefton were inside the main building and were quickly spirited upstairs to the Officer's Mess. A welcome pink gin awaited them all.

A Steward suddenly appeared and spoke quietly into McCandless's ear. He led Ribchester and Sefton out of the Mess and down a corridor into a small dining room. After ushering the three officers inside he closed the heavy wooden door behind them.

A large picture window offered a perfect view of the three submarines, their home for the last ten weeks and, beyond them, the Gareloch who's dark blue waters were framed by the seasonal brilliance of the purple coloured heather that would last for such a few short weeks.

A dining table set for six people faced them. On the far side by the window sat a middle aged Chinese gentleman. None of the officers recognised him. Another, much older Chinaman stood up and walked slowly towards McCandless, right hand outstretched.

'Hello, my old friend Brucie. Long, long time no see!' It was Jimmy Leung now in his late seventies. McCandless was absolutely stunned. He had not seen him since June 1997 when they had met at the Talk of the Town and learned of the Excelsior Agreement. They shook hands warmly. Jimmy did not want to let go but slowly but surely his emotions subsided sufficiently for him to introduce him to his friend. His name was Kelvin Kwan. McCandless in turn, introduced his two fellow officers and the five men sat down at the table, the naval officers on one side the two Chinese on the other. The vacant space between them.

A Steward brought leek and tattie soup and oaties. The men talked.

The soup plates were cleared away and three Stewards brought five gleaming platters covered with silver lids onto the table. At a nod from one of them all five lids were lifted simultaneously.

'Ayee –ah!!' shouted Jimmy. 'Grousies!'

It was grouse. Five roast grouse. They should have realised – it was the 12th of August, the Glorious Twelfth. The first day of the grouse shooting season. You tend not to think of such things beneath the Atlantic.

Another Steward brought a whole litre bottle of Grouse whisky and placed it onto the vacant setting between Kwan and Leung and left the room, closing the door behind him.

There appeared to be a card of some kind tied around the neck of the bottle. Curious, McCandless leaned forward and read the hand written inscription.

It read:

This is just in case I don't make it.
A toast – to the Operation!
Best wishes. Gordon Bedford.'

Some asshole. Some guy.

That evening Kelvin Kwan and Jimmy Leung entertained Bruce McCandless to dinner at their hotel in Glasgow, the Kelvin Park Lorne on Sauchiehall Street. It was always a bit of a joke whenever Kelvin stayed there. The receptionist, a friendly blonde called Eileen Ann Macintosh, genuinely thought that Kelvin owned the hotel and always made a great fuss of him. He never enlightened her. But there again he thought she was the granddaughter of the famous architect and she never enlightened him.

After dinner the three of them drank aperitifs in the Rennie Mackintosh Bar. They brought apologies from John Ross who had expected to join them in Glasgow but sadly he couldn't make it. Anne's mother had taken a turn for the worse in her nursing home in St Kilda and John had done the honourable thing and flown down to join her.

The men talked about business and the future until well into the early hours.

Next morning after breakfast McCandless bade farewell to Kelvin Kwan and Jimmy Leung as a hotel car took them to Glasgow Airport for onward connections to Hong Kong. Out of habit McCandless still called Glasgow Airport 'Abbotsinch Naval Air Station' which is what it used to be. Back in his room, the Jura Suite, he opened a sealed envelope that had been delivered by courier. It was from Fitzgerald and was the first non-encrypted communication he had ever received from him. It must be very, very urgent for Peter to have done that. He need not have worried. It was simply a request to call him on his home number that evening at five o'clock Eastern Daylight Time.

After checking out he drove the hirecar straight to Edinburgh having decided to forego the fishing on Lewis. Just over an hour later he was buying the landlord of the Tilted Wig pub a drink courtesy of Kelvin Kwan who didn't make it to Edinburgh this time.

At ten o'clock he made the call to Fitzgerald. It was a call that was to change his life.

By midnight the girl of his dreams was singing to him. In English or Italian it mattered not. It was *his* turn to sleep the sleep of the blessed and the saved.

51

Edinburgh Castle, Scotland

The regimental Celebration Dinner for the Operation had been well planned in advance with true military precision.

Officially, of course, it did not take place. The world's press would have had a field day. The Regiment would be in total disgrace and the British Government's blood would still be on the U.N. carpet long after it had been thrown out of the Security Council. There were no Government officials present. This was a private function. Very private. The dinner had been Ferguson's idea and the Regiment's slush fund had met the expenses for all those attending from afar. He wanted to give all those who had assisted the Regiment a taste of their honour and history. In that he succeeded.

The endless dining table was covered in the Regiment's silver, some of it the spoils of wars going back as far as the battle for Quebec in the 18th century. Battle Honours hung from the dark panelled walls as stark reminders of bygone glories. Crimean War. Boer War. First World War. Second World War. Suez. Aden. Only one was missing. Officially there had been no 'battle' in Hong Kong. Instead, a Scottish artist had painted in oils a huge picture of the Union Flag and the Regiment's Standard being ceremoniously lowered in Hong Kong at midnight on the night of 30th June 1997. High in the night sky, a million miles above Victoria Peak, like gems of the Milky Way were two silver regimental insignia radiating light into the cosmos forever. One was for Macleod. The other for McLaren.

All officers and invited guests stood behind their dining chairs whilst the regiment's padre gave a blessing for what they were about to receive. All eyes turned to the one female present as she took her seat, the officers on either side of her adjusting the chair as she sat down and smiled a quiet thank you. Dinner commenced as a swarm of stewards descended on the assembled with silver trays of silver goblets. More wars. More spoils. More claret.

Shortly into the proceedings Major General Alan Ferguson rose from his chair at the head of the table.

At sixty five he was a campaigner of the old school. Still possessed of stature and a muscled physique, as everyone else was seated, his six feet looked more like six three. His dark green formal tartan shimmered like a sea of emeralds as the light from the crystal chandeliers bore down from the starry firmament. His receding silver hair, gravelled Midlothian lilt and slow deliberate demeanour gave him the air and gravitas of a descendant Caledonian Chieftain. This was his time.

He started off by thanking everybody for coming – a long way for some people. He expounded on the success of the Operation from the Regiment's viewpoint. Revenge had been sweet and served cold. The Communist Chinese Politburo had appointed a new, more liberal, President within hours of the attack and it had not proved necessary to use more than one Tomahawk *on this occasion*. His tongue seemed to linger on the last three words. John Ross looked up from his Scottish smoked salmon. Kelvin Kwan's face, as usual, was expressionless.

Susan Elizabeth Braukman (nee Bedford) was representing her late Father. Betty had insisted. At forty five she was a picture of pure elegance. Her shoulder length natural blond hair was tied back with a silver and pearl choker. The matching string of Mikimotos, a twenty first birthday gift from Daddy, glistened on the appropriate navy blue dress she had bought specially for the occasion. She was the only female present at this most masculine and secret of functions. The attention she was receiving from the officers initially made her feel shy but as the evening progressed she gained the confidence and composure that had epitomised the late Commander.

Ferguson continued his resume of what had happened three months ago. Hamish McLaren wiped a tear from his eye when the Major General mentioned Stanley Military Cemetery. Although invited, Mrs Moira Macleod had declined to attend. The emotion would have been too much and Ferguson had understood. He had detailed a senior officer earlier that day to take a bouquet of flowers to Devonbanks Cottage in Pitgober.

After all present had eaten their fill of salmon, roast Aberdeen Angus and Scottish raspberry pavlova, the stewards brought decanters of port to the table. Ferguson asked everybody to stand. He proposed three toasts. The Queen, the Regiment and the Operation.

The atmosphere relaxed.

Susan Braukman was seated on Ferguson's immediate right.

'I hear you have a son at Harvard, Ms Braukman. What line of business is he going into when he graduates, may I ask? Computers? Electronics?'

'No, Sir.' replied Susan, maintaining her perfect manners and persona.

'Actually, Trevor's joining the Navy in the fall. He's got a place at Annapolis. His Grandfather would have been very proud of him.'

Jimmy Leung's normally inscrutable eyes sparkled like three carat diamonds.

In her suite at the Caledonian Hotel later that night, Susan looked out across Princes Street and over the glen to the battlements of the ancient castle itself where she had dined only hours earlier. As her eyes moved forever upwards beyond the granite outcrop to the splendour of the edifice itself, she marvelled at the solidity and dignity of what she had been privileged to attend. She would not have missed it for the world.

52

Beijing, China

Li Shau Kee had never been so happy. Indeed, all the Gods had been kind to him. The signs had been good when, almost three months ago, Jiang Zemin's spittle had obliterated the sun on the ceramic replica of the Kiulung. And now Zemin's own sun had set. For ever. For the tenth time that day he opened the plain white envelope that had been especially delivered to him that morning by hand. Inside was a slip of paper.

It was computer generated and printed in German. Li didn't have to be a linguist to understand it. It was printed in the universally acknowledged language of money. Headed up OstenBankPrivat S.A. in three adjacent columns it simply read: ...3 Juli 2007 ... LSK2007 US106,205,475.88

Li looked up at the Portraits of the Patriots. To the right of Chairman Mao was a new picture He was dressed in full Royal Naval uniform in the rank of Captain. The dolphins on the badge betraying his speciality. For the first time since the Long March, a Gweilo, a foreign devil, had become a Patriot.

Li was eating alone. A little time to himself for quiet reflection and then it would be time for lunch. More noodles. The same electric fan rotated through the same arc and he pondered slowly on the events of the last few weeks that represented only a tiny blip in the vast history of the Middle Kingdom. It was time for change and a real Great Leap Forward that echoed the words of Mao himself but that this time would bring freedom and prosperity to her teeming millions. One day.

Li never saw that day. Like all the rest, he did not live into his nineties. In fact he did not even make his mid eighties. By mid afternoon he was dead. Poisoned via the lunch he had just consumed and utterly betrayed by the servants he trusted the most.

At six o'clock Beijing Time precisely, National Television cancelled its remaining programmes for that day and viewers were told to stand by for a major Government announcement. In the TV studio the final arrangements were made to the man about to make the most serious television broadcast in the country's history. His dyed jet black hair was combed back to perfection, his non reflective make-up applied to his chubby cheeks and his immaculately tailored suit was brushed like a mannequin in a tailor's shop window. A final wipe with a tissue to his oversize black rimmed spectacles and he was ready.

The studio digital clock counted down the seconds to the start of the broadcast. Five. Four. Three. Two. One. The large red LCD started flashing. On air! On air!

'Fellow countrymen of the Motherland. Once again I am speaking to you as your Leader. I can now reveal to you all the Plot that almost brought our country to an end.....'

It was Jiang Zemin!

53

In Washington DC and Langley Virginia the news was stunning. At the White House the President called together his newly appointed Secretary of State and National Security Advisor and convened a meeting of the National Security Council for the next day. Fitzgerald and Bellringer would both be present.

The President and his Chief of Staff sat through a recorded transcript of Zemin's two hour monologue that expert interpreters had dubbed into English. They watched and listened to it three times. It was reminiscent of Fidel Castro at his worst both in its length and in its brazen boastfulness. Jesus. What a nightmare. Zemin rambled on about how all enemies of the State had been eliminated and how China could now become the major economic power in the whole world. For too long the world's 'cities' in the shape of the US and Western Europe had controlled the international purse strings but now it was the turn of the 'countryside' to have their say. It was Maoism of the worst propagandist sort but this time it was being performed on the world stage and the whole world was listening. And boy, did Zemin know it. The aborted invasion of the Spratly Islands was now ancient history and in any case the world was unaware it had even been attempted save for a few people who weren't going to say anything anyway.

Zemin was strutting his stuff like no Chinese leader had ever been able to do before. The International Olympic Committee had just delivered him, free of charge, a four aces poker hand and nobody else at the table had a chance. He was starting to look like the President of the Planet.

Nauseated beyond words the American President turned off the monitor. During the third viewing of the sickeningly painful transcription he had made a momentous decision. Several months earlier Zemin had outplayed him over the spyplane saga. He would not forget that. No Sir. If Zemin wanted a duel with him for the rest of his Presidency then that was fine by him. All he had to do was make sure he got a second term from the American people. With that secured he would still be President during the 2008 Olympics. He cast his mind back to the 1980 Moscow Olympics when the US had persuaded many countries to boycott the Games. Yes Sir. There was gonna be plenty of time and scope to create Mr Zemin a whole lot of problems. A whole lot of problems. He would also make sure, come what may, that Son of Star Wars would go ahead whatever the fiscal cost. The latest test to knock out a missile over the Pacific had been a complete success. Yes Sir. Continued development of the National Missile Defence System would get right up Zemin's nose. It will go ahead. He, the forty third President of the United States would make sure of that.

At Langley, Virginia James Bellringer was feeling quite unwell at the news of Zemin's reincarnation. Thank goodness the CIA's hand in the 'assassination' had been completely hidden. Both he and Fitzgerald did not yet know that the President had changed his mind again on Son of Star Wars. They soon would.

At Crypto City the news was not quite so stunning. Fitzgerald and Eagleburger had known for three days that Zemin was still alive but only they in the United States had been privy to this most staggering of developments. The news had come via DSD in Melbourne, Australia who had picked up SIGINT from Hainan. Those guys were really on the ball and to Fitzgerald, after Fort Meade, DSD was the most crucial component of UKUSA. Even more so now that world attention would refocus once again on Asia.

The encrypted briefing from Melbourne had informed him that Zemin had not been killed in the attack by Jamil ibn Salim. The plane that had been brought down was in fact an identical back-up plane chartered from the same airline in the same colours. Within several minutes of the stinger missile attack on the first plane Zemin's airplane, already in the air en route from Macau, turned through one hundred and eighty degrees and flew southwest to the same air force base in Hainan where the crippled US Navy Aries spyplane had been forced to land a few months earlier. Zemin had stayed there for his own safety and in total secrecy whilst his own loyal cohorts in Beijing and Hong Kong sought furiously to discover the extent of the treachery. They had bade their time. But when they struck it was fatal and clinical in its delivery.

Fitzgerald had to decide quickly whether to tell the President how much he knew. Jamil was dead for sure but with Zemin now alive he would be gunning for Son of Star Wars and it would boil down to a war of personalities between him and the President. The Middle East was calmer than it had been for years but if China represented a new and greater threat, economically and militarily, to America then the President would still push ahead with the project that could bankrupt the nation. Let alone his beloved NSA.

He had a duty to protect the nation and UKUSA before the President.

In bed that night he lay awake and mentally tried to prepare himself for tomorrow's crucial meeting in Washington. How much should he tell the President? By the time he had finished his breakfast the next morning he had made up his mind. He had decided to tell the President nothing. Absolutely nothing. Eagleburger concurred. They were of one mind. Around the world their own organisation was working well. Far better than any individual Government. In the Southern Hemisphere DSD in Australia was operating like clockwork. And soon, very soon, they would have their own man as the Director of GCHQ in England. Three components all working together in unison with a common aim. In his mind Fitzgerald dubbed it the Triangle of Trust.

He would protect the National Security Agency and its overseas partners at all cost. They were the cerebral centres of intelligence for the whole of the Free and English speaking World. They were beyond negotiation. As Clement Arrigoni had mused almost a century ago, in China you were either a peasant or a mandarin. To Fitzgerald, the future might be China's but *they*, that is the NSA and her partners, *they*, would be *The New Mandarins*.

EPILOGUE

South China Sea
425 Nautical miles East
South East of Ho Chi Minh City

Chris Todd leant over the side of his chartered boat, the Singapore Registered *King of Kinabalu*. Time was running out for him and he knew it.

A keen student of maritime history for years, he had followed the fortunes of one of his fellow Australians who had successfully searched for and found the wrecks of two ancient cargo boats, the *Geldermeison* and the *Tek Sing*. Both subsequent salvages had earned the treasure hunter, Mike Hatcher, a fortune. The ships had been loaded to capacity with Chinese porcelain bound for the markets of Amsterdam and Batavia, now known as Jakarta, the capital city of Indonesia. Todd had followed up the *Tek Sing* story with the utmost diligence travelling to both Foochow in Southern China and to the London Museum to further his research.

The last trip to Foochow in March earlier in the year had turned up new evidence on the Tek Sing. This new information had cost him some amount of money to a corrupt official in what remained of the Fukien Peoples Marine Department. The loss of the *Tek Sing* in 1822 when she hit a reef during a typhoon had been catastrophic in terms of the loss of human life. In addition to the precious cargo of over 1,000 tons of the finest porcelain, aboard had been more than 1,400 Chinese citizens emigrating to a new land for a better future for themselves and their families. Whilst some 200 were rescued, ironically by a British opium trader heading for China, over 1,200 poor souls had lost their lives. When this information became public in 1999 it had been dubbed *China's Titanic*.

However, the information that had cost Chris Todd five thousand US dollars 'tea money' to the Marine Department officer was potentially worth a thousand times more. The loss of the most valuable cargo ever to have left China on the *Tek Sing* had caused financial hardship to thousands. The cargo had been manufactured by scores of small family owned factories who would take the newly made bowls and plates to municipal kilns for firing then subsequent export. That lost revenue had to be recouped quickly. Todd now knew that the cargo was replaced within three months on a second ship, name unknown, that had sailed for Batavia on the same route but this time after the end of the dreaded typhoon season. Like its predecessor the Tek Sing, it didn't make it to its destination. The corrupt official in Foochow had told Todd that the Department of Historical Artefacts in Beijing were hoping to launch their own search and salvage operation in 2002 based on old nautical charts recently discovered in archives in the city of Amoy. Illicit copies of those charts were now in Todd's possession.. He would have to act quickly.

Todd had postulated that in much better weather, almost guaranteed to be typhoon free, it must have come to grief on uncharted reefs. Over several months of extended research on charts, new and old, and coupled with the illegally bought information in Foochow, he had, he was certain, narrowed the search area down to about twenty square miles.

Mortgaging his substantial property in Perth, Western Australia, to the bank he borrowed a hundred thousand dollars to finance the search. The *King of Kinabalu* and her Malaysian crew were costing him a thousand dollars a day. He had been searching for ninety days. A few more days were all the time and money he had left. The boat would have to go back to Singapore and he would have to return to Perth to sell his lovely house overlooking the Swan River.

On the last day, Todd was almost philosophical. Nobody could have tried harder. He had dubbed the ship he was looking for the *"Hop Sing"* after the Chinese butler on the old cowboy TV series Bonanza. If he ever found the *Hop Sing* he would have his own bonanza! He took a final drag on his "roll-up" and tossed the butt over the side. They would have one more trawl with the caesium gas magnetometer, a miniature torpedo looking capsule towed behind the boat, on the shallowest sector of his projected sinking position. Then that would be it. The end of the day. Shit.

The weather was fine and clear and the boat sailed at ten knots on a north south vector for half an hour on the last search ribbon on the chart. With about a mile left to run the crew member manning the magnetometer's screen suddenly shouted out. 'Look, look! Mr Todd you come quick! Big contact, *big* contact! Todd raced up the ladder from the main deck to the bridge. Sure enough there was something big down there at about 180 feet. In fact it looked *too* big for the "Hop Sing". But using this type of kit was not an exact science – more of an abstract form of art. Todd ordered the boat to slow down to five knots and make a one hundred and eighty degree turn and onto the reciprocal course so that they could double check. Sure enough, fifteen minutes later there it was again. The dark shadow on the recording paper like a cancer sufferer's lung.

The King of Kinabalu hove to and dropped anchor. They only just had enough chain. The water was one hundred and eighty five feet deep according to the echo sounder. Todd was a historian, not a diver. He ordered his two most experienced divers out of his team of four to prepare to dive onto the contact. Excitement was high. Fifteen minutes later the two men went over the side.

It took the two men only four minutes to reach the target. It would take them a lot longer to get back. The budget did not run to a decompression chamber and on returning to the surface the two divers would have to make two 'stopovers' en route to avoid the potentially lethal bends caused by nitrogen dissolving in the blood. They would be below the surface for at least fifty minutes. For Todd and the remaining crew it seemed like fifty hours. He smoked all the "roll-ups" he habitually made at breakfasttime to last the whole day.

Eventually, the men broke the surface and were hauled aboard up the rope ladders. Exhausted they fell on the deck panting loudly whilst the others helped them remove their tanks. One of them, Ramul, tossed a large bible like book onto the deck. He'd found it in air lock. It was bound in dark leather and although it looked unaffected by its time in the sea water during the rise to the surface to attempt to open the book would not be wise at this juncture. The crew gathered round to look at it. The senior officer clutched it to his chest and looked up into the clear blue sky. It was a Holy Koran. 'Allah be praised.!" But just a minute – there were no Holy Korans on Chinese cargo junks.

Todd questioned Ramul, instantly depressed. It could not be the "*Hop Sing*".

'Mr Todd, Sir. It is a cargo ship, all steel hence the huge magnetic deflection. It was Cyprus Registered, in Limassol.

It's called the Aphrodite. There are skeletons of crew. I took this dog-tag.' He threw a gold necklace type chain onto the deck. It has only recently met its end. I am not an expert on marine damage assessment but if I had to put money on it I'd say it had been torpedoed. There were at least three distinct holes in the hull two starboard, one port. The screw was on the sandy bottom some sixty meters distant.

Todd shrugged his broad shoulders. Oh well, he'd just have to go back to teaching history until he could raise enough dough to try again. Some day. He tossed the Koran to Ramul. Here, you keep this, mate, as a souvenir. You're a Moslem aren't you?'

Kuala Lumpur, Malaysia
10th October

On reaching Singapore, Ramul had paid his fee from Mr Todd into his bank. He felt sorry for him. He had not complained at his misfortune and had paid the crew their dues as agreed before the trip. They had shared a beer or two before Todd flew back to Perth and the dreaded meeting with the bank. They exchanged addresses in case Todd wanted to try again one day.

Ramul studied the Koran he had salvaged. It seemed very old to him and was enscribed with gold leaf Arabic lettering on the cover. Was it a name, a place? He didn't know. He had two weeks to kill before his next job and decided to visit the Islamic Library in the Old Quarter of Kuala Lumpur on the mainland six hours drive away. In any case he could do with the break.

The Library's curate, Dr.Iqbal, was excited with what Ramul had brought him to see. His telephone call the day before had come as a surprise but he said he would help if he could.

'Mr Ramul, I don't know where you obtained this Koran – that is your business. But I can tell you that it is almost certainly an old family owned Koran and that it was printed in the Lebanon, probably in the 17th or 18th Century. Quite possibly in Tyre. I have only ever seen one like it before. They are very rare and extremely valuable.' Donning gossamer surgical type gloves Dr.Iqbal used a very fine pewter paper knife to gingerly prise open the cover to reveal the first two pages. His eyesight was not good and he reached into a drawer in his desk for a large brass rimmed magnifying glass. He bent forward to read the Arabic handwriting on the inside cover. The ink had been affected by immersion in sea-water but not to the extent that it had become illegible. As he read the writing one word at a time he translated from Arabic to Ramul's native Malay.

'*Presented to our Brother in Arms, Jamil ibn Salim, for his devotion to the Palestinian People, Gaza City, 1200 in the year of the Prophet.*

'Mr Ramul, where on earth did you obtain this magnificent and Holy Book.'

Ramul told him the whole story about the Tek Sing, the "Hop Sing " and the Australian, Mr Todd. Dr. Iqbal listened attentively.

'With your permission, Mr Ramul' said Dr. Iqbal, squinting at his battered old wristwatch, 'I should like to make a call to associates in Beirut. Now let me see we are five hours ahead, it's Saturday today so there should be somebody available to help.'

He reached for a dusty brown notebook from his desk drawer, opened it and using the magnifying glass dialled a string of numbers as he ran the glass along the open page. He waited. It took some time to get through. For the next two minutes he spoke only in Arabic and Ramul became a little restless. Iqbal finished his conversation and wrote a series of numbers into his notebook. The final word he spoke – *shokran* – meaning thank you, was the only word that Ramul understood.

'Mr Ramul, that was the Islamic Library in Beirut, our Head Office so to speak. I have been asked to call another name on this other number in ten minutes time. Meanwhile let me get you some refreshment – I have been very rude.'

Ten minutes later Dr. Iqbal dialled the new numbers. The 'Good morning, Mr Salim' were the only words that Ramul could follow. The call lasted more than fifteen minutes and was interspersed from time to time with Iqbal reading the writing on the inside cover directly to the man at the other end of the line. Iqbal paused, holding the palm of one hand over the telephone handset, 'Mr Ramul, Mr Salim would like to know if you are available to take the Holy Book to Beirut in two days time. All expenses will be paid and a substantial reward will be paid to you for the Book's safe return.

'Dr. Iqbal, if by so doing I can make somebody happy, I will. Gladly.

The necessary arrangements were made. Dr. Iqbal thanked Ramul for coming to see him and bade him a safe and pleasant journey to the Lebanon.

Corporate Headquarters
Al-Aktar Aviation Corporation
Beirut, Lebanon
12ᵗʰ October

The twelve hour journey via Amman on Royal Jordanian Airlines had actually been quite relaxing. Mind you, First Class usually is. It was early afternoon, Beirut Time, and the black Mercedes was at the airport to meet Ramul as promised. He had never before been outside South East

Asia and the blue of the Mediterranean and the dry, almost arid landscape contrasted sharply with the luscious shades of green seas and jungles of his native Jahore Province of Malaysia. It was a short fifteen minute drive north into downtown Beirut and the Mercedes slowed as it pulled into a private semi-circular drive in front of an imposing office building of obviously recent construction.

As the car pulled to a halt outside the main tinted glass doors Ramul could see the giant letters AAA from the top of the eight storey building reflected in a huge ornamental pond within the semi-circle of the drive. The pond was in the shape of an inverted crescent like a moon at these latitudes. Of course, it was a depiction of the Red Crescent. The Palestinian Red Crescent.

An aide wearing white gloves rushed forward to open the rear door of the Mercedes and Ramul alighted, clutching his briefcase. He was staggered. Between him and the main door must have been a dozen or more smartly dressed men all waiting in a line. All were wearing black suits and, without exception, dark glasses. The first one stepped forward and shook hands with Ramul, introducing himself as Ali ibn Salim. He spoke good English, knowing that Ramul spoke almost no Arabic. Dr. Iqbal had briefed him well.

Like royalty at a formal reception, Ramul walked down the line of men, Ali ibn Salim introducing each one by name in turn. Ramul felt like a King. The *King of Kinabalu* perhaps. The last man in line was shorter and much older with silver hair and seemed to stand up with difficulty. Ramul noticed a walking cane propped against a nearby wall and guessed correctly that it was his but determined not to use it at this moment. His name was given simply as Abdullah and Ramul could see that he was almost in tears.

The introductions completed, the entourage walked inside the palatial marbled interior and the blessing of shade and air conditioning although Ramul was unaffected by the drier heat and low humidity. Minutes later they were all sat around a huge circular table heavily inlaid with the Islamic marquetry that only Artisans of the Faith could deliver. On the table were flagons of juices from a dozen fruits, brass pots of coffee, dates, olives and pineapples. Ramul was seated between Ali and the old man, Abdullah. He felt nervous and comfortable all at the same time.

Ali addressed the gathering in Arabic. Only he and Ramul spoke English.

'Brothers, I welcome Mr Ramul to the bosom of our family. Only I know why he is here with us today. Now I will tell all of you.' He spoke slowly and deliberately for nearly three minutes. There were gasps of astonishment from the men. One sobbed. Several shouted out loud but of course Ramul could not understand. Ali turned to Ramul and speaking in English asked him if he would kindly present the contents of his briefcase to Abdullah. Ramul reached down to his black executive Echolac which had seen better days and placed it flat onto the table the twin combination locks facing him. Quickly he spun the dials. The left one, 835, was the Registration No. in Singapore of the King of Kinabalu, the right one, 704, was his Mother's birthday, the fourth of July. The locks sprung open and he lifted the lid. As he did so a dozen pairs of eyes craned forward. He lifted the Holy Koran carefully from the case and turning to his right passed the heavy book to Abdullah. The old man's arms started to shake and the man on *his* right helped him lower it safely to the table. Slowly and with total reverence he opened it. He started to cry. Just a little at first, then the trickles from both eyes turned into Rivers of Jordan, ran down both cheeks and onto the Holy Book itself.

'You must excuse my father, Mr Ramul. But he is naturally emotional at this moment. Jamil was his first son. My half-brother.'

Abdullah ibn Salim *had not died* on day one of the Yom Kippur War. He had survived and married again. Ramul was almost overcome himself.

'Then, Ali, assuming you are the eldest of the sons, I must also give you this. He reached into the back of the Echolac behind the folds restrained by the studs. Ramul passed him the solid gold necklace bearing Jamil's name in Arabic letters. It was Ali's turn to cry as he held it tightly to his chest and uttered a short prayer to the Prophet. Then he laid it on the table like a jeweller would display an expensive piece in a shop window. He inadvertently placed it upside-down. Ali started to shake with horror and disbelief. Jaggedly scratched on the back in almost childlike writing that looked as if it had been done with a sharp piece of metal and in great haste were three letters.

Those letters were ... C...I...A...

Effected in the last dying seconds of his life, it was Jamil's last message to the material world.

ABOUT THE AUTHOR

Mark Harland has lived and worked in the Near, Middle and Far East.

He is a former pupil of St. George's Army School, Hong Kong.

His other works include:

Novels:
Your Country Needs You
A Very Special Relationship
Her Place in the Sun

Non-fiction:
MALTA: My Island
One Thousand days in Hong Kong
Sunburnt Pom's Tales of Oz
From UK to Belgium and back

Mark currently lives in North Yorkshire.

www.mvhbooks.com